# There's Trouble Brewing

# There's Trouble Brewing

## NICHOLAS BLAKE

PERENNIAL LIBRARY
Harper & Row, Publishers
New York, Cambridge, Philadelphia, San Francisco
London, Mexico City, São Paulo, Sydney

This work was originally published by William Collins Sons and Company in 1937. It is here reprinted by arrangement.

*Designed by Susan Hull*

First PERENNIAL LIBRARY edition published 1982.

ISBN: 0–06–080569–2

82 83 84 85 86 10 9 8 7 6 5 4 3 2 1

*To*
Joyce and Teddy

*All the characters, places and business firms in this book are entirely fictitious. My best thanks are due to H. Sandeman Allen, Esq., F. W. Hands, Esq., and K. Mead, Esq., for assistance on technical points.*

# CONTENTS

# I
## April 23, July 16

*Dogs begin in jest and end in earnest.*
PROVERB

EVERY dog, they say, has its day. Whether Truffles would have assented to this proposition during his lifetime is highly doubtful. Not for him the elusive rabbit, the ineffable dungheap, the hob-nobbing with loose companions at street corners that for upper-class dogs represent the illicit high-spots of cloistered lives. Truffles, like everything else that Eustace Bunnett had to do with, was kept very much at heel. One might have supposed that a wife, a brother, a brewery and a town council would have provided Mr. Bunnett with sufficient exercise for his lust for power. But that would be to underestimate both the late (though far from lamented) Eustace Bunnett and that most insidious of human vices of which Edmund Burke said so justly, "Power gradually extirpates from the mind every humane and gentle virtue." No, Truffles had a dog's life, in every possible sense of the phrase. Even the natural and almost boundless servility of his species must have been pretty heavily strained by the demands of his master.

Yet Truffles, too, had his day. Whether it was ade-quate compensation for a lifetime of alternate whipping and pampering, I cannot pretend to decide. At least it ended in posthumous fame; and posthumous fame is no doubt the next best thing to a happy life. Truffles achieved the ambition of all downtrodden creatures. His pusillanimous and shifty-looking terrier face appeared in every illustrated newspaper in the United Kingdom, ousting from the front page the not altogether dissimilar features of Hitler, the neurotic-bulldog expression of Mussolini, the sealed lips of Mr. Baldwin, and the unconcealed charms of bathing beauties. In death, as in life, Truffles and his master were not divided. Side by side with the dog's face appeared that of Eustace Bunnett—the petulant mouth, the pince-nez which only called attention to the cold and self-satisfied eyes, the whole expression of meanness, suavity, self-importance, and latent ruthlessness. And as for the headlines!

But we anticipate, as the small boy said when he was sick on Christmas Eve. When Nigel Strangeways received the invitation, he naturally had no inkling of the sinister circumstances in which it was going to involve him. Had he had such an inkling, he would have accepted the invitation with much more alacrity: Nigel would go anywhere if a problem in crime was promised, whereas he would normally have run miles to avoid a literary society—and it was to address the Maiden Astbury Literary Society that he had been invited. Here is the letter, filed by him later as exhibit one in the Bunnett case:

*3, Pound Street, Maiden Astbury, Dorset*

DEAR MR. STRANGEWAYS,—*As secretary of the local literary society (a poor thing, but our own!), I am venturing to ask whether you would come down and give us an address. We have been studying your delightful little book on the Caroline poets, and our members are all eager to have the privilege of meeting its author. The desire to "see Shelley plain" is a very human failing, after all, and perhaps will excuse the presumption of this request. I know how busy you writers are, but I'm sure you would feel recompensed by our enthusiasm. I'm afraid we cannot offer you a fee: I expect the funds could rise to your expenses, though, if necessary! Do come if you can—any date in June or July would suit us.—Yours sincerely,*

SOPHIE CAMMISON

*P.S.—We live in the middle of the Hardy country.*
*P.P.S.—My husband met you at Oxford, and would be so glad to renew the acquaintance.*

"Crikey!" said Nigel, inspecting this communication bleakly over his early morning cup of tea. "This is what comes of dabbling in literature. Why ever didn't I stick to the straight path of crime?"

"What comes of dabbling in literature?" asked Georgia from the adjoining bed.

"Oh, *you're* there. You know, I just can't get used to waking up and finding a woman in the room."

"It's a damn sight better than waking up and finding a fer-de-lance in the room, and that's what happened when I——"

"Spare us the reminiscences, please. Keep them for *Three Thousand Miles Through the Bush on a Tricycle*, or whatever you're going to call your travel book."

"You're sweet. I'm glad I married you," said Georgia.

"Well, you go instead then."

"What on earth are you talking about?"

"This," said Nigel, holding up the letter. "Some dastardly hag wants me to go down to Dorset and address her blasted literary society. A literary society! I ask you."

"Let me see." Goergia took the letter.

"Note the skittishness," said Nigel. "Sophie clearly has rather protuberant eyes of a washed-out violet colour, and spits at you when she talks. Her friends say, 'Poor Sophie is so artistic, you know!' She is the type of virgin that——"

"What's all this about 'virgin'? Her postscript says she is married."

"Oh, I hadn't got that far. Anyway, I never read postscripts—either they're unnecessary or they've got a catch in them."

"Well, it's a post-postscript, actually. The PS. says they live in the middle of the Hardy country."

"A fact already adequately communicated by the address at the top of the page."

"The PPS. says her husband knew you at Oxford."

Nigel sat up in bed. "Ah, now that *is* interesting."

"You remember him?"

"Yes, vaguely. I don't mean that, though. What's interesting is the fact that this frolicsome hag only mentions him in a postscript. She is evidently jealous about him and henpecks him unmercifully, at the same time telling all her girl friends that Herbert has no soul and does not understand her. Her mission is to bring culture, spiritual values and whatnot into Herbert's life—and, if I remember anything about him, she's undertaken a pretty tough job. Still, she's probably got him down by now. Wives always do."

"Oh yes?"

"Yes."

"Well, I don't believe a word of it. I'll lay you evens that Sophie Cammison is a highly intelligent woman with a figure as well developed as her sense of humour. She wrote this letter with her tongue in her cheek, and she's pulled your leg right out of its socket."

"How anatomical you are," said Nigel. "So you expect me to go down there without a fee—the funds could rise to expenses, exclamation mark—just to win a beggarly quid off you?"

"Not win, lose."

"Very well, that settles it. I'll go, just to prove you're wrong. It'll be interesting to see how old Cammison has turned out, too."

"Ah, the human interest always gets you, doesn't it? You're the editor's dream come true." Georgia wrinkled up her nose at him.

"Now that I come to look at you in the cold light of morning, you really are exactly like a monkey," said Nigel.

"Darling Nigel!"

"Well, only fairly like a monkey. A literary society! Human interest! Pah!"

But indeed that absurd bet with Georgia was to lead Nigel into a very great deal more human interest than he could possibly have bargained for. . . .

As the train puffed through the lush July landscape of Dorset, Nigel took out Mrs. Cammison's letter again. He was feeling more reconciled to the visit. Georgia, whose odd craving for the most solitary and uncomfortable parts of the world had won her fame as an explorer, was off wandering amongst the outer Hebrides. So he might as well be in Dorset as anywhere else—even if it was to involve him in reverent pilgrimages to Mellstock and Egdon Heath with the kittenish Cammison creature. For there could be no doubt that Georgia was wrong there. Sophie Cammison, Nigel reflected as he studied her letter again, would be one of those kittens that keeps a very useful set of claws concealed behind her playful pattings: she was the sort of woman who had to be bossing something; if it wasn't a literary society, it would be flag-day committees, the Women's Conservative League, Rescue and Prevention, the Society for the Preservation of Home Crafts, Country Dancing, or some other of those innumerable activities that give idle women a pretext for interfering with other people's lives. Well, she was not going to get her claws into him.

In due course a ramshackle station bus bore Nigel up the steep, narrow main road of the little Dorset town and deposited him outside 3, Pound Street. It was a solid, dignified little house, its Ham Hill stone glowing apricot in the evening sunlight. A brass plate on the door read "Herbert Cammison, F.R.C.S." Of course: Nigel remembered now that Cammison had been studying medicine: in his youth he had been just the moody, wild, cynical type of lad that by some incredible alchemy turns out a model of professional etiquette and bedside manner. No doubt the Herbert Cammison who one night had strung every chamber-pot in college on a rope over the quadrangle was now incapable of saying boo! to a stethoscope. *Tempora mutantur,* murmured Nigel as he crossed the threshold, *nos et mutamur in illis.* The hall was dark, cool, stone-flagged. The maid took his suitcase and showed him into the drawing-room. Nigel's determination to show Sophie Cammison at the outset that he did not stand any nonsense was badly wrecked. Failing to notice the two steps that led down into the room, he fell into her presence rather than arrived. As he picked himself up, blinking in the strong light, he heard an amused voice say:

"It's all right. Everybody does that the first time. I'm always telling Grace to warn people."

Nigel shook hands with the owner of the voice. Mrs. Cammison was a robust shapely creature, red-cheeked and blue-eyed, the picture of health: she might have been any age from twenty-five to thirty-five, and looked like a Victorian painter's idea of a milkmaid except for her chic dress and the horn-rimmed spectacles that went so incongruously with her fresh face. Nigel muttered involuntarily:

"I believe Georgia was right after all."

"'Georgia was right'? That's your wife, isn't it?"

"Yes. It's a long and rather discreditable story."

"Do tell me. You can tell me while you're having tea. You haven't had it yet, have you? I'm sorry I couldn't meet you, but Herbert wanted the car this afternoon."

Nigel ate heartily, as always, and Mrs. Cammison regarded him with the amiable satisfaction of a mother who observes that her son has recovered his appetite. After a bit she said:

"Well now, what is this discreditable story?"

"Well, you see," said Nigel, picking his words gingerly, "it was your letter. I—er—formed one opinion from it about what you'd be like, and Georgia formed another."

"It doesn't seem a very long story."

"No, perhaps not. That's because I'm leaving out the er—discreditable details."

"I can imagine them."

"I sincerely hope you can't. But seriously, you're not a bit like your letter."

Sophie Cammison's eyes twinkled. She replied comfortably:

"And you're not a bit like a celebrated amateur detective."

"Oh, dear," said Nigel disconcerted. "You know about that?"

"I read the newspapers. They were full of you last year over that Chatcombe case.* That was when you met your wife, wasn't it?"

"Yes. What do you think an amateur detective ought to look like?"

"I'll tell you that if you tell me first what you thought *I* was going to look like."

"Well, on your own head be it," Nigel told her. Mrs. Cammison threw back her head and laughed with hearty enjoyment. No man is quite invulnerable against a woman's laughter, when she is laughing at his ideas—even if the ideas are only half serious. A little piqued, Nigel said:

"Why did you write such a misleading letter, then? You've lost me a quid over it."

"Oh, I just thought it was the sort of style that would appeal to a writer. If he was a fool, I mean, it would flatter his vanity: if he wasn't, he'd see through it."

"And I didn't see through it, therefore——"

"Oh, I didn't mean that—really, I didn't," exclaimed Mrs. Cammison, flushing deeply. It made her look a little overblown, a little stupid. But she isn't stupid really, thought Nigel: her physical self-

* c.f. *Thou Shell of Death.*

8

confidence has made it unnecessary for her to learn finesse: she is sophisticated in her intelligence, but ingenuous at heart. Clever—the letter shows it—in a superficial, mischievous way, like an ape. Probably a good mimic.

He said, "Now it's your turn to expose your misconceptions."

"Well, I suppose my idea of a detective is based on Sherlock Holmes, Father Brown and Poirot."

"A curious composite figure he must be! Long and short, fat and thin——"

"Now don't interrupt. He has piercing eyes, that see exactly what you are thinking. He is always making sinister deductions from one's most innocent remarks. And of course he's wildly eccentric. Are you wildly eccentric?"

"It's very difficult: some of my friends complain that I'm too eccentric, others that I'm not eccentric enough."

"You look quite ordinary to me."

Nigel, who prided himself normally on his unobtrusive appearance, now found himself faintly resenting this remark. Really, it's strange the way this artless creature gets beneath my skin, he reflected: perhaps because everything she says is so transparently honest. He was driven, as a sort of self-assertion against this downrightness of hers, to adopt a flippant tone.

"And how is crime in these parts? Have you any nice murders for me to solve? Or a spot of blackmail, perhaps? I am always willing to oblige."

There was the slightest pause. Then Sophie Cammison said:

"Oh, no, I'm afraid not. We're a very law-abiding lot. By the way, Mr. Bunnett is coming round after

9

the meeting, and one or two others. He is anxious to meet you. I hope you don't mind."

Actually, Nigel minded a good deal. It is one of the impositions, however, that an author has to put up with—this "one or two people coming round after the meeting" and bombarding him with questions, opinions and manuscripts when he is already reeling with fatigue. Nigel said politely that it would be a pleasure. So that was that.

It was only when he was dressing for dinner an hour later that this conversation returned to Nigel's mind. There was something in it that had bothered him. What? Mrs. Cammison had talked about detectives "making sinister deductions from one's most innocent remarks." That was quite true, of course: and still more true of pauses, hesitations in answering a question. Ah, now he'd got it! There had been a slight but quite unnecessary pause after his flippant remark about "crime in these parts." And then, when Sophie had answered, "Oh, no, I'm afraid not"; her voice had been almost too normal—as though she were consciously mimicking her own normal voice. Then she had abruptly changed the subject. Of course, she *was* abrupt. It was her natural manner. But Nigel believed that, when a person deliberately changes the subject, there is often an unconscious association between the original subject and the new one. Still, it was difficult to see any connection between crime and a few people coming round after the meeting, apart from the criminal act of subjecting a jaded author to such an ordeal. One person was mentioned by name—who was it now? Oh, yes, a Mr. Bunnett. A relation, perhaps, of the composer of Bunnett's "Magnificat in F," or whatever the key was, so beloved of ambitious village choirs.

As it happened, the mysterious Mr. Bunnett's name cropped up at dinner, though in a context very far removed from church music. Nigel was a firm believer in first impressions. He thought that you could find out more about a person in the first ten minutes than in the next ten days, because then the mind was unprejudiced, the intuition like a smooth wax tablet ready to take a clear imprint. So, while he sipped his sherry and talked trivialities with Mrs. Cammison, he was closely observing her and her husband. It was not easy to recognise in this swarthy, taciturn doctor the harum-scarum undergraduate of ten years ago. Cammison's face was peculiarly unrevealing, his voice quiet and non-committal. Two vertical furrows above his nose might indicate worry or concentration. There was a sort of stealthiness about his movement, like a cat's, and at the same time a suggestion of perfect nervous co-ordination. His hands were very quiet and very sensitive—a surgeon's hands. They seemed to handle knife, fork and glass of their own volition, as though they could go on working if their owner was asleep or dead. Nigel only saw Herbert Cammison smile once during dinner and that was at his wife during a lull in the conversation: it was a smile of curious warmth and complicity.

The relations between these two were obviously of the best. There was none of that slightly petulant, semi-affectionate verbal sparring in which ill-assorted couples are apt to indulge before strangers. Nor did they compete with each other at all for their guest's attention. Nigel was wondering idly why Sophie Cammison, with her dark hair and high colouring, wore such insipid pastel shades instead of something more crude and barbaric, when the name of

Bunnett cropped up. Cammison had asked him would he have beer or whisky. Nigel chose beer. As he fingered the bottle, he saw it was labelled, "BUNNETT'S BREWERY, MAIDEN ASTBURY, DORSET."

"Is this something to do with the man I'm meeting tonight?" he asked, and was instantly aware of a tension in the atmosphere, a guarded deliberation in the way Mrs. Cammison answered:

"Yes, he owns the local brewery." She went on quickly and smoothly, "Mr. Bunnett wanted to meet Mr. Strangeways, so I asked him with a few others to come round after the meeting."

"Oh," said Herbert Cammison. "I see."

On the face of it, one couldn't imagine two more ordinary remarks: but Nigel somehow felt that Mrs. Cammison's tone implied, "Don't show surprise, Herbert: leave me to manage this," and her husband's answer a more than superficial acquiescence.

"Well," said Cammison in his usual sombre tones, "here's luck." He raised his glass and waggled his little finger at Nigel—a gesture that suddenly bridged the gulf between Oxford and Maiden Astbury. "I wonder are we drinking Truffles to-night," he added.

"Drinking truffles?" asked Nigel in amazement.

"Herbert!" Mrs. Cammison remonstrated. "Don't be so disgusting! Anyway, that brew wouldn't have matured yet."

"I don't mind. It would add body," said Herbert equably.

"What on earth is all this about? An old Dorset recipe?"

"Not exactly," Cammison answered. "Truffles fell into one of the open coppers a week or two ago.

12

Eustace Bunnett's dog. A happy release for the abominable little beast, I should call it. Bunnett made the hell of a to-do about it, I believe."

"A happy release?"

"Yes," said Cammison crisply. "I suspect Eustace Bunnett of sadist tendencies. Amongst other things."

"Herbert!" his wife exclaimed. It was something more than the conventional "shocked" expostulation.

Herbert replied grimly:

"Well, perhaps 'suspect' is the wrong word. We all know——"

"Do you mind people asking questions after your address?" Sophie interrupted hastily. Nigel grimaced.

"That's part of the bargain, I'm afraid," he said.

When dinner was over they walked along to the hall. It was a dusty, fusty, depressing place, smelling of varnish and stewed tea—the centre, Nigel imagined, of all Maiden Astbury's more gruesome activities, from jumble sales to inquests. The intelligentsia, so to speak, of the town was already assembled. Nigel was introduced to a strapping great woman of aggressively civic aspect who might have sat, suitably draped, for a statue of the Goddess of Public Works ("this is Miss Mellors, our president"), and followed in her wake up to the dais. The Goddess of Public Works breathed heavily on him, took out a bottle of eau-de-Cologne, liberally lustrated herself and boomed at Nigel:

"Glad you could come. Good turn-out to-night. Feeling nervous?"

"Paralysed. However, I've fortified myself with some of your Mr. Bunnett's excellent booze. Good stuff, isn't it?"

"Indeed? 'Good' is not the word I should apply myself. I am vice-president of the Blue Ribbon Society. We aim to stamp out liquor-drinking."

"Oh," said Nigel, reflecting that anything Miss Mellors stamped on would stand little chance of survival. He fidgeted with his notes and began to scrutinise the audience. Lower-middlebrow, he decided, was the prevailing tendency: he began to wonder whether a lecture on the post-war poets was quite their dish of tea. Still, it was too late to do anything about it now. The front row was occupied, reading from left to right, by two ladies with ear-trumpets huge as cornucopias; a small boy sucking a lollipop and looking mutinous, as well he might be, Nigel considered, after being dragged to a party like this; a bucolic woman—his mother, presumably, who looked as if she would be more at home with fatstock prices than with sprung rhythm; an old gentleman with hand already cupped expectantly to ear; two nuns; three empty chairs; a beaming curate.

"Do—er—all these people belong to the Literary Society?" he asked Miss Mellors timidly.

"Oh, no. We threw the meeting open to the public. Coffee and sandwiches are being provided afterwards."

"Oh," thought Nigel, "so that accounts for it. She might have put it a little more tactfully, though. Bread and circuses, with me figuring as the circus, I suppose."

"Only respectable people are admitted, of course," said Miss Mellors.

"Of course."

As Miss Mellors rose to introduce him—in words that were neither few nor remarkably well-chosen, Nigel resumed his study of the audience. His eye

14

was attracted by a gentleman in the third row who was regarding him coldly through a pair of pince-nez: Nigel took an instant dislike to him; his roundish face and small, petulant mouth contrasted disagreeably with something mean, ascetic and arrogant in the eyes. Without removing his gaze from Nigel, the man made a remark to a faded, pathetic-looking little woman by his side, twisting his mouth towards her contemptuously. She looked up at him as she answered, the white of her eyes showing in an expression horribly fawning and docile—as though she were his dog. Some distance behind, Nigel caught sight of his host and hostess, Herbert unsmiling, self-contained as ever, his wife grinning mischievously at Nigel. Away to the right sat a young man in a stained tweed coat, a khaki shirt, and side-whiskers, manifestly trying to dissociate himself from the whole proceedings. The contemptuous pout of his lips reminded Nigel vaguely of somebody—who could it be, now? Beside him sat another young man, who appeared to be already asleep: "the local press, no doubt," said Nigel to himself. Miss Mellors was whipping herself up to her peroration, speaking in an affected mimsy sort of voice that she reserved presumably for cultural pronouncements: Nigel preferred her normal, unmitigated boom.

". . . and I am sure we all feel privileged to have such a distinguished author with us to-night. Mr. Strangeways' fame in another field is well known to us. No doubt, as an eminent detective, he will be able to give us some clues as to this modern poetry, and I feel sure that most of us need them. Ha! ha!" ("Hear, hear!" unexpectedly roared the old gentleman with his hand cupped to his ear.) "Well, you have not come here to listen to me, so without more ado I will call upon Mr. Nigel Strangeways to give us his delightful lecture. Mr. Strangeways."

Nigel rose and gave them his delightful lecture. . . .

When it was over, and the coffee and sandwich binge had ended, Miss Mellors called for questions.

A gentleman with a white moustache and mottled complexion instantly rose and launched into a philippic against the alleged bolshevist tendencies of the younger poets. His speech ended on a note of interrogation; but as it had contained only rhetorical questions, Nigel had to content himself with replying that there was no doubt a great deal in what the last speaker had said.

A rather pretty young woman got up, blushing, and said that there seemed to her to be no music in modern poetry.

Nigel quoted a number of passages to refute this heresy.

A considerably less pretty young woman, with protruding teeth and a theosophical glint in her eye, asked:

"What about the music of the spheres?"

This was the first question—in the strictly grammatical sense—that Nigel had received: but, as he did not know the answer, he had to remain silent. At this impasse, the young man in the khaki shirt brought relief.

"What is your opinion of surrealism?" he asked truculently.

Nigel translated his opinion of surrealism into comparatively uncensorable language. The young man then showed signs of making a fighting speech, but was quelled simultaneously by a nasty look from Miss

Mellors and by the uprising of the gentleman to whom Nigel had taken an instant dislike.

"Mr. Bunnett," said Miss Mellors.

"So *that* is Mr. Bunnett," thought Nigel: "I might have guessed."

All heads turned as the local brewer adjusted his pince-nez and gave a dry cough.

"I don't think," he said in a dry, crackling voice, "that we can profitably concern ourselves with surrealism. We may not be experts on artistic questions"—his little mouth twisted sideways towards the last speaker—"but at least we can recognise stark lunacy when we see it."

"Hear, hear!" exclaimed the mottled gentleman.

Mr. Bunnett removed his pince-nez and pointed them at Nigel.

"Now, sir. You were saying, I think, that modern poets feel themselves bound to the truth, to the exploration of reality, however ugly or painful it—and often, I fear, the poetical results too—may be. Now this is my point. You may think me an old fogey, but I read my Tennyson, my Browning, my—er—Shakespeare, and I don't want reality in my poetry. There is quite enough of it in ordinary life. If I want reality, I look at the butcher's book."

Mr. Bunnett paused meaningly. The faded woman beside him tittered, a signal for polite laughter from the rest of the audience.

"No, sir," proceeded Mr. Bunnett, his voice throbbing, rather as though he had pulled out a vox humana stop; "what I ask the poet for is Beauty: I ask him to make me forget the ugliness and difficulties of this world, to lead me into a fairy garden."

"I am sure, sir," rejoined Nigel in his politest and most non-commital voice, "that no modern poet

*17*

would wish to lead you up the fairy garden path."

There was an instant of anxious silence, as the audience sought to assess the exact significance of this remark. Then a colder silence set in like the Arctic night, broken only by a sound—which might have been a snore or a snort—from the local press.

"It evidently doesn't do to sauce your Mr. Bunnett in this town," said Nigel as he walked back with Mrs. Cammison to her house.

"No," she replied evenly: "he is highly respected, as they say." Suddenly she began to chuckle, and waggling an imaginary pair of pince-nez at Nigel, rasped in the most exact imitation of Mr. Bunnett's tones:

"I ask the poet to lead me into a fairy garden." Her voice changed. She was saying, half to herself, "A fairy garden. Yes. Perhaps it's not so incongruous. The fairies were malevolent spirits, weren't they?"

Nigel hesitated, decided against the question he would have liked to ask, and said lightly:

"You're a remarkably good mimic."

"Yes, so they tell me. You ought to see this street in moonlight: there are lovely shadows. The full moon is just over, though."

What a queer mixture of straightforward and mysterious this woman was! Her talk of moonlight and shadows for some reason put Brahms' "Sapphic Ode" into Nigel's head. He began to hum it gently. He was still humming it when they stopped at the front door and Sophie Cammison put her hand on his arm and said:

"Nigel. Don't sauce Mr. Bunnett any more, will you?"

He had never heard her voice sound more neutral

and equable. Nor was there anything in her words to explain the little shiver that ran up his back, as though the spirit of fear itself had laid one icy and deliberate finger upon him.

Five minutes later Mrs. Cammison's comfortable, untidy drawing-room was filled with people. Miss Mellors occupied the greater part of one sofa. Nigel was introduced to Eustace Bunnett and the pathetic-looking woman, his wife; then to the young man in the khaki shirt, Gabriel Sorn; then to several others, whose names he did not catch. Herbert Cammison was attending to the drinks, pouring them out with noticeable dexterity and holding the glasses up to the light as if they were test-tubes. He turned to Miss Mellors, his dark face quite expressionless.

"Whisky, sherry, a cocktail or tomato-juice, Miss Mellors?"

"You naughty man!" she laughed roguishly; "are you trying to make me break the pledge?"

The doctor was evidently a favourite.

"Mrs. Bunnett?"

She started a little, and said breathlessly:

"Oh, me? Sherry. Just a little sherry, please," then looked round apologetically at her husband.

"Are you sure you wouldn't rather have some ice-water, Emily?" asked Eustace Bunnett in his precise, crackling voice, jingling a bunch of keys in his pocket. There was a moment's embarrassing pause. Then, simultaneously, Dr. Cammison said dourly:

"There is no ice-water," and Emily Bunnett, catching Nigel's eye, flushed painfully and said:

"No, dear, I think I will have some sherry."

Nigel observed a faint contraction of Bunnett's cheek muscles. He wondered how long ago was the last occasion on which Mrs. Bunnett had asserted herself: no doubt she would be made to pay for it later: Nigel found himself disliking the brewer more and more.

For a while the conversation was general. Then Gabriel Sorn came up to Nigel and began talking about surrealism. He talked well. Soon the others were listening. When Sorn realised this, his enthusiastic, rather naïve manner changed. His mouth twisted into a theatrically cynical expression, and he said, "Of course, the advantage of the method is that you are not responsible—not consciously—for anything you create, and therefore you're not open to criticism."

"Aren't you betraying your beliefs now?" asked Nigel gently. The young man gave him a startled, almost respectful glance; then took a gulp at his whisky—he had been drinking pretty heavily—and exclaimed:

"It's not the first time. I spend my life betraying them. Didn't you know that I am the brewery bard?"

Eustace Bunnett took off his pince-nez and opened his mouth, but Sorn forestalled him.

"Oh, yes," he went on wildly, "you must have seen some of my—occasional verses, shall we call them?

> 'North, south, east and west,
> Bunnett's beers are still the best.'"

Eustace Bunnett cut in, his voice suave as ice:

"Mr. Sorn does some of our publicity work, Mr. Strangeways, amongst his—er—other duties."

"Well," said Nigel, "it certainly gives you a public. I'm all for poetry being popular. Get the ordinary man used to the idea of verse—on hoardings, the

20

films, anywhere—and there'll be more chance of his wanting to read serious work."

"I don't agree," said Sorn: "poetry can never be a popular medium again. It will have to appeal to a small circle of highly-trained, sensitive persons. I——"

"Now, Gabriel," Mr. Bunnett interrupted, "we can't have you monopolising our distinguished guest. Run along and talk to Mrs. Cammison."

Sorn's fists clenched. Nigel was terrified for a moment that there might be a scene. Then the young man's shoulders drooped; he kicked the fender childishly and moved away. Mr. Bunnett clearly disapproved of his employees muscling in on the limelight. He now straddled his short legs in front of the fireplace, made a movement with his hands as though straightening an invisible piece of blotting-paper on an imaginary table before him, and said:

"I have a little problem for you, Mr. Strangeways— in your detective rather than your literary capacity."

Nigel received the impression that everyone in the room had been frozen into immobility, in the middle of a word or a gesture: it reminded him of the children's game called "Grandmother's Steps." Mr. Bunnett had his audience where he wanted them.

"Yes," he proceeded, "I am sure it would interest you. A fortnight ago, on the second of this month, to be precise—my fox-terrier, Truffles, disappeared. He was found later when my men were cleaning out one of the open coppers. The flesh, of course, had been all absorbed, but we identified him by the metal tag on his collar."

Eustace Bunnett paused impressively.

"But where do I come in?" asked Nigel.

"I understand that you are interested in crime," said the brewer in a measured, perfectly serious voice: "there is not the least doubt in my mind that THE DOG WAS MURDERED."

The guests, who had been fidgeting a little, were now frozen again. Nigel noticed Dr. Cammison standing rigid with a bottle poised above a glass.

"But," Nigel stammered at last, "but isn't it much more likely that the dog fell into the open copper by accident, chasing a rat or something."

Mr. Bunnett raised a censorious hand.

"If you will allow me to tell you the facts. Truffles accompanied me to the brewery every morning. There was a basket for him in my room, and he was attached to the leg of the chair by a strong steel chain. I had occasion to go out for a few minutes that morning. When I returned, I found that the brute was gone. He had not slipped his collar. Someone had unfastened the catch of the lead."

"Well, granted that was so, you surely don't suspect one of your employees of deliberately stealing the dog and throwing him into the open copper. No doubt someone unleashed him for a joke and he wandered out and met his death accidentally."

"The sides of the open copper in which he was found, Mr. Strangeways, are six foot high, and Truffles was old and very far from active. (No wonder, thought Nigel, after a lifetime on the lead.) I questioned my employees, but could not pin the guilt on anyone."

Eustace Bunnett's voice hushed. His lips scarcely moved as he added:

"I am exceedingly anxious to find out who did it."

Nigel was genuinely appalled by his tones. As

though seeking to give the brewer an opportunity for justifying them, he said:

"You were very fond of Truffles?"

"The animal was my property, Mr. Strangeways."

A short silence while the company digested this.

"It seems to me a lot of fuss to make about a dog," said Miss Mellors unexpectedly. "Why didn't you call in the police while you were about it?"

"I did," replied Mr. Bunnett frigidly. "They declared themselves unable to take any action. That is why I am asking Mr. Strangeways."

Nigel surreptitiously pinched himself. Yes, he was awake, incredible as it might seem.

"You wish me to conduct an inquiry?" he said. "But the whole thing is"—he was on the point of saying "utterly farcical," but remembered Sophie's request that he should not sauce Mr. Bunnett again, and amended it to "most irregular."

Mr. Bunnett smiled at him. At least, a sort of twinkle appeared in his eyes, though his mouth remained singularly mirthless.

"I did not imagine a little 'irregularity,' as you put it, would be any great obstacle to one who declares himself an admirer of modern poetic metres. I am prepared to give you full facilities for questioning my staff, and a free run of the premises, of course. My little problem should help to keep your hand in till your next big murder case turns up."

Mr Bunnett's request was so bizarre that Nigel felt strongly tempted to take it up. But no, it was all too sickening—this dried-up, vindictive creature with his lust for domination.

"I'm afraid, sir, I really can't——"

"Oh, for God's sake do. None of us will get a moment's peace till the thing is cleared up." It was

Gabriel Sorn who had interrupted. Nigel heard a heartfelt appeal beneath his repressed, edgy tones.

"Very well, then," he said, "I'll take it on. But I assure you, Mr. Bunnett, that I am still convinced it was an accident."

"I shall be happy if you succeed in convincing me," replied the brewer. "Now, let me see, I shall not be at the brewery to-morrow morning. If you will come along about tea-time, I will meet you and arrange for you to be shown over the place. I don't know whether you accept fees for this sort of thing: I dare say not, but——"

"Twenty-five guineas retaining fee, and a refresher of five guineas a day is my minimum charge."

Mr. Bunnett stared at Nigel incredulously, but Nigel's face was perfectly serious and businesslike.

"Really, Mr. Strangeways, that is a bit—I mean, I had thought of a little honorarium, say——"

"I cannot consider anything less, Mr. Bunnett."

"Oh—er, very well then."

It was the first time Nigel had seen Eustace Bunnett look disconcerted.

# II
## July 17, 8 a.m.–5.15 p.m.

*As he brews, so shall he drink.*
BEN JOHNSON

NIGEL awoke to the remorseless chattering of a multitude of sparrows, and the long-drawn notes of the priory clock booming eight. He went to the window and looked out. The roofs of the town stretched downwards away from him, grey-tiled, mossy, sharply-pitched; there was a curious attractiveness in their irrelevant angles, that seemed like a choppy grey-green sea frozen into immobility: their architects, no doubt, had never heard of town planning, but the relationship of house to house was fixed by a sure instinct. Brilliant sunshine blessed the town, while the wooded hills beyond were veiled in mist that promised a scorching noonday. Nigel wondered idly where the brewery was. That brick chimney over there might be it. It was difficult in this fresh sunlight to take seriously either Mr. Bunnett or the fantastic problem that he had proposed. Last night Nigel had gone to bed convinced that the brewer was one of the nastiest characters and quite the most dangerous that he had ever met. Now, he attributed this rather hysterical judgment to the unsettling influence of the Maiden Astbury Literary Society. He was thinking up some well-chosen phrases in which to describe this body to Georgia as he came down to breakfast.

"I hope you are quite recovered," said Mrs. Cammison.

"Recovered? Oh, yes, thank you. The ordeal was not so bad as I expected. But, look here, is it all right—my staying on a few days more? I could easily——"

"Stay as long as you like," said Herbert Cammison.

"But are you seriously going to take on this ridiculous business about Truffles?"

"Well, I seem to have let myself in for it. I must have been drunk last night. Still, I've always wanted to see over a brewery. 'Simple pleasures,' as Oscar Wilde said, 'are the last refuge of the complex'— and what simpler pleasures could there be than seeing your Mr. Bunnett's face when I told him my fee?"

"Yes, he doesn't like paying out money. Half the equipment in the brewery is obsolete, but Mr. Bunnett is too old-fashioned and too much of a skinflint to have it replaced. But look here, young Nigel, what do you propose to do if you do find out that someone was responsible for bumping off Truffles?"

"Well, tell Bunnett, I suppose—I mean, it is rather a bad show chucking a harmless beast into an open copper just because you dislike its owner."

"Wait a minute. You may or may not realise it now, but Bunnett is a thoroughly vindictive man. No one so close with money would consent to pay the exorbitant fee you demanded—just in order to prove a wild suspicion—if he was quite sane. I am telling you, in all seriousness, that Bunnett is not

26

altogether sane. Like other unloved persons who happen to possess almost unlimited power, he has a marked persecution mania. His belief that someone 'murdered' his dog is a symptom of that mania. At the same time, he knows he is making a fool of himself—so his motive for finding a victim is even stronger."

"Yes, I see all that: so what?"

"Do you know what Bunnett will do to anyone you may succeed in pinning the guilt upon?"

"Sack him, I suppose."

"That will merely be the preliminary," said the doctor grimly. "He will do his level best to hound the chap out of existence. He will make it impossible for him to get another job, in the first place. And if you think he will let the chap live comfortably on the dole, you're very much mistaken."

"Damn it," Nigel protested, "I can't really swallow that. It's too melodramatic even for my sensation-loving mind."

For the first time he saw an expression of impatience on Cammison's face.

"You know as well as I do that people with a lust for power plus a persecution mania live in a world of melodrama. I could tell you things about Bunnett——"

"No horrors at breakfast, please," interrupted Sophie in that deceptively neutral voice of hers. It was enough to take the tenseness out of the atmosphere, though. Herbert's face was impassive again and he spoke more lightly.

"Well, promise me anyway that—if you do find out a culprit—you won't do anything about it till you've had a talk with me."

"O.K. That's fair enough. I could always hand back Eustace his cheque, if you convinced me that I ought to hold my tongue."

"I'd convince you all right, young Nigel."

Herbert seemed about to amplify this; but a glance from his wife, which Nigel intercepted, silenced him. Gazing noncommittally down his nose, as was his habit when reflecting on the behaviour of present company, Nigel sought to interpret that glance; there was entreaty in it—and something very like panic, too. Oh, well, let it go. But Nigel's memory was far too retentive to let anything go for good.

He began asking Herbert about his work in Maiden Astbury. Though a specialist in surgery, Cammison had preferred to take up a general practice. His contempt for the Harley Street type was blistering—"all spit, polish and pompousness," he called them; "all you need to get on there is a good tailor, a posh-looking butler, and nerve enough to make people pay a hundred guineas for advice that any G.P. could give them for two. Racketeers in tail-coats! The only thing to be said for them is that it is the rich they rob."

When Cammison spoke about his own work, which he did without hesitation, complacence or false modesty, his swarthy, impassive face lit up with an expression almost of fanaticism. His eyes seemed to be looking right through Nigel into some vision of the future as he inveighed against social conditions—the under-nutrition of children throughout the industrial areas where he had first worked, the cynical way in which some employers of labour attempted to evade health regulations—"and you needn't go to the industrial areas to find that sort of thing. Why, in this very town"—Cammison broke off abruptly:

then said, "For the price of a few battleships, we could give you a healthy nation. We have the knowledge, the skill, the material resources; but those in power prefer to use them for destroying their competitors and safe-guarding their own profits."

After breakfast Dr. Cammison went off on his rounds and Nigel strolled about the town. Returning at midday, he found his hostess sitting in the little garden at the back of the house: Nigel fetched a deck-chair and sat down beside her.

"Your husband is a remarkable man. He must do a lot of good here."

"Yes, I think he does. He finds himself up against things, though."

Nigel waited for her to amplify this, but she said no more.

He studied her handsome, ingenuous face; the horn-rimmed spectacles that somehow made her look as though she were playing a part in an extempore charade; the large, capable hands knitting away at a child's jersey. A baffling creature—it seemed as if nothing could possibly ruffle that humorous maternal composure. Nigel leant back and said quietly:

"Why are you afraid of Mr. Bunnett?"

The large, capable hands paused for a moment, then resumed their knitting. Without turning her head, she replied:

"That would be a long story."

Nigel was reminded of what he had said at tea yesterday—"It is a long and rather discreditable story." He asked lightly:

"Not too discreditable, I hope?"

"Some people would think it so," Sophie Cammison replied with disarming frankness. She looked straight at him as she added, "You wouldn't."

Nigel felt at the same time rebuked and gratified.

"You must forgive me," he said. "I am incurably inquisitive about other people's affairs."

A little summer breeze fluttered the rambler-roses and swept the lawn with the shadows of overhanging leaves.

Nigel said, "Excuse this harping on old Bunnett, but I can't imagine him as the owner of a brewery. However does he manage to keep his employees, for one thing?"

"Oh, that's Joe."

"Joe?"

"His younger brother. He's the staff-manager. They'd all do anything for him. He really acts as a sort of buffer between the staff and Eustace. He's always trying to get Eustace to modernise the plant, and so on, but Eustace is terribly conservative."

"I should say that Eustace would turn down any suggestion merely because it came from someone else."

"Yes, I expect that's true."

Nigel was conscious again of that guarded note in her voice.

"I should like to meet Joe."

"He's just gone off on holiday. He keeps a cabin-cruiser down at Poolhampton. He was going round the Lizard, up the Welsh coast this time, I believe. It's the sort of thing I'd love to do."

"A motor-cruiser?"

"Oh, no. Joe despises them. He hasn't even got an auxiliary engine. He says no sailor worth his salt needs an engine. We've often told him it was rather dangerous—without one, I mean."

"Sounds as if he ought to have been a sailor."

"He would have liked to. But I believe his brother

made him come into the brewery when he was quite young."

"So Eustace has Joe under his thumb, too?"

Mrs. Cammison considered this.

"Yes," she said, "I'm afraid he has, a bit. Joe is the hail-fellow-well-met sort—frightfully popular with everyone, and quite brave physically. But I expect he's a bit of a moral weakling. We're very fond of him."

A very revealing little statement, in more ways than one, thought Nigel. He found himself liking Sophie Cammison more and more.

At 4 p.m. Nigel was walking with his ostrich stride and preoccupied air through the main gates of the brewery. To his left was a great brick-face, oozing steam here and there, with a few windows set irregularly, high up, their panes not all intact. The familiar smell of malt permeated the air. Farther on there was a raised platform, and backed against it a lorry into which men were rolling barrels. Climbing on to this platform, beyond which was an office with ALL INQUIRIES HERE placarded on it, Nigel could see to his right a long tunnel: barrels were proceeding towards him along this tunnel, moving with the portly, dignified gait of a civic procession. Nigel repressed a strong impulse to take off his hat to them. Lost in admiration, he did not at first hear the shout from the foreman.

"Stand away, sir!"

Nigel looked up to where the man was pointing, and leapt convulsively aside. A huge crate was descending rapidly towards the spot where he had been standing, twirling round at the end of a chain. The foreman winked.

"Unhealthy spot, this, sir. Tackle broke the other day."

"And was anyone underneath?"

"Not half there wasn't. Old George got knocked out. Bust his shoulder, it did, and bleedin' lucky it wurn't his head."

"Well, I suppose you've got a new tackle now, after that."

"Not we. Patched up the old 'un, that's all. When Mr. Joe comes back, though——"

At that moment the foreman's attention was distracted, and, after a last glance at the barrels gliding on the conveyor, Nigel went into the office.

"Mr. Bunnett?" said the clerk. "I don't think he's on the premises now. I will just inquire."

"He said he would arrange for me to be shown round this afternoon. Perhaps Mr. Sorn will know about it."

The clerk took up a house-telephone and indulged in some spirited back-chat with a disembodied squeak at the other end of the wire.

"He's not in, sir. Mr. Sorn is coming round to attend to you."

The clerk showed no marked inclination to resume work, and regaled Nigel with hot tips, dead certs, and intimate news from the stable. Shortly Gabriel Sorn appeared, looking unexpectedly efficient in a white sort of umpire's coat. He led Nigel through a variety of passages and swing-doors, the last of these opening into the most hellish din Nigel had ever heard.

"The bottling-room," Sorn shouted in his ear.

Bottles on all sides. Marching sedately along conveyors, turning corners, jerking under the filling and corking apparatus, lying meekly down to have labels stamped on them, the bottles looked at least as human as the slatternly girls who, with sullen, mechanical movements, helped their progress and fed the machine. For a moment Nigel thought of these marching armies of bottles as glass gods, and the girls as devotees performing an endless and uncouth ritual for their worship. Then, half-deafened by the roaring machinery and the rattle-clash of glass, he allowed himself to be led away.

He followed his guide up a steep ladder into a sort of signal-box, ten feet above the floor of the building. There he was introduced to a tall, lean, despondent-looking man, with the biggest and blackest eyebrows that Nigel had ever seen.

"Mr. Barnes, our head brewer."

"Pleased to meet you, sir."

"Well, we might as well have some tea before I conduct you through the inferno," said Sorn.

He handed Nigel a cup of tea and a plate of dry biscuits. Mr. Barnes scratched his chin, poured out a glass of beer, scrutinised it with sombre curiosity, as though he had never seen the stuff before, and sipped at it delicately.

"M'm. Turned out nice, this brew," he said dreamily: then suddenly tipped the rest down his throat.

"How you can drink that stuff at four o'clock in the afternoon beats me," said Sorn.

"Never could fancy tea. Poison, that's what it is. Turns your insides to leather. A tannin process, as you might say."

"Joke," said Sorn.

Nigel looked out of the plate-glass window of the signal-box. Two men were sitting on a barrel down below, chatting in a desultory way. Nigel remembered the chattiness of the foreman and the clerk.

"Is this a slack time or something?" he said. "Some of your chaps don't seem to be bursting themselves with effort."

Mr. Barnes laid a finger to the side of his nose.

"When the cat's away——"

"Old Bunface hasn't turned up to-day," amplified Sorn. "You'd see them jumping to it all right if he was snooping about."

Nigel noticed that Sorn was quite a different person inside the brewery. Last night he had been prickly, argumentative, very much on his poetic dignity, self-conscious: here he seemed more at home, more sure of himself, easier to get on with, but possibly less interesting. Clearly he kept the surrealist poet and the brewer's pupil in two separate compartments, and the latter was much more interested in his work than the former would have cared to admit.

"I expected that Bunnett would be here to give me the dope on the Truffles case," said Nigel.

"Oh, he'll probably turn up soon," said Sorn unconcernedly.

"Hasn't been around at all to-day, has he?" said Mr. Barnes.

"No. What of it? Do you *like* him hanging about? Count your blessings, Mr. Head Brewer."

Gabriel's voice sounded unnecessarily irritable.

"That's right," said Mr. Barnes uncomfortably—torn, no doubt, between loyalty to his employer and his own feelings of relief.

"Hanging about is one of old Bunface's most repulsive characteristics," Sorn went on. "He has to be standing over his workmen all the time. He'd wear carpet slippers, only there's such a racket in here he doesn't need them."

"Steady on, Mr. Sorn! You shouldn't say that," remonstrated the head brewer, his black eyebrows rising half-way up to his forehead and giving him a fleeting resemblance to George Robey. Sorn's lower lip jutted out pugnaciously. Nigel was worried again by the young man's likeness to—who could it be, now?

"Well, what about Ed Parsons?" Sorn demanded truculently.

"Oh, well," said Mr. Barnes, "he was feeling poorly that day, see. That's what it was—he was ailing."

"Bunk!" Sorn turned to Nigel. "Ed Parsons is the chap in charge of the lorry-loading. Well, one day he was out there and Bunnett came along and stood behind him. Ed knew he was there, but he wasn't going to look round. Bunnett just stood there, staring at Ed with those beady little reptile eyes of his, saying nothing. Ed couldn't stand it after a bit—he was sick on the spot, vomited, threw up—that's Mr. Eustace Bunnett for you." Sorn's voice had become almost shrill.

"There ain't no sense raking up past history, Mr. Sorn," said the head brewer: "let sleeping dogs lie, that's what I say. Anyways, we'll maybe not be having the governor here much longer."

"What's that? What the devil do you mean?" exclaimed Sorn sharply.

"Rumours has come to my ears," replied Mr. Barnes darkly. "I will not specify my informant, but rumours has come to my ears that there may be an amalgamation. A big Midland firm, whose name I will not mention, is desirous of buying out Mr. Bunnett."

"You don't say?" Gabriel Sorn's voice was insouciant, but Nigel noticed a sort of twinge pass over his face; the young man swallowed hard, before he said:

"Well, Strangeways, if you're ready, we'll have a look round."

Nigel was supplied with one of the long white coats, since a tour of the brewery was apt to leave its mark on one's clothes.

They left Mr. Barnes meditatively pouring out another glass of beer, and climbed down from his eyrie. Along a passage, up another ladder, and they were standing on a platform beside two vessels. One was like an enormous washtub, the other was a copper sphere resembling nothing so much as the body of a stratosphere balloon. Sorn pointed to the latter. "The pressure-copper," he said; "the malt extract and the hops are boiled up together in it. We're extra busy just now. Three separate boilings to-day— the process takes almost two and a half hours. This copper's only been put in lately—the pride of the brewery. Joe had the hell of a fight with Eustace to get it installed."

He turned to the enormous washtub. "This is the old open copper. Much more wastage here—evaporation. This is the one Truffles got slung into."

So Nigel was now on the scene of the crime. He could only just see into the open copper by standing on his toes. It certainly didn't look as if an elderly dog of sedentary habits could have jumped in.

"They'll be drawing off soon. At five o'clock they clean the pressure copper."

Nigel wondered how anyone could get into that copper orb; then he noticed a manhole high up in the side of it.

Gabriel Sorn led him right through the different processes, talking technicalities which Nigel made little attempt to take in. Not being of a mechanical mind, he was less impressed by scientific marvels than by odd, irrelevant details, such as the great, woolly dollops of foam scattered over the floor in one place, the pungent smells he encountered—steam, hops, yeast, malt, and heaven knew what besides, the eerie atmosphere of the whitewashed vaults below the brewery, with hundreds of barrels lying side by side on the sandy floor, one or two occasionally fizzing quietly to each other. In an alcove here there was a rusty iron gate.

"That's the well, through that gate. It was sunk soon after they built the brewery. The town water supply didn't make good beer. The chemical quality of the water makes an enormous difference."

Sorn dropped a stone in. One—two—three—plop. Nigel counted. A good place to get rid of a person, he thought. The same thing, though, occurred to him several times during their tour. In fact the whole brewery seemed a series of temptations to anyone murderously inclined. There were the vats for rejected beer, left unattended for months: a beautiful way of disposing of the body. Or the fermenting vessels. Sorn clambered over the rail of a staircase on to a huge circular wooden platform, and beckoned Nigel to follow him.

"This is one of the fermenting vessels under our feet. If you slide back the lid and peer into it, you will pass out in thirty seconds. It's full of $C.O.^2$."

Nigel intimated that he would take Sorn's word for it.

Pipes, pipes, pipes. The whole brewery seemed as full of complicated intestinal tubes as the human body; writhing sinuously round corners, disappearing into the ceiling, tripping you up—and all, no doubt, gurgling with lovely beer.

"Decent," thought Nigel.

The heat in some of the processes was terrific. After visiting the boiler-room Nigel began to wish that he had some of the lovely beer gurgling inside himself. He wiped the sweat off his forehead.

"Want to cool off?" said Sorn. "Follow me."

They went up and down some more of the ubiquitous ladders, through a room stocked with enormous one and a half hundredweight sacks, till they reached a very solid-looking door. Before opening it, Sorn pressed a switch at the side.

"The emergency bell," he explained. "A chap locked himself in here one evening by mistake. He just managed to keep alive by running up and down. After that, Bunnett *had* to get a safety-device installed."

When the solid door swung aside, Nigel soon understood why. They were in the cold-storage room. The cold did not strike you in the face as you entered, for there was no draught; but after a few moments, you began to feel it insidiously creeping into your bones. Glittering with frost, the cold-storage tanks stood white and monstrous. Sorn had shut the door behind them, and the silence, after the confused roaring of machinery with which Nigel was still dazed, was like the frozen silence of the Ice Cap. Nigel found himself talking in a whisper. Sorn was explaining the method of regulating the temperature, and Nigel—who felt he could not really compete with any more scientific data—was running his finger idly up and down a frosted groove in the tank nearest the door, when it encountered a small, solid object at the base of this groove. There was a little pocket of deep frost there, Nigel's eye registered, and the object lay on top of it—its surface was a little frosted, but it was not buried. Almost unconsciously he took up this object, and presently dropped it into his pocket, where it was destined to lie forgotten for several days—and thus to add materially to the difficulties of the grotesque problem that even now awaited Nigel outside the cold-storage-room door.

While he had been showing Nigel round, Sorn's manner had been efficient and impersonal; obviously he was accustomed to functioning as a guide—the descriptive phrases came fluently, absent-mindedly almost, off his tongue, like runs from the bat of a Wally Hammond when he has passed his fifty. But Nigel got the impression that, behind this mechanical flow of details, Sorn's mind was engaged upon some quite different matter. Once or twice he seemed to surprise in the young man's eyes a look of—fear, was it? Anguish? Or some more complex battle of emotions? Nigel wondered suddenly whether it was not Sorn who had killed Bunnett's dog. He said:

"Well, I suppose I ought to be doing something to earn my fee."

"What? Oh, Truffles. Yes," said Sorn absently.

"On the other hand, I can't do much till Mr. Bunnett tells me some more of the facts."

"No. I can show you the—er—the scene of the disappearance, if you like," said Sorn, opening the solid door and standing aside to let Nigel pass. "We'll go up to Eustace's room. He may have turned up by now."

But they did not, as it happened, go up to Eustace's room. While Sorn was locking the door behind them, they heard a muffled shouting somewhere away to the right. It made Nigel realise that the roar of machinery had dwindled to a mild hum. He looked automatically at his watch: three minutes past five; work must be nearly over for the day. A wild-eyed man rushed up to Gabriel Sorn, said something breathlessly, of which Nigel could only hear the last two words—"pressure-copper," and hurried away again with Sorn at his heels. Nigel followed. A few seconds later he was climbing again on to the platform where the coppers stood. Mr. Barnes was already there, blasphemously addressing a small knot of men below who had been trying to get up on to the platform. Beside him stood another man, whose dirty blue dungarees accentuated the pallor of his face. The manhole of the pressure copper was open. Mr. Barnes jerked his finger at it. Sorn clambered up and looked in. Nigel could see him stiffen, recoil, and sway as if he was about to faint. They helped him down, and Nigel took his place.

The inside of the copper was dark, but not so dark that Nigel could not see the livid thing that smirked up at him. It was a half-disjointed skeleton: but not, this time, the skeleton of a dog. What was left of the skeleton was wearing the soaked and tattered remnants of a dinner-jacket and boiled shirt.

Nigel dragged his eyes away from the unpleasing spectacle, and jumped back on to the platform. Mr. Barnes and the cleaner were staring at him with the helpless, rather pathetic look of people faced by an emergency outside their normal experience.

"Have you phoned for the police and a doctor?" asked Nigel, realising as soon as he had said it that no one could stand in less need of a doctor than that man of bone inside the copper.

"Yes, sir," said the head brewer, "I just told Percy to——"

"Look here, we must get him out, we can't——"

Sorn was very near to hysterics. Nigel took him by the shoulders and shook him hard.

"Pull yourself together," he ordered.

Sorn passed a hand wearily over his forehead; then stared strangely at Nigel, his body going rigid again. He whispered, with the over-deliberate, unnatural seriousness of a drunken man:

"Do you know who that is in there?"

"No," said Nigel, "but we may be able to find out."

He stood irresolutely for a moment. Then, muttering to himself, "No point waiting for the police," told the cleaner to get an electric torch and search inside the copper for any articles that might be lying about. "Don't disturb the—er—body, but if there's anything in the pockets you can fetch it out. And put on these gloves before you go in, we don't want to multiply the fingerprints on the outside of the copper."

"Fingerprints," said Mr. Barnes dubiously, scratching his chin. "You mean this here is murder, like?"

"No one got through that manhole by accident, and you don't suppose anyone would commit suicide in such a fantastic way, do you?" replied Nigel a little irritably.

"That's right," said Mr. Barnes.

"Shall I send a man to look in the hop-back?" he added.

"The hop-back?" asked Nigel mystified.

"That's right. Where the wort drains into. Any small articles would slip through the outlet pipe when the wort was drained off, see?"

"Right. No, on second thoughts, you'd better not." Nigel realised that any clues which might be found had better be found under his own eye.

A hollow, booming sound proceeded from the copper as the cleaner moved about inside. The watchers heard a stifled gasp. The lethargic Mr. Barnes sprang with unexpected alacrity to the manhole. The cleaner passed up an object to him.

"Look here, Mr. Barnes, this is the governor's watch—fastened in his waistcoat, it was." He spoke in an urgent whisper, but somehow it reached the ears of the men below, and was taken up in hoarse mutterings—

"The guv'nor."

"The guv'nor!"

"It's the guv'nor in there."

"They've found 'is watch."

"Someone chucked the guv'nor into the pressure copper!"

"*Oo* d'yer say chucked 'im in?"

Nigel studied the faces of his companions. The head brewer seemed bemused, his brain trying to catch up with things. Gabriel Sorn looked as if he was working out a calculation on which his life depended.

The cleaner scrambled through the manhole, blinked a little, then drew from his deep overall pockets a fountain-pen, a pair of pince-nez with most of the glass missing, some loose change, and an electric torch. Nigel made him lay them on the floor in a row.

Mr. Barnes reached down his hand towards the pince-nez; then drew it slowly back, as though the pince-nez were a dog of uncertain temper.

"Those are Mr. Bunnett's spectacles, I'd swear to it," he said. "And that's his fountain-pen, too—a Waterman. That proves it."

"I'm afraid it isn't so simply proved as all that," said Nigel. He realised that his companions were badly shocked. Particularly for a nervous type like Sorn, repression would be dangerous. Nigel started talking in a dispassionate lecturer's voice:

"To establish identity, it is necessary——"

But his fidgeting audience did not have to listen long. A tramp of feet was heard. A large, pale-faced police inspector advanced with unhurried stride; beside him was a sergeant; and close behind, to Nigel's surprise, Dr. Cammison. The inspector climbed cumbrously up the ladder, fixing the little group with suspicious, irritable eyes. Nigel suddenly knew that the inspector was going to say, "Now then, what's all this about?" Sure enough, the inspector did. No one else seemed prepared to answer this fairly simple question, so Nigel did.

"A body in the copper."

The inspector glared balefully at Nigel; then, baffled by his serious expression, said:

"A body, eh? Well, we'll come to that." He produced a notebook and asked in louder, bullying tones:

"Who found it?"

The cleaner gulped and replied, "Me, sir."

"Name?"

His name and address were taken, then Sorn's and the head brewer's. The inspector turned, with a look of crafty suspicion, to Nigel.

"And your name, sir?"

"Nigel Strangeways."

"One of the employees here?"

"No, I——"

"Ah, I thought not. And may I ask what is your business here?"

Nettled by the man's pompous, aggressive voice, Nigel replied solemnly:

"Well, I came to see a man about a dog."

As the inspector's jaw dropped and an angry flush appeared in his face, Nigel could not resist adding:

"But it seems that, in the words of the poet, the man it was who died."

# III
## July 17, 5.15–7.50 p.m.

*When shall this slough of sense be cast,*
*This dust of thoughts be laid at last,*
*The man of flesh and soul be slain*
*And the man of bone remain?*

A. E. HOUSMAN

"YOU came to see a man about a dog?" said the inspector when he had recovered his powers of speech. "Do you expect me to take that seriously, or are you being humorous at my expense?"

The pedantry of the phrase made the inspector seem really dangerous for a moment. Nigel was annoyed with himself for falling to the temptation of pulling his leg.

"No, quite serious. I oughtn't perhaps, to have put it like that." Nigel proceeded briefly to explain the commission that Mr. Bunnett had given him.

"Mr. Strangeways is a private inquiry agent. He has assisted the police on several occasions. His uncle is an Assistant Commissioner," explained Dr. Cammison, who had been watching the proceedings with the very faintest occasional twitch of a muscle in his impassive face.

"Very well," said the inspector coldly. "We'd better get to work. My name is Tyler, by the way, and this is Sergeant Tollworthy. Who is the deceased?"

"The body is unidentifiable—at least as far as I can tell," Nigel said. "But certain articles have been found in the copper that Mr. Barnes has identified as belonging to Mr. Eustace Bunnett. There they are."

When the name of Bunnett was mentioned, Sergeant Tollworthy was heard to ejaculate a wish that the Deity should strike him pink, and even the inspector seemed a little shaken. He soon recovered himself, though.

"These articles shouldn't have been touched," he said, looking censoriously at Nigel. "Who removed them?"

"The cleaner," said Nigel quickly. "I take full responsibility for that."

The inspector turned brusquely to the cleaner, and addressed him in the loud, hectoring voice that he apparently reserved for members of the working-class.

"You did, eh? Describe their positions."

The cleaner licked his lips nervously and said:

"Well, sir, they was like this. The watch chain was fastened through 'is waistcoat button-hole; the watch was dangling at the end of it. The money was in his trouser pocket and the electric torch in his coat pocket. Fountain-pen clipped on inside pocket. The spectacles had got caught by that thing that goes round your ear—caught in the side of his head, sir, see?"

"And that's all you found?"

"Yes, sir."

"Quite sure?"

"'Ere, what's the——?"

"Frisk him, Sergeant."

Inspector Tyler was taking no chances. The cleaner had to submit to a thorough examination of his pockets and person.

"Here, you," said the inspector when it was over, "give me that torch. I'll take a look inside now."

The little group of men on the platform stood still and silent as he climbed awkwardly through the manhole. It somehow impressed them that he should climb straight in without even a preliminary glance at the appalling object that sprawled there. They heard his feet shuffling inside. Then silence. He seemed to be in there an interminable time. Sorn was fidgeting with his fingers. At last the inspector's face reappeared at the manhole; he was paler even than usual, and beads of sweat stood out below the peak of his cap. With ponderous, deliberate movements he climbed out; then stood for a moment, brushing at his uniform. At last he turned to the head brewer.

"Hmm. That venthole, outlet pipe, whatever you call it—where does it lead to?"

"Into the hop-back," said Mr. Barnes. "If it's clues you want——"

"Tollworthy, get someone to show you this hop-back and make a thorough search of it. Now then, who's in authority here?"

"I suppose, in a manner of speaking, I am," said Mr. Barnes, "seeing as how the governor's been done in and Mr. Joe's away holidaying."

"Very well, I shall want a private room for the examination of witnesses presently. Will you see about that? I dare say Mr. Bunnett's would do."

"Oh, the governor would never allow that," exclaimed Mr. Barnes, in shocked tones. The influence of Eustace Bunnett died hard. The inspector disregarded his protest.

"If you want to make a preliminary examination, doctor, you'd better do it now. I don't imagine it'll be of much use, though. There's not much left to examine," he added grimly. "Don't move it, please, sir. Our photographer'll be here in a minute."

Dr. Cammison hesitated for a moment, as though to say something, then disappeared into the copper.

"Now," said Inspector Tyler, "when was Mr. Bunnett last seen?"

"He's not been here to-day," said the head brewer.

"Are you sure of that?"

"Positive certain. The clerk at the inquiry office will tell you he's not been in. We'd've known if he had been about all right, don't you worry."

"Mr. Bunnett was never what you'd call an Unseen Presence," added Gabriel Sorn.

The inspector turned a suspicious glare upon him for a moment. Sorn did not stand up to it too well.

"What time do the employees arrive here in the morning?"

"Five a.m.—the first of them."

"I'll need to see those men. Are they on the premises?"

"No. They'll have hopped it by now."

"Well, send for them, please."

The head brewer descended the ladder, and was heard to tell one of the men below that the Lord God Almighty wanted to see so and so, so and so, and so and so in the brewery, double-quick. To cover up this revelation, which did not seem altogether gratifying to the inspector, Nigel said:

"Mr. Bunnett was at a party at the Cammisons' last night. He left with his wife, between 11.0 and 11.15. That fixes one end of it. He told me then that he was not going to be at the brewery in the morning, but would meet me here at tea-time."

The inspector's small, light-blue eyes gazed speculatively at Nigel.

"Were you not surprised when Mr. Bunnett did not keep his appointment?"

"Only moderately. I thought he would be turning up any moment. Mr. Sorn was kind enough to show me round."

"And Mr. Bunnett left no message for you?"

"Not that I know of."

"Hmm. Very queer." The inspector seemed to radiate an atmosphere of suspicion that permeated, like a damp fog, everything he said and the bones of those who listened to him. Nigel put him down as an ambitious man whose ambitions had not been achieved quickly enough and were going sour on him.

"The first job," the inspector was saying, "is to establish identity and fix the time of death as near as we can."

"And that's not going to be a pushover," said Herbert Cammison dryly, emerging from the copper. "The flesh has all been digested, so we shall have no help in the way of birthmarks. The lower jaw and a number of small bones have become detached—we shall find them all, no doubt, but it will take some time to articulate the skeleton; luckily the clothes have held it together a bit. If there is any congenital deformity of the bones, or a mended fracture—say, I shall find it when I make my thorough examination, and it might give you a pointer. All I can tell you at the moment is that the remains appear to be of similar height and physique as Bunnett, the clothes are his, and the hair resembles his in colour. As you noticed, the body had got caught over the steamcoil inside the copper. The heat of that pipe alone would have been enough to burn away all the flesh that was touching it. Incidentally, it was the body's being caught up on this coil that prevented it sinking to the bottom of the copper when the stuff was drawn out and so blocking the mouth of the outlet pipe. Where are the teeth, by the way?"

"The teeth? Ah, I noticed that," said the inspector slowly.

"Bunnett, I know, had a complete set of artificial teeth—full upper and lower sets. The upper jaw and the detached lower jaw of the skull in there are both toothless. You've got to find those teeth. They would be the best means of identification."

"I shall attend to that, sir," said the inspector, a little testily. "Now what about the time of death?"

"Can't help you. Nor will the post-mortem. The organs are simply not there for us to examine. All I can say is that the body must have been in that copper six hours at the very least to have been reduced to this state."

The inspector turned to Mr. Barnes.

"Do they open that manhole before they let the stuff in—the hops and so on—in the morning?"

"No."

"And what time does the boiling process commence?"

"Eight a.m."

"Which means that—as far as we can tell at present—if the body is Mr. Bunnett's, it was put in there some time between 11.15 last night and eight o'clock this morning."

Conscious of an attentive audience, the inspector was talking himself into a better temper.

"Mr. Barnes, I shall want the name and address of your night-watchman. . . . Thank you. Now, Dr. Cammison, there's nothing more for you to do here at present. I wonder if you would mind ringing up

50

the wid—Mrs. Bunnett. You are the family medical man, so it will come more natural like from you. Don't alarm the good lady. Just ask her when her husband left the house this morning—you can make some excuse for the inquiry—Mr. Strangeways was wondering why he had not kept the appointment—something like that."

"Very well," said Cammison.

"Just a moment, doctor," said Tyler, "before you do. Does there seem to you any likelihood at all that this is a case of suicide or accident? It hardly seems worth asking, but——"

"Accident, out of the question," replied Cammison curtly. "Suicide? It would mean that the unfortunate fellow got inside, bolted the manhole—which can't be done from inside—or if it had been left open someone would have noticed it this morning before the stuff was poured in—and then lain down and waited to be boiled alive. The same applies to his having jumped in some time to-day, after the boiling process had started: the manhole would have been found open and it would have been reported."

"No one reported to that effect, Mr. Barnes?" asked the inspector.

"No. I'll make inquiries to-morrow, if you like, and find out for certain."

"If you please."

"No, you can take it from me, suicide is just possible theoretically, but humanly quite impossible," said Cammison.

"That's as I thought," said Tyler. "And the same goes for the body, eh? Theoretically, I mean, it might be somebody else, but practically it's pretty certainly Mr. Bunnett's?"

"I wouldn't go so far as that," replied Cammison,

relapsing into professional caution. "There's one more thing, by the way. The murderer could not have got the victim through that manhole without first rendering him unconscious. If it was a drug, poison, or anaesthetic, I shan't be able to help you. If it was anything that would affect the bone-structure—a blow on the head, say—my examination might be able to give you a lead."

Herbert Cammison went off to telephone. Shortly after, the photographer and fingerprint man arrived and set to work. Nigel stared at them absent-mindedly, trying to recall something that was at the back of his mind. The copper. Boiling. Ah, yes!——

"Sorn, didn't you say that there were three separate boilings in this copper to-day?"

"Yes."

"Of two and a half hours each?"

"More or less. Yes."

"Look here, Inspector. Cammison said the body couldn't have got into that state unless it had been undergoing the boiling process for six hours at least. That implies it must have been there during all three boiling periods. Therefore it must have been put in before the first one—before eight o'clock this morning—whether it is Bunnett or somebody else."

"Yes, sir. That seems correct enough. I didn't know there were three separate boilings. I thought the copper was working continuously all day."

There were other implications of this point, Nigel felt, but his brain was too tired to unravel them. At this moment Sergeant Tollworthy appeared, flushed, dirty and triumphant. His honest yeoman's head was set squarely on a brick-red neck. He was carrying something carefully in his handkerchief. He opened the handkerchief to reveal the grisliest objects—except for the corpse itself—that had turned up so far in this case. Two dental plates, warped, battered and distorted, with a few of the teeth still in position. In the handkerchief lay also a number of loose teeth, a signet ring and some small bones.

"Recognise this ring?" Tyler jerked his head curtly towards Mr. Barnes.

"That's the governor's all right. His crest, see?"

"Must have slipped off the finger-bone when the flesh was eaten away. Sergeant, let the ambulance men get the body out now. I'll be back at the station in half an hour. . . . Ah, there you are, doctor. What does she say?"

Nigel was conscious of a tensening in the atmosphere. Mr. Barnes' black eyebrows were drawn together. Gabriel Sorn was staring fixedly at the back of his right hand; even the inspector seemed to have shed some of his official skin, and was looking excitedly inquisitive. Herbert Cammison's face was impassive as ever, though; in the same tones that he might have remarked, "See that the patient is kept warm, he has a slight touch of fever, nothing to be alarmed about," he said:

"Mrs. Bunnett tells me she has not seen her husband to-day. He did not appear at breakfast."

"Not at breakfast?" exclaimed the inspector. "D'you mean to say the deceased was missing from his home all day and his wife has taken no steps about it?" He glared ferociously at Cammison, as though the doctor were responsible for Mrs. Bunnett's unnatural behaviour.

"It would seem so," Herbert replied imperturbably. "But you'd better ask her yourself. If you like, we'll step over there now. I'll break the news of this discovery to her, and then—if she is in a fit state to be questioned—you can interrogate her."

The inspector gave a few more instructions, then prepared to depart.

"I must ask you to remain on the spot, Mr. Barnes," he said. "When I have interviewed Mrs. Bunnett, I shall be returning to look over her husband's private office and interview those men. Will you please hold yourself in readiness."-

Mr. Barnes looked more despondent than ever.

"That's all right. I shall have to be getting in touch with the excise authorities. A whole day's brewing wasted—it's enough to break your heart."

Which, thought Nigel as the head brewer walked away, considering the character of Eustace Bunnett, was perhaps the most sensible view of the day's occurrences that could be taken. Nigel himself was torn between disgust and curiosity. Eustace Bunnett was better dead—there could be no doubt about that, and Nigel had no desire to hound down the person who had eliminated him. Yet he felt himself somehow involved. It was not only the business of Truffles. He could not forget the strange reticences of Sophie Cammison, and that even stranger moment when she had laid her hand on his arm and asked him not to "sauce Mr. Bunnett any more"; it had been as though the spirit of Fear itself had laid a finger upon him. What was this fear that Sophie had communicated? But no, he thought, impatiently shaking back the lock of tow-coloured hair that drooped over his forehead; it's all moonshine, hoo-haa. I'll have nothing to do with it.

"Well, I'll be getting along," he said.

"Won't you come over with us?" asked Cammison unexpectedly. The inspector frowned. "Very irregular, sir; I don't know that I could——"

"But look here," Cammison interrupted. "Strange-ways is in on this already. The business of Truffles may be connected with Bunnett's death—or who-ever's death it is that you're investigating."

"Oh, come, sir. That's straining things a bit. There's no call for mystificating this job any further," replied the inspector with irritating superiority.

Cammison said patiently:

"It *may* be coincidence, of course. But it's at least odd that, within a fortnight, first a dog and then its master should be killed in the same way. Isn't it possible that Truffles' death was a *dress-rehearsal for Bunnett's*?"

Even the inspector had to be impressed by this unnerving suggestion—all the more unnerving for being put forward in Cammison's calm, business-like tones.

"Well, sir, there may be something in that," he said. "But I like to do things regular, and——"

"Great Scott, man, this is a murder, not a case of traffic-obstruction. If you want to regularise the position, ring up Sir John Strangeways at the Yard to-night, and he'll give you Nigel's bona-fides."

So in the end Nigel found himself walking out of the brewery with the other two. He noticed that he was the only one not to be consulted; both Tyler and Cammison apparently took it for granted that he was an eager—if amateur—bloodhound straining on the leash. Oh, well, let it go. The Bunnetts' house was only a minute's walk from the brewery, a preten-tious red-brick affair on the outskirts of the town, asserting itself crudely against Maiden Astbury's mel-low, time-honoured dignity; a fitting habitation for its late owner, thought Nigel.

Dr. Cammison left them in the morning-room,

while he went to speak with Mrs. Bunnett. The inspector sat solid and upright, his hands on his knees, looking straight in front of him. Nigel prowled restlessly about, fingering the furniture absent-mindedly. There was a studio portrait on the mantelpiece that attracted his attention; the head and shoulders of a middle-aged man; a roundish face, heavily brilliantined hair parted in the middle, a military moustache that only half-concealed the weakness of the small, too amiable mouth. The eyes held an expression half-apologetic, half-hearty. Nigel felt that this was the sort of man who would retain in civil life a temporary military title—yes, he would enjoy being called "Captain so and so"; he would probably address you as, "Well, chaps, how's things!" order drinks all round, and tell you a not very subtle dirty story. He would, without realising it, fear unpopularity more than anything else, but he would be popular—particularly with his "social inferiors." As to profession—he might be an unsuccessful chicken-farmer or a successful commercial traveller. He would, Nigel fancied, be exceptionally plausible when making excuses.

"Know who this is?" he asked the inspector.

"That's Mr. Joe Bunnett—Mr. Bunnett's brother."

"Good Lord! He's not a bit like Eustace. At least, the whole expression is different. There *is* a resemblance in feature, when you come to look at it."

What struck Nigel as more odd, however, was Sophie's having said that they were very fond of Joe; he really didn't look a bit their sort. Nigel was still pondering this when Dr. Cammison appeared at the door.

"Mrs. Bunnett is ready to talk to you now. I've told her that we are very much afraid her husband

56

has met with his death. It would be desirable to keep off the unpleasant details."

"How is she taking it?" asked the inspector.

"Well, it is naturally a severe shock to her," replied Dr. Cammison. Nigel sensed some reservations behind this noncommittal statement. Even the inspector eyed Cammison curiously, as though expecting him to amplify it. The doctor, however, silently led the way to Mrs. Bunnett's drawing-room. While the inspector was expressing his condolences, Nigel studied Emily Bunnett. Her dazed eyes, feverishly flushed cheeks and trembling hands; the untidy mass of grey hair, a loop of it falling over her ear; the dowdy disarray of her dress, and the quivering at the corners of her long, weak, down-curving mouth—it all reminded Nigel of, what could it be? Something very different from the sorrowing widow. Yes, she was exactly like one of those repressed, lonely, queer old spinsters who suddenly, for no apparent reason, after a blameless lifetime, break out one day and get drunk and screech out blasphemies in the middle of the street and sorely embarrass the policemen who have to remove them. Nigel had seen just such a one, years ago, being dragged off through an applauding crowd in Pimlico.

Inspector Tyler was saying:

"Now, ma'am, you say you have not seen your husband since you both returned here about 11.20 last night. You went straight to bed. Your husband, who occupies a separate room, said he had a little work to do. You went to sleep at once and did not hear him go up to bed. Is that right?"

"Yes, sir."

That "sir," and a touch of commonness in Mrs. Bunnett's accent—quite different from the timid but ladylike tones of last night—startled Nigel. Eustace Bunnett must have married "beneath him"; his death had freed Emily from all his careful "training": now, at last, she could be herself again; this was the real Emily Bunnett.

The inspector, too, had been a little disconcerted by that word "sir." Its effect on him, though, was that unconsciously he reassumed something of the loud aggressive voice in which he had spoken to the cleaner at the brewery.

"You're telling me that, although your husband did not come down to breakfast, although later you found his bed had not been slept in, you took no action whatsoever about it? You did not even ring up the brewery to make inquiries?"

As though the bullying note in his voice reminded her of Eustace, reminded her that she was supposed to be "a lady," Emily Bunnett answered in her old, genteel tones:

"Yes, no, I mean. You see, my husband very much resented interference of any sort. He wouldn't like—wouldn't have liked the idea of my fussing about him. If he'd found out that I'd been making inquiries at the brewery, I mean, he'd have been very angry."

"But surely, when his bed had not been slept in—after all, didn't that strike you as—unusual, shall we say?"

Mrs. Bunnett's fingers twisted about her handkerchief. Her cheeks flushed a deeper red. At last she raised her head and said in a tiny, defiant voice:

"Well, it wasn't unusual. So there. It had happened several times before."

"What the devil——"

Dr. Cammison interrupted the inspector's outburst, saying quietly:

"You mean, your husband used to—go to other women?"

"Yes." Mrs. Bunnett's voice was almost inaudible. "And if he couldn't get them here, he used to go off and stay with women in Paris on his holidays. He never troubled to conceal it from me. He despised me too much to take the trouble——" Her voice broke, and at last she was weeping.

They did not stay much longer. Joe Bunnett's return from his holiday was imperatively necessary, but Emily knew no more of his movements than that he had sailed from Poolhampton and would be cruising around Land's End and up the Welsh Coast. Tyler would have to notify the various possible ports of call, and leave it at that. The Bunnetts' servant deposed that she had heard the master and mistress come in about 11.20 last night, and then had gone to sleep. The inspector inquired the name of Bunnett's dentist, so that the sets of false teeth might be identified. After one or two more questions, they went out. The time for the post-mortem was arranged, and Tyler took a curt leave of the other two.

"Mrs. Bunnett didn't look too broken-hearted. And I don't wonder," said Nigel as they walked up the steep, narrow street. "A deliverance from bondage— that's what it must be for her. When Israel came out of Egypt!"

Herbert Cammison looked at him sharply.

"The first thing she said, when I told her that we feared her husband was dead, was 'Dead? Eustace dead? You're telling me the truth? Is he really dead at last? I can't believe it.' It was the shock, of course; she was not responsible for what she was saying," he added meaningly.

"Of course not," said Nigel without expression.

"It gave me a turn, I can tell you. She looked as if I'd brought her a present. Flushed; her hair tumbling down; pathetic. You noticed her accent, too, I suppose?"

"Yes."

"Funny. I'd never suspected it. Well, that's that. And see here, young Nigel, none of this to Tyler. That man's too ambitious. All he's going to be concerned about is to make an arrest—and as quickly as possible. He'd clap Mrs. Bunnett into jail on the strength of what I've just told you. Tollworthy's a good sort. I've played a lot of cricket with him. But we'll have to watch our step with Tyler, believe me. There's only one word for that man——"

Dr. Cammison stated the word.

"A meiosis, if anything," said Nigel.

# IV
## July 17, 8.55–10.30 p.m.

*One Pinch, a hungry lean-faced villain,*
*A mere anatomy.*
SHAKESPEARE, *Comedy of Errors*

"Do you really like drinking your coffee off the floor?" asked Sophie Cammison. "There is a little table beside you."

Nigel took up his cup from the floor and held it in his lap. He was sitting with his back against one of the arms of his deep arm-chair and his legs over the other. The carpet beside him was littered with cigarette-ash. Sophie glanced at it and sighed, half-vexed, half in resignation. Nigel really was an untidy creature. What was the use of leaving ash-trays about at every possible strategic point of the house, when he just ignored them? It was odd that she should still be able to get fussed about such a ridiculous little thing, after what Herbert had told her while she was dressing for dinner. Eustace Bunnett was dead, and here she was fussing over cigarette-ash. Dust unto dust; ashes unto ashes. She could scarcely believe it yet.

"What are you thinking about?" asked Nigel.

"I was thinking how silly it was of me to mind about your cigarette-ash when—well, when all this has just happened."

"Cigarette-ash? Oh, I say, I really am very sorry. What an awful mess I've made. I am quite bestially untidy."

Nigel's face looked comically concerned, like a small boy's who is about to burst into tears. He writhed out of the chair, nearly upsetting his coffee-cup in the process, took coal-shovel and brush out of the fireplace and began to sweep up the mess. Mrs. Cammison studied him over her knitting. He was entirely absorbed in what he was doing; his clumsy movements both touched and irritated her. How childish men were in their absorption over tri-fling things! It was impossible to imagine that this flushed awkward creature, who was so ineptly wield-ing brush and shovel, had ever followed a murderer through the distorted-mirror-world of his imagina-tion, had written a book on the Caroline poets, had married one of the most remarkable women of her age.

"Why do you do it?" she asked suddenly.

"Do what?" said Nigel, twisting upright on his knees and glancing at her quizzically. "I should have thought this was the least reparation I could make for ruining your nice carpet."

"I don't mean that," said Sophie, a little annoyed by the implication that she was one of those rabidly house-proud women, "I mean, why do you mix your-self up in crime?"

"Sometimes one can't help getting mixed up," he said lightly.

Sophie Cammison's fingers paused a moment in their knitting. When they commenced again, it was unlike their usual mechanical movements, Nigel thought: it was as though she had flashed a message to them—Go on! Knit, I tell you. Knit! You mustn't break down just now! She said:

"But that's only sometimes. Why did you ever take it up?"

"Oh, something to do, I suppose. It seemed to be the only profession for which a classical education fitted one."

"Now you are laughing at me. I'm quite serious."

"So am I. It does. If ever, in your salad days—as one of my comic uncles calls them—you were compelled to do a Latin unseen, you'll know that it presents an accurate parallel with criminal detection. You have a long sentence, full of inversions; just a jumble of words it looks at first. That is what a crime looks like at first sight, too. The subject is a murdered man; the verb is the modus operandi, the way the crime was committed; the object is the motive. Those are the three essentials of every sentence and every crime. First you find the subject, then you look for the verb, and the two of them lead you to the object. But you have not discovered the criminal—the meaning of the whole sentence yet. There are a number of subordinate clauses, which may be clues or red-herrings, and you've got to separate them from each other in your own mind and reconstruct them to fit and to amplify the meaning of the whole. It's an exercise in analysis and synthesis—the very best training for detectives."

"But, really," exclaimed Sophie, rather overwhelmed by all this, "it sounds dreadfully dry and cold-blooded. You're leaving out the human element altogether."

"Oh, no, I'm not," said Nigel dogmatically. "Of course it's only an analogy, and no analogy holds true at every point. But to return to classical education. You learn to write Latin and Greek compositions in the style of certain authors. The first thing you learn is that all the best authors are constantly breaking the rules of the grammar-books; each has his own idiosyncracies; and that is equally true of the criminal—the murderer in particular. To write a good Latin or Greek composition requires more than a superficial gift of mimicry; it requires that you should get right inside the head and the skin of your model. You've got to try and think and feel like Thucydides or Livy or Cicero or Sophocles or Virgil. Similarly, a detective has to get right inside the character of a criminal if he is successfully to reconstruct the crime."

Mrs. Cammison looked at her guest in amazement. Did he really believe all this nonsense, or—no, she realised it now—he was talking away just to keep her mind off things, off that appalling vision of Eustace Bunnett sagging, a mess of bone and hair, inside the copper. Did he know how that vision was haunting her mind? Well, he had enabled her to forget it for a few minutes and she should be grateful for that. But did he also suspect the infinitely more horrible thing, that, as yet, she had not dared even to admit into the daylight of her mind—that she fought to repel, eyes tight closed, refusing so much as a glance at its dreaded features? Suddenly she felt frightened of Nigel. She wished that Herbert was here; but he had been called away to a case in the middle of dinner.

"You do knit a lot, don't you?" said Nigel. "You must have a packet of nephews and nieces."

"Yes," said Sophie. Then, answering the question that she felt (quite mistakenly) must lie behind Nigel's remark—"Herbert and I decided not to have children till—till we were more settled."

"How long have you been married?"

"Nearly three years. We married when Herbert bought his partnership here."

"You would make a very good mother, I should think."

Sophie felt she could not bear this line of conversation any longer. She might burst out weeping any moment. It was to kill this weakness that she said rather strenuously:

"But I don't see why you want to hunt criminals. I'm sure you can't enjoy it. You don't have to for a living. Do you believe in Justice or something?"

Nigel was gazing non-committally down his nose. "Hallo, what's this?" he said to himself. "What is making her attack me like this? What is she trying to hide from me—or from herself?" He said to Mrs. Cammison:

"I don't believe in justice in the abstract. Some crimes are 'just' and some actions are criminal. I suppose I do it because criminal investigation gives one an unique opportunity of studying people in the nude, so to speak. People involved in a case— particularly murder—are always on the alert, on the defensive, and it's when they're trying to cover up one part of their mind that they expose the rest. Even quite normal people start behaving in the most abnormal way."

"You sound quite inhuman," Sophie said in a trembling voice.

"No. There's nothing inhuman about curiosity. And mine is only trained, scientific curiosity. I'm sorry, though; I'm upsetting you, talking like this. I'm not a monster, really. To tell you the truth, I've pretty well made up my mind not to touch this Bunnett affair. Whoever did him in had every excuse, I should think."

"You're probably right there," said a deep voice from behind Nigel, "but I shouldn't talk too soon about giving the case up."

Dr. Cammison had entered, unnoticed by the other two. His square-jawed face, with its black jowl, swarthy complexion and deep brown eyes—together with his silent, unobtrusive, beautifully controlled movements as he closed the door and came up to them—made Nigel think of a black panther. His eyes regarded Nigel, bright and unwinking.

"Well," said Nigel, "how you do chop and change. Only this morning you were telling me to lay off the Truffles case. And now——! Ah, well; as old Tacitus said, *Supervacuus inter sanos medicus* or—we may roughly translate it—'When the doctor is amongst sane people, he appears even more vacuous than usual.'"

" 'Rough' is scarcely the word for that translation," said Dr. Cammison, his white teeth flashing in one of his sudden, rare grins.

"But Truffles dead is one thing and Bunnett dead is another."

"Adequately, if somewhat sententiously expressed."

"You see, a considerable number of people would have liked to see Eustace Bunnett liquidated—I apologise for the unfortunate accuracy of the term."

"So what?"

"So——"

"*Herbert!*"

The anguish of Sophie Cammison's voice struck Nigel like something solid hurled at him. He found himself for a moment quite breathless. Even Herbert's composure was ruffled. He looked doubtfully at his wife.

"It's all very well, my dear," he said slowly, "but——"

"Look here, you two," said Nigel, recovering himself. "I didn't want to gate-crash into your private troubles. It was obvious to me, from the moment I arrived, that Sophie had something on her mind—something to do with Eustace Bunnett."

"I thought—I don't see how you could think that," she interposed hurriedly.

"Whenever his name was mentioned, you had to steel yourself to behaving quite normally. And it showed. The one person a mimic cannot mimic successfully is his normal self."

"This is all getting rather metaphysical," said Dr. Cammison. "It's no use, Sophie. We've got to tell him. For all you know, we may be needing his help before long."

"His help?"—Understanding dawned in Sophie's eyes. She gripped the arms of her chair. It was the only way she could stop her hands shaking. Herbert leant over the back of her chair and put his hands on her shoulders. He began to talk, a touch of professional pedantry in his words.

"I had a good deal to do with Bunnett, one way and another. Soon after we came here, he wished to consult me. It was very awkward. Annerley was his doctor, and medical etiquette—as you know—does not permit one to treat another man's patient without his permission. I told Bunnett this, of course. He said that Annerley was a—er, that he was not satisfied with Annerley and that I would be a fool not to take the case. His money was as good as anyone else's. All that sort of thing. I told him—rather stiffly, I suppose—that we did not do things that way. It must have been the first time anyone had opposed him for years. He got very angry, raved about medical mumbo-jumbo, and so on. I thought that would be the end of it. But the next I heard was that he'd had a row with Annerley and refused to have anything more to do with him. Then he came to me again. Annerley was very decent about it. So that was that. I took Bunnett's case. He thought he'd got a gastric ulcer or peritonitis or something: in a regular panic he was. It was nothing of the sort, of course. I put him on a diet—the same diet, no doubt, that Annerley would have recommended, and he very soon recovered. Unfortunately, he then began to get matey with us, always inviting us down to dinner, sending cases of wine—that kind of thing. I couldn't stand the fellow personally, and I was beginning to hear things about the brewery that I liked still less. I couldn't imagine what his motive was, making up to me like this. Then it became painfully apparent. He, er——"

"He began to get fresh with me," said Mrs. Cammison. "Horrible little man! It was ludicrous, though; I couldn't help laughing at him."

"And Bunnett was not the sort of person calculated to enjoy the joke, was he?" said Nigel.

Herbert Cammison regarded him seriously. "No. He was not. And I may as well tell you at once that I think whoever removed him ought to be given free beer for the rest of his life by the State. He was the worst kind of anti-social pest, and decent society would clap him straight in jail—well, his type simply wouldn't be able to exist in a properly-run community. However, that's beside the point. His—er—advances to Sophie were only a symptom—of secondary consideration, really, compared to——"

Sophie Cammison chuckled. She was almost her own old equable self again for a moment. "Darling," she said, pressing her husband's hand, "I'm sorry my honour comes so low in your scale of values."

"Your honour can take care of itself—very efficiently, I should say," he replied with unimpaired gravity. "The employees at the brewery were less invulnerable. Anyway, after a bit Bunnett laid off Sophie—temporarily, at any rate. It was just then that I began to find out things about the brewery. A number of my panel patients were employed there, and there were far too many accidents and cases of occupational sickness. It's not my business to listen to gossip; on the other hand, I don't believe that a doctor should refuse to concern himself with social conditions. He ought to be at least as interested in preventing disease as in curing it."

"Hear! Hear!" said Nigel. "How admirable these quaint old Chinese beliefs are."

"We'll take what I heard first," proceeded Dr. Cammison, in the preoccupied tones of one lecturing a group of students over an operating-table. "I heard that Bunnett always employed married men where possible, so that he could have a stronger hold over them. I received the impression that his employees were really frightened of him—he was perpetually turning up in different places and standing silently behind them while they were at work—it got on their nerves, one of them told me, so that they began to get flurried and make mistakes; and then, of course, Bunnett had them where he wanted them."

"Yes, Sorn told me about a case of that this afternoon. Someone actually being sick—what was his name? Ed Parsons."

"Yes, and there was more to Ed Parsons' case than you know. Well, those are just examples. I heard a good many more. Of course, there are always chaps who can't live without a grievance, and no doubt some of what I heard was exaggerated. But there must have been a sizeable fire where one got such a hell of a lot of smoke. Things came to a head, as far as I was concerned, when I was called in to attend one of their lorry-drivers who had had a bad smash on Honeycombe Hill—just outside the town. From the evidence given in court afterwards, it was perfectly obvious that the driver had been overworked, compelled to run to an impossible schedule, and had dropped off to sleep through sheer exhaustion. Bunnett, being who he was, got off with the minimum fine: he celebrated the occasion by sacking the driver. That sort of thing goes on constantly, of course: it pays the employers—they gain more over the time and labour-saving than they lose over an occasional fine. Actually it wasn't the injustice of this sort of thing in the abstract that compelled me to take a hand; it was the effect of hearing that poor chap, in delirium after the accident, saying over and over again, 'I can't make it! Christ, I'm sleepy! It's bloody murder! I can't make it! The governor'll turn me off! It's bloody murder, that's what it is! I'm sleepy! Christ, I'm sleepy!'

"I'm tough as doctors go, Nigel, but that got me down. I tried to forget it, but I couldn't. The chap getting sacked on top of it was the last straw. I went to see Joe—Eustace's brother, you know: he runs the transport side. I as good as told him he was a murderer. He took it damned well—we've been friends ever since, actually; said he'd told his brother again and again it was asking for trouble making his drivers run to a schedule like that, but it hadn't had any effect. Poor Joe is a damned good sort, but Eustace always had him where he wanted him. However, this time Joe thought that—if he had a doctor's statement behind him (my name wasn't going to be brought in, of course)—he might be able to make some impression on Eustace. I thought I might as well be hung for a sheep as a lamb, so I got Joe to show me over the brewery—I wanted to see exactly how far people had been exaggerating over the conditions there. Believe me, there hadn't been much exaggeration. I gave the place a pretty thorough look-over, from the hygienic point of view. I won't bother you with details: but the ventilation was appalling, and one didn't have to be a technical expert to see that the machinery and apparatus were nearly worn-out and thoroughly dangerous. Bunnett was the sort that has to squeeze the last ounce of work out of his machines as well as his men."

"But surely there are government inspectors who——?"

"There are ways and means, young Nigel, of dealing with that difficulty. Eyewash and palm-grease, applied in equal proportions, will work wonders. And Eustace was an expert at applying them, I've no doubt. Well, I sent in a detailed report to Joe—about the conditions in the brewery, their effect on the health of the employees, etc., as well as about the lorry schedule. He was as keen as I to improve conditions all round. And he bearded brother Eustace with it. The next thing that happened, as far as I was concerned, was a note the day after requesting me to go round and see Eustace at the brewery. Eustace was sitting at the end of the long table in the boardroom, straightening a piece of blotting-paper in front of him. At least, I imagined it must be a piece of blotting-paper till he took it up in one hand, tapped it with his pince-nez, and said, 'I take it you are the author of this—er—document.' It was my report! Typed and unsigned, but he'd tumbled to it quick enough.

"After that, of course, there was hell to pay. He

asked me by what right I interfered in another man's business. I told him that it was every citizen's duty to see that the laws were not broken. He asked me to state any laws *he* had broken. I quoted parts of the factory acts. Then he asked what I proposed to do about it. So I told him that, unless some changes were made pretty quick, I'd raise such a stink that even he, the omnipotent Eustace Bunnett, would have to knuckle under. He sat there for a while, fidgeting with a paper-knife and darting an occasional glance my way out of those cold little lizard's eyes of his. Then, to my surprise, he caved in. Said that I didn't look the sort to accept a handsome remuneration in return for a policy of non-intervention in the future—here he made a significant pause, but I was not nibbling at the bait. 'Very well, then,' said he, 'you win. Give me six months to make the alterations suggested in your report, and then I think you'll be able to come back and give us a clean sheet—hem, ha, sniff'—you know the sort of noises he made. I pointed out that it did not take six months to revise a lorry-running time-table. He hemmed and sniffed a bit, but finally promised to see to that at once. And he did. When Joe told me that the schedule had been altered, I felt convinced that I'd really put Bunnett on the spot. But——"

"But you found out the great truth," interrupted Nigel, "which inexperienced troops always have to learn—and pay for—that veterans are never so dangerous as when they give ground."

"Yes. Served me right for thinking I could run the whole show single-handed. Six months later, to the very day, Bunnett asked me to come and see him again. As I went through the brewery up to his private office, I looked around me—and it didn't look as if reconstruction had been done at all. So you can imagine I was not in too good a temper when I arrived in the Presence. Bunnett sat at his desk, pursing up his fat little mouth at me and rubbing his hands—they made a noise like a lizard's tail slithering over a stone wall. 'Ah, doctor,' he said, getting down to business at once, 'if I remember rightly, on your last visit here you said that it was every citizen's duty to see that the laws are not broken. Now I am sure, Dr. Cammison, that—as I prophesied last time you came here—you will see your way to giving us a clean sheet.' Even then I didn't know what he was driving at. He leant back in his chair and said, 'Kate Alpace.' Then I knew I was done."

"Kate Alpace?" asked Nigel, mystified.

"She is my sister," said Mrs. Cammison. "It was before we came here: when we were living in the Midlands. She had a lover and became pregnant. She asked Herbert to perform an abortion."

Herbert Cammison said, "I don't approve of abortion, as a general rule. But I happened to discover that there was insanity in Kate's young man's family. So of course I did it for her. Well, as you know, it's a criminal offence—penal servitude if you get found out."

"And Eustace Bunnett had found out?" said Nigel.

"Yes. He must have spent the six months I'd given him to improve his own business in making inquiries about me. Some shady private-inquiry agent, no doubt. That gives you an idea of what Bunnett was like, doesn't it? Heaven knows how his agents discovered it; it's irrelevant, anyway. The point was, if Bunnett had broken the law, so had I."

"Sort of stalemate," said Nigel.

"Worse. Exposure would have cost him pretty heavily in fines: but it would ruin my whole career. He was really in a strong position. Well, I generally have pretty good self-control, but that time I lost my temper. I told Bunnett exactly what I thought of him. Unfortunately, I also told him that people like him ought to be exterminated."

"Unfortunately?" asked Nigel. "You mean——?"

"Yes," said Cammison. "One of Bunnett's pleasant little practices—I forgot to mention it before—was to have one or two spies on the premises: it's not unknown in big business: the employer pays one of his employees to report to him any dissatisfaction, strike rumours and so on, he may hear in the shop. I'm terribly afraid that one of Bunnett's spies was listening-in on my little outburst."

"It looks as if I'd better stay on," said Nigel.

"You certainly had," said Dr. Cammison grimly. "Unless by any chance you were sitting outside my bedroom door all last night."

Nigel glared at him perplexedly.

"You see, otherwise there is no proof that I didn't visit the brewery last night and liquidate Bunnett."

"It will be awkward if the inspector turns up that row you had with Bunnett, certainly. Still, no doubt there are plenty of other people who had equally strong motives for doing him in."

"Very comforting you are, I must say."

"Oh, do stop talking about it as though it was a chess problem!" exclaimed Sophie Cammison. "Don't you realise that——"

"It's all right," her husband said gently; "I realise everything, don't you worry. And, by the way, young Nigel—as I *am* incriminating myself, I'd better do it thoroughly. Since that interview with Bunnett, So-

74

phie and I had been living in—to put it mildly—a state of considerable uncertainly. For some time, he did nothing. But a few months ago, he started getting uppish with Sophie again. He as good as told her that he could ruin my career if he liked—and would, if she was not a bit more forthcoming. Yes, I know, it all sounds like a threepenny novelette; but there it is: Bunnett was not distinguished for literary good taste, anyway—as you discovered at the meeting. The point is, when Sophie told me about it I went to see Bunnett and informed him that—career or no career—I'd see him dead before I let him get away with that sort of thing."

"And now you have—er—seen him dead," said Nigel meditatively. "Yes, the situation is certainly a trifle daunting. However; courage, mes enfants. I will apply the gigantic resources of the trained mind. You reconstruct the anatomy, Herbert, and I'll reconstruct the crime. And then, Sophie," he added, "you can start knitting a wardrobe for your own children."

# V
# July 18, 9.15–11 a.m.

*Watchman, what of the night?*
ISAIAH (xxi, 11)

AT exactly 2.17 the next morning Nigel had woken up with a bizarre, a wildly fantastic idea in his head. After breakfast he drew Herbert Cammison aside and said:

"Look here, I had an idea last night. Supposing that skeleton isn't Eustace Bunnett at all."

"Well, we don't know it is yet. But all the evidence points to it. Where is Bunnett, anyway, if it wasn't him in the copper? And why shouldn't it be?"

"It just struck me that it was a curious—an unnecessarily elaborate way of getting rid of him. I mean, why not just kill him and be done with it? Why go to all that trouble to destroy his identity—and yet leave his clothes and watch and ring and everything on him?"

"That's very simply explained. By putting the body in the copper, the murderer would succeed in effacing anything that would give us a clue to the method of the crime—that is, unless it was a blunt instrument affair. All traces of poisoning, say, or strangling, or even stabbing probably, would be destroyed."

"Oh, heavens!" groaned Nigel. "Of course. These

midnight inspirations always look cock-eyed in daylight. I don't know why that didn't occur to me at once, though."

"Besides," continued the doctor, "if the remains were not Bunnett, yet are dressed up to make us believe that they are him—I'm getting ungrammatical—the deduction would be that it was Bunnett who did the murder. Unless there is a third party, X, who killed Y, and then persuaded Bunnett to exchange clothes with the corpse. And why should X do that—or Bunnett, for that matter?"

"X might have killed Bunnett as well."

"Now you're just asking for complications."

"That's true. Well, then, suppose for the sake of argument that there's no X. Bunnett would be the murderer then."

"But, my dear good Nigel, *why*? Why should he want to kill anyone—and kill himself in the process, which is what he'd be doing by dressing up the body to look like himself?"

"Search me!"

"I should think so! But seriously, Eustace Bunnett was the last chap to commit murder. Murder—even most unpremeditated murders included—is the last resort of the person who can't get his own way by any other means. Now Bunnett wielded, in his business, his personal relationships, and in this whole town, almost absolute power. He could get what he wanted, when he wanted, without killing anyone in the process—beyond an occasional lorry-driver. The only thing here he didn't get was Sophie: I was the obstacle to that: are you going to suggest that it's really me who was boiled in the copper?"

"All right, old boy, all right! Pax!" Nigel's irregular and somewhat discoloured teeth showed in a placatory grin. "As a matter of fact, I hadn't much confidence in my midnight inspiration all along; I was just wondering idly whether it could be put across on the inspector, supposing that he——"

"Supposing he started to get after me? Well, you could try it on him; but——"

Herbert Cammison grimaced and made a thumb-down gesture. "Well," he said, "I must be off to try and put Humpty Dumpty together again. Good hunting!"

"Good jig-saw!" responded Nigel politely.

As Nigel was walking down town towards the brewery half an hour later, he perceived Miss Mellors forging in his direction with purposeful strides. He glanced round furtively to see if there was any shop door into which he could retreat: no, nothing but private houses: he stood his ground, with the dour fatalism of the prairie-dweller who beholds the thundering herd galloping down upon him and can only hope for a speedy and conclusive kick on the head. At a distance of twenty yards Miss Mellors, raising simultaneously her ash-plant and her bull-like head, bellowed:

"Hoy! Mr. Strangeways! I want a word with you. Don't run away now!"

Nigel submitted to a handshake which nearly wrenched his arm out of its socket.

"Now, what's all this I hear about an accident down at the brewery, eh?"

"A—er—body was discovered there yesterday evening. It seems likely that it is Mr. Bunnett's."

The effect of this communication was devastating. Miss Mellors' huge and sanguine face grew suddenly pale. She seized Nigel's arm and exclaimed in an absurd, croaking little voice:

78

"But that's ridiculous. He's away cruising. In a boat," she added rather unnecessarily.

"Not Joe. Eustace Bunnett—that is, as far as we can tell at present."

Miss Mellors recovered herself very quickly. "My dear man," she expostulated in her ordinary, booming, loudspeaker voice, "my dear man, either the body is Eustace Bunnett or it isn't. There's no use making a mystery about it."

"I'm not making the mystery. It's the body—I mean, there isn't a great deal left of it, you see."

"Come along! You needn't be mealy-mouthed. I'm not a green girl, you know. You mean, the body was battered out of all recognition," said Miss Mellors, not without relish. "The work of a maniac, eh?"

"Not battered," replied Nigel, slightly irritated by the accusation of mealy-mouthedness: "boiled to rags, if you want to know."

"Really, now, that's most interesting," she boomed affably. "Tell me all about it."

Nigel gave her a short and guarded résumé of events. "A pretty ghastly business," he concluded.

"Ghastly business? Tripe. Don't be so conventional, young man. That Bunnett was a scoundrel, and had it coming to him. I'd have horse-whipped him long ago myself, only he was below my weight. I will say nothing about his private life"—Miss Mellors proceeded to discourse on that subject for a good ten minutes—"but apart from all that, the fellow was a poisoner."

"A poisoner?" ejaculated Nigel, considerably shaken. "Dash it all, I can't quite believe that."

"Strong drink, young man, is poison. You may not be aware of it, but——" Miss Mellors gave an outspoken and exceedingly physiological lecture on the

79

effects of alcohol. She concluded by reciting, in sombre but penetrating tones, emphasising the metre with taps of her ash-stick:

*"Ha! see where the wild-blazing Grop-Shop appears,*
*As the red waves of wretchedness swell,*
*How it burns on the edge of tempestuous years—*
*The horrible lighthouse of Hell!"*

"Well," said Nigel, "that may be so. But killing an odd brewery proprietor here and there is not going to have any effect on the drink trade. Presumably Joe will be carrying on the business, and——"

"Indeed he will not. Not if I have any say in the matter."

"And what say *will* you have in the matter?" Nigel was emboldened to ask. If it were possible for a Goddess of Public Works to blush, one might say that Miss Mellors did blush. She changed the subject quickly, saying:

"What was Bunnett doing in the brewery in the middle of the night, anyway? Snooping around, I'll be. Serves him right. Live and let live, I say," she added, somewhat inconsistently. "Well, cheerio!"

But that, of course, *was* the question, Nigel reflected as he proceeded on his way. How did the murderer get Bunnett into the brewery? The answer was to be supplied very soon. Nigel was stopped by a constable at the brewery gates. On giving his name, he was told that the inspector would like to see him in Mr. Bunnett's private office.

"Pursuant to Dr. Cammison's suggestion, I got into communication with the Yard last night. Sir John Strangeways vouched for you personally, so your position in respect to this case is now regularised," said the inspector. Nigel wished he would not talk this bogus sort of officialese: no doubt, it was meant to impress him with Tyler's superior education; oh, well, the main thing was that he now had some official standing.

"Well, how's things?" he said.

"We have just opened Mr. Bunnett's private safe. We found this, which may be of interest to you, sir." The inspector handed across a sheet of cheap, lined notepaper, on which was written, in block letters:

*Dear Sir,—If you want to know where your bottled beer and sugar goes to, go to the brewery to-morrow night about 12 and ask the night watchman.*

A WELL-WISHER

"Oh," said Nigel, "so that's what took him to the brewery. I was wondering. Envelope there too?"

"Yes, sir. Postmark, Weston Priors—that's a village about fifteen miles away. Dated July 15th, 7.30 p.m."

"I take it that the bird who wrote this is the murderer: which implies that the murderer had a pretty fair knowledge of the workings of the brewery—though we could have told that without this letter."

"Just so, sir," said the inspector, with a complacent superiority that Nigel found exceedingly irritating. "But there's one possibility that you've overlooked. And what is that possibility? This, Mr. Strangeways—the letter might be a bonerfidee anonymous letter; Mr. Bunnett, acting upon it, might have gone to the brewery and caught the night watchman pilfering; that might have led to an affray in which Lock—that's the watchman—killed Mr. Bunnett; whereupon, to conceal the evidence of his crime, he disposed of the body in the copper."

"H'm!" said Nigel politely; "that's certainly an idea. It seems to me to have two rather salient drawbacks, though."

"And what might they be?" asked the inspector, leaning back in his chair so that a roll of fat appeared above the back of his collar.

"First, the fact that this alleged well-wisher stated the day and hour at which Bunnett should come to the brewery suggests that he proposed to be waiting for him there. An ordinary anonymous letter-writer would have no object in stating the exact time. If the night watchman was a pilferer, he would be just as likely to be pilfering one night as another. Second, if the watchman did kill Bunnett, why didn't he put the body into one of the boiler furnaces? That would have destroyed all evidence of his crime completely; Bunnett would have disappeared and there would be no reason to suppose that he had ever gone to the brewery that night—the watchman couldn't know about the anonymous letter, of course."

"Ah, but if every criminal always did the most sensible thing, the Force would have to go out of business. Still, I'll allow there may be something in what you say. Now, sir, I had a talk with this Lock before he went on duty last night: and I found out one or two items of interest. First, he's a new man—only taken on a couple of months ago. Second, he works to a sort of time-table."

"Time-table?"

"Ah. He's supposed to visit every part of the brewery—the various store-rooms and processes, if you follow me, at stated times during the night. It's part of his job to see that the temperatures are kept right, the taps running proper, and so forth. He has a clock in a leather case on his wrist, that's set by radio time every evening. There's a schedule upon the wall of the little cubby-hole where he sits when he has a spare moment, showing what times these inspections must be made. Now, Mr. Strangeways, do you see the significance of that?"

"Well, you mean that—if he was doing his job properly—we should know exactly where he was at any time of the night."

"Yes and no, sir, yes and no. I looks at it this way. If he was doing his job properly, he should have been on one of his tours of inspection between 11.30 and midnight. Why then didn't he see Mr. Bunnett and the murderer—supposing there was a third party on the premises? You'd think he'd at least have heard a scuffle or something."

"I'm not so sure about that. The brewery is a big place, remember. If Bunnett was trying to catch out the watchman in some petty pilfering, he'd take good care not to be seen or heard. As to the murderer, he'd take equally good care to carry out his dirty work at a time when Lock was in another part of the building. As far as I can see, it only goes to show that the murderer had an exact knowledge of the way things worked in the brewery—which at least limits your number of possible suspects a bit."

"That's theory, sir, just theory, if you'll pardon me saying so. What I want is facts."

"Of course. And so say all of us. Have you got that schedule here?"

The inspector passed it across; then told the constable at the door to ask Mr. Barnes would he step this way for a minute. Nigel took up the schedule. The important period, if the anonymous letter was really part of the murderer's plan, must be around midnight: between 11.30 and 12.30 say, allowing a wide margin. The watchman's tour of inspection ended at midnight, he noticed; so it would be after midnight that Bunnett might expect to catch him out knocking back the bottled beer. For that reason, if it was the watchman who had killed him—presuming, of course, that he had not been getting down to the bottled beer before opening time—so to speak, the murder would have been committed soon after midnight. But that applied with equal probability if the murderer was not the watchman: he would be less likely to attack Bunnett while Lock was going his rounds than when he had retired again to his cubby-hole. However, as the inspector said, it was all theoretical. Nigel hastily made a copy of the schedule and was handing it back when the head brewer entered.

"This man Lock, now," said the inspector without preamble: "you say he's entirely trustworthy?"

"That's right. An old army man, he is. Had a job at Roxby's before he came to us."

"Had any small thefts lately—bottled beer, say, or sugar?"

Mr. Barnes raised his massive eyebrows, and his lugubrious face took on an appearance of what might almost have been called animation.

"Funny you should mention that. About three weeks ago, when we were checking up, we found there was a sack of sugar and a couple of crates of the light ale missing. How did you come to hear about it?"

"Information received," replied Tyler curtly. "Why weren't we informed about it at the time?"

"Ask the guv'nor, buddy, ask the guv'nor. Thought he'd do a bit of detecting like on his own. 'Barnes,' he says to me, 'Barnes,' he says, 'these local bobbies are no catch,' he says, 'if we're going to find out who's been lifting the stuff, we'll have to do it for ourselves,' he says."

"Well, go on," said the inspector, not without heat; "I haven't all day to listen to your reminiscences."

"So the guv'nor laid a little trap," continued Mr. Barnes blandly. "The stores was checked every night and morning for a week, see, so if Lock had been lifting anything we should've noticed, see. But there wasn't nothing missing then. Mind you, I'd have no objection to Lock taking a glass of beer at night— when the mood came on him, as you might say. But the guv'nor was a bit close that way. Soon after, his dog got into the open copper and he was rampaging about that, so the other business lapsed."

"Who did put Truffles into that copper, by the way?" asked Nigel mildly. "Now that his owner has— er—gone the same way home, there doesn't seem any point in keeping it dark any longer."

"Nor doesn't there seem any point asking about it in that case," replied Mr. Barnes, bending a glance of uncommon shrewdness in Nigel's direction. "Let the dead bury their dead, is what I say. But I couldn't tell you, sir, even if I wanted to. The guv'nor held an inquiry, mind you—fair turned the bleeding place upside down: but nothing came of it. Everyone could prove they was at work then—everyone except the accountancy office staff, that is, and myself and Mr. Joe."

"The office staff being?"

"Lily—that's my daughter—Mr. Bunnett's secretary, she was, and a couple of clerks."

"Um. I must have a talk with them some time."

"Well, gentlemen, if you've finished with me for the present, I'll be slinging my hook. The wheels of industry must be kept turning. So long." Mr. Barnes raised his eyebrows at them and slung his hook.

Inspector Tyler's temper was by no means improved by this interview. When the night watchman entered the room, Tyler said harshly:

"Now, then, Lock, what's all this I hear about your pilfering the brewery stores on the side, eh?"

"I don't know what you've heard, sir, but it's certainly not true."

"Never have a bottle of beer at night, eh? Must be a bit of temptation with all that lying around."

"Not for me, sir. I'm a teetotaller—ever since I left the army. Can prove it, sir."

The inspector sat back in his chair and fingered the anonymous letter. He said:

"Well, there's more things can be done with beer than drinking it—and with sugar, eh? What did you do—sell 'em to your friends?"

"No, sir. I don't know what you're trying to put on me—unless it's that theft as took place end of last month."

Lock had been standing at attention, very straight—a stalwart, grizzled man with many wrinkles at the corners of his steady eyes.

"What have you to say about this?" asked the inspector, pushing the anonymous letter to the far side of the desk. Lock took a brisk, military step forward, bringing up one heel against the other with a click, and took up the letter.

"Don't understand this, sir. That sort of scrounging—it wouldn't be worth while in a job like mine. You have to be honest—though I says it, as shouldn't—for a watchman's job. Ask my old regiment, or Roxby's—them's my last employers. They'll give me a clean sheet all right, I'll back."

"H'm. That's as may be. And you still assert that you performed your midnight round of inspection the night before last, and heard or saw nothing suspicious?"

"That is so, sir."

"Doesn't it strike you as peculiar that a murder should have been committed on these premises and you should know nothing about it? Have you no ideas at all how it happened?"

"No, sir."

"Yours not to question why, yours not to do—er—but it was Mr. Bunnett who died, wasn't it?" said Nigel in a friendly voice. "Y'know, Inspector, I'm inclined to believe him. I wonder, Mr. Lock, would you mind my looking at your hands."

The inspector started slightly; then said:

"What's all this? Palmistry? That's a new one on me."

"It's not the palms so much as the backs of the hands that interest me at the moment."

"That's all right, sir," said Lock, stretching out his hands.

Nigel peered at them closely, pulled up the sleeves and studied the man's wrists, then sat back in his chair.

"O.K.," he said. "Parade dismissed—as far as I'm concerned. I expect Mr. Lock will be wanting to go to bed."

"What's all the funny business about hands?" said the inspector suspiciously when Lock had turned smartly about and marched out of the room.

"You had an idea that Bunnett might have surprised Lock pilfering, that there was some sort of a struggle, Bunnett was killed or injured, and Lock put him into the copper. Well, now. If Lock drew a knife on him, you would have found traces of blood—or of cleaning up—on the scene. Did you?"

"No, sir. We went all over the brewery last night

pretty carefully, and I admit there was no sign of that. But——"

"If Lock hit him over the head with a blunt instrument—or if anybody did—Cammison would probably have seen traces of it during his first examination. If he'd strangled Bunnett, there would have been scratches on the backs of his hands—quite likely marks on his face, too. There weren't. The only other possibility is that he should have used his fists, knocked him out: I don't think it's in the least likely that, if Lock had merely injured him, he would have gone on to murder him. After all, he hadn't enough at stake to justify that."

"A lot of 'ifs,' sir. I don't think you've proved anything."

"Not your sort of proof, possibly. But all that is comparatively unimportant. You know what's the worst crime in the army, don't you?"

"Why, I suppose——"

"Striking a superior officer. With all those years of discipline and tradition behind him, I'm prepared to assert that it was as good as impossible—physically and psychologically impossible—for Lock to have assaulted Bunnett. His immediate reaction, *if* he'd been caught knocking back an illicit glass of beer, would have been to spring to attention. And anyway—he's obviously an honest, trustworthy type of man. I've no doubt at all you'll find dozens of other people with infinitely better motives for putting Bunnett out of the way."

"You may be right," said the inspector, fingering his chin.

Just how right Nigel was, particularly in his last remark, was to be demonstrated sooner than either he or the inspector could have imagined.

# VI
## July 18, 1.30–4.35 p.m.

*Let's choose executors and talk of wills.*
SHAKESPEARE, *King Richard II*

HERBERT CAMMISON, Sophie and Nigel had just sat down to lunch—or, to be more accurate, Sophie and Nigel had sat down, while the doctor was carving a chicken with the somewhat sinister absorption of one who is operating for an appendix but anticipates some intriguing complications. When the remains of the patient had been removed to the kitchen and Herbert had helped himself to potatoes, salad, salt, butter and a glass of water with a deliberation that very nearly drove Nigel crazy, he said:

"Well, Felston and I have been working on that skeleton."

"I hope you had an enjoyable time," said Nigel politely. "And can these dry bones live? Will they sit up and answer to their name, if I may so express myself?"

"You may, young Strangeways. Up to a point, they will. We haven't any doubt that it's Bunnett."

"Oh, Herbert." Sophie no longer attempted to conceal the fear in her mind. She looked pathetically young and vulnerable, Nigel thought—almost like her own daughter might look at the age of fifteen, with those absurd horn-rim spectacles and her child-like fresh complexion.

"You mustn't worry, Sophie. I didn't kill him, as it happens, and the percentage of people wrongly convicted for murder is really very low."

Dr. Cammison began talking about their next holidays. Sophie seized on the subject with pathetic eagerness. No one was at all deceived; but it passed the lunch-time as well as anything might. After lunch Nigel took the doctor aside and asked for details.

"No signs of violence on the skull. No bones broken. The height corresponds pretty accurately with Bunnett's—five foot seven: of course, one has to allow a certain margin of error in a reconstruction like this."

"How much?"

"A couple of inches, at the very most. The hair, as I said originally, is the right colour. Tripp is still working on the dental plates, but he's pretty certain they're the set he supplied Bunnett with. Felston agrees with me that we've enough data to presume death. By the way, I rang up Tyler and told him our conclusion: he's going along to interview Grimshaw—that's Bunnett's solicitor—at three o'clock: the will: he's agreeable to your going along there, too, if you want."

"H'm. I wonder. . . . That man seems to have come over all respectful like. I'm not sure I don't prefer him with the gloves off."

"Tyler? A common or garden bully. Plays up to anyone in authority. Your uncle did that for you."

"Dear, dear! And I had been thinking it was the effect of my own masterful personality. Talking of which, by the way, what are your reactions to our Miss Mellors?"

"Just what do you want to know?"

"How keen is she really on her temperance stuff, for instance? Take it in her stride, so to speak, or a fanatic? What is there—or was there—between her and Joe Bunnett? How d'you think she'd shape as a murderer?"

"My dear Nigel!" Herbert Cammison for once looked startled. "What shocking ideas you do have! Ariadne Mellors a murderer! Come off it!"

"*What* Mellors?"

"Ariadne. Addie for short."

"Blow me down with an anchovy! Ariadne. Well, well, well. But this one walked out on Bacchus. However, one thing at a time. A fanatic?"

"No," said Herbert carefully. "I shouldn't say so. It's the organising part she's really keen on, more than the faith itself."

"Just like the Bishop of——?"

"I have no information about bishops," said Herbert with a twinkle in his eye.

"Well, what about Joe Bunnett?"

"Joe?"

"Yes, she gave me the impression this morning that she has him on a string."

"Oh, I don't think so. They're good friends. Are you trying to deduce a romance between them?"

"Not exactly. Who would know about them, though?"

"Well, we've not been here long enough. You might ask Barnes. Sophie *might* know, as a matter of fact: Joe has opened up to her occasionally. People do."

"Yes. I can imagine that."

Half an hour later, Nigel and Inspector Tyler were closeted with Mr. Grimshaw. "Closeted" seemed the only possible word, for the solicitor's office was exiguous and his long, sprawling legs took up most of the floor-space. While the formalities were being conducted, Nigel watched Mr. Grimshaw with fascination: his ears wiggled as he talked, which drew attention to the ginger-coloured hair that sprouted out of them; he also had a habit of munching before every sentence, as though the words would sound better if they were chewed up small.

"Now, Mr. Grimshaw, I don't think I need keep you long," the inspector was saying. "In an affair like this the question of motive has to be considered. That is why I am interested in the late Mr. Bunnett's will. Perhaps you would be good enough to inform me who the chief beneficiaries are, sir."

"Hum—mum—mum—nyah, I think we need have no hesitation about that. No. There are times when the law must have precedence over the lawyer. Mum-nyum. Mind you, in the ordinary course of things I should not countenance such an eeregularity; but, er—mnyum, desperate events reequire desperate remedies."

Looking, presumably, as desperate as he knew how, Mr. Grimshaw unfolded a document with a sharp crackle that made Nigel start, struck it negligently over the face, then peered at it with some distaste.

"M'm—yum, I should make it clear at the outset that I was not altogether satisfied with certain clauses in the will—as a man, not as a lawyer. In fact, I ventured—with considerable deefeedence—to remonstrate with Mr. Bunnett on these points. But, as you know, my client was a headstrong man, accustomed to having his own way, so of course I had to bow to his wishes. But really" (here the ears wiggled molto agitato) "the deeposeetion of the property is most peculiar. Most peculiar. It is as follows. Hum-mum-chumble-yum. Eustace Bunnett's share in the brewery is bequeathed to his brother, Joseph Bunnett, provided that he be unmarried at the time of the testator's death. Out of Eustace Bunnett's personal estate, an annuity of £100 is to be paid to his wife, Emily Rose Bunnett. There are a few minor bequests. The whole of the reseedue of his estate is bequeathed to Mrs. Annabel Sorn, provided she shall not have married again."

"Sorn!" exclaimed Nigel and the inspector simultaneously.

"Just so," munched Mr. Grimshaw, leaning back in his chair and gazing at his visitors with undisguised consternation.

"I considered the provision made for Mrs. Bunnett to be most inadequate—I speak," he added hastily, "in my private, not my professional capacity. But my client did not take my remonstrations in good part. By no means."

"Who is this Mrs. Sorn? Does she live here? A relation of Gabriel Sorn?" asked Nigel.

"Um-yum. She is domeeciled in the South of France. I have her address here." Mr. Grimshaw passed a slip of paper to the inspector. "My client averred that she was an old friend of his. It was to do her a kindness, I understand, that he took her son into the brewery."

"Oh, so Mr. Sorn is her son, is he?" said the inspector with visible relish. "Well. We shall see. Now, sir, can you give me any idea how much this Mrs. Sorn stands to gain by the will?"

"Let me see, now. It is impossible for me to tell you precisely, of course. But I should say that, when all the other bequests have been settled, death duties paid, and so on, Mrs. Sorn should receive something in the neighbourhood of £50,000."

"A tidy packet," said Nigel. "And what about Joe?"

"My late client held a controlling interest in the brewery. That interest now passes to Joseph Bunnett."

"And what has Joseph's position been so far?"

"Nyum-nyah, I believe that he was paid a salary as manager of the transport and the tied houses. He also had shares in the business."

The inspector took the names of the lesser legatees—the head brewer's was amongst them, thanked Mr. Grimshaw and made to depart. The solicitor munched a polite farewell. As they reached the door, Nigel turned and said:

"By the way, have you any idea why Eustace put in that proviso about his brother not being married?"

"Professionally speaking, no, my dear sir. But, if I may say so as a private indeevidual and without prejudeece—without prejudeece, of course—I should say that it was due to my late client's somewhat domineering tendencies. Please note, I am making no assertions. But when Mr. Joe returned from the war, an attachment sprang up between him and a certain young lady in this locality who must be nameless. It was shortly after this that my client inserted that proviso in his will. Hum-munch. I make no assertions, I repeat. But you may think it legeeteemate to draw a certain inference."

"And how did Miss Mellors take all this?" asked Nigel guilelessly. Mr. Grimshaw's ears performed an almost complete revolution.

"Hum-mum-chumble-yum," he exclaimed uncomfortably, "Really, my dear sir, I fear we are going outside our terms of reference. I really cannot admit——"

"Very well. We'll have it stricken from the records. Many thanks. Good-day."

"What's all this about Miss Mellors?" said the inspector when they were outside.

"In love with Joe Bunnett. Or was. Gave me two hints of it this morning. Nearly passed out when I told her Bunnett was dead—thought I meant Joe. Also said that Joe wouldn't be carrying on the brewery business if she had any say in it: which means, presumably, she *would* have a say."

The inspector's round and pasty face took on an unpleasing expression. It was, thought Nigel, like seeing a saucer of milk go sour before your eyes.

"Meaning, sir, that Joe Bunnett had been prevented by his brother from marrying Miss Mellors. So Miss Mellors and Joe conspire to murder Eustace, thus removing the obstacle to their marriage and gaining for Joe the controlling interest in the brewery."

"And they always say the police have no imagination! No, I don't mean all that. If Miss Mellors and Joe were in a conspiracy to murder Eustace, why should she come over all queer when I tell her that Bunnett's dead?"

"Ah, it takes them different ways. Don't you be so sure, Mr. Strangeways. I shall have to go into this."

"Joe's on the high seas, anyway. Or isn't he?"

"I've not contacted him yet, sir" (Nigel shuddered inwardly at the word), "but I'm expecting a report from the Poolhampton people any time now. Tollworthy is going round inquiring as to the whereabouts of everyone connected with Mr. Bunnett on the night of the murder. May not be much use. People would normally be in bed by that time of night, and that's about the most difficult alibi there is to break."

"Yes," said Nigel to himself, remembering Herbert Cammison, "and about the most difficult alibi to prove, also."

They were walking along a narrow street of mean houses away from the centre of the town, a street that every fifty yards or so gave itself a shake and set off again in a different direction. The street was dreadfully hot, and afforded disagreeable evidence of terminating in a cattle-market. Nigel thought longingly of his own flat that looked out upon a démodé but clean and beautiful London square. Just as the stench grew almost intolerable and an open piece of ground covered with whitewashed pens appeared, the inspector stopped at a squalid red-brick house.

"What have we come here for?" Nigel asked. "I really don't want to buy any fat stock at the moment."

"Maybe you'd fancy a pig in a poke," said Tyler with the challenging complacent air of one who has made a joke rather too subtle for the inferior wits of his audience.

"I'll buy it then. What is it?"

"This is Mrs. Bolster's house," said the inspector, banging again on the door, "where Mr. Sorn lodges."

"Here? Gabriel Sorn? God help us! But why? I didn't know he was a koprophil as well as a surrealist."

The door opened and a woman, who answered very aptly to her name, appeared.

"Good-afternoon, Mrs. Bolster. Is your lodger in? I'd like a word with him."

"Mr. Zorn's out just now. He always goes for a walk on Zaturday aafternune. He'll be back to tea any minute now, though."

"We'll wait for him, then. May we step inside?"

"Surely. This way, gentlemen, if you please."

Mrs. Bolster let them pass and closed the door behind them. The passage was almost pitch-dark and impregnated with a complex and peculiarly noisome odour, of which one could predicate nothing but that its basis seemed to be rotten fish.

"Will you wait in the parlour?" she asked.

"No, I think we might as well go straight to Mr. Sorn's room. One thing, Mrs. Bolster. I'm investigating the murder of Mr. Bunnett, and we have to find out—just as a matter of routine—the whereabouts of everyone connected with him on Thursday night. Mr. Sorn was at a party till 11.15 or so. I suppose he got back about half-past?"

"Yes, sir. Haaf-paast to the tick, it was. Our Bertha had the toothache fair cruel that night and I was zitting up with her. Very poorlee she was."

"I suppose you locked up after him, then?" said the inspector, looking a trifle dashed.

"Oh, no, sir, he always locks up himself. He often goes for walks at night, you see, sir. Many's the time I've toold him the night air's no good for man or beast, but he will do it. A queer gentleman in his habits, but he pays up his rent regular."

"Did he go for one of his walks on Thursday night?"

"That I cannot tell you, not for sure. I thought I did hear him go downstairs again, me being awake with our Bertha, who was poorlee that night. Walking very quietlee he was, as he always does at night, not being wishful to wake us up. A very conziderate gentleman, Mr. Zorn, I will say that."

"I'm sure he is," said the inspector heartily. "You didn't actually hear him go out, then?"

"No, sir, I caan't say as I did. Oh, dearie me! I was forgetting. I must be fair mazed. Why, it was only laast night, when I brought in his supper, Mr. Zorn says to me, 'Bolster,' he says, that being his way of called me, and I always said it was disrespectful, but you can't pick and choose with your lodgers nowadays, 'Bolster,' he says, 'I hope I didn't wake you up last night when I came in.' I told him I was awake with our Bertha along of her being poorlee with the toothache. So Mr. Zorn he says he hadn't felt too happee in his inzides that night so he'd gone downstairs to fetch a book in case he couldn't go to zleep. So I must have heard him, see, when he was fetching the book."

"Yes. That was it, no doubt," purred the inspector. "Well, now, if you will show us Mr. Sorn's room, I don't think I need trouble you any more."

The most noticeable thing in Gabriel Sorn's room was an extraordinary, confused, scurrying, metallic noise—as though one had walked into a kind of mechanical ant-heap. That, indeed, was the only noticeable thing, for the room was even darker than the passage outside.

"An infernal machine, that's what it must be," thought Nigel fatalistically. "Sorn has left it here to blow up the incriminating evidence and the detectives. Neat, if unfortunate."

Mrs. Bolster drew back the curtains, saying:

"Mr. Zorn must've been writing at his poetree before he went out. Always makes it up easiest in the dark, he says."

"Like developing a photograph? Quite a sound principle," said Nigel, his eyes tight shut against the imminent explosion and the painful dazzle of the sunlight that was now pouring in.

"Ah, quite a lot of things can get done in the dark, eh, Mr. Strangeways?" said the inspector with ponderous significance.

"Please, Inspector! We are not in the smoking-room now," protested Nigel, slowly opening his eyes. "Wouldn't it be a good plan to put the bomb into a bucket of water—before it blows us all up, I mean."

"Bomb!" exploded the inspector. "Bomb! What's all this about a bomb? You got a touch of the sun, sir?"

"Oh, I beg your pardon. The error, I perceive, was mine. So Sorn is a chronometrophil as well as a koprophil. I wonder how many there are."

Nigel began to walk around the room, counting the clocks in it. "Reading from left to right," he said, "we have a grandfather clock; a cuckoo clock; two timepieces of Swiss origin, very rare and curious, depicting respectively a gnome hammering an anvil and a coach with its rear wheel revolving in jerks; on the mantelpiece a marble clock, weighing probably a ton, surmounted by a pair of all-in wrestlers who are clearly not trying very hard; also two travelling clocks; a wall clock, done in fretwork, with most of its entrails dangling out; a more modest clock, coyly peeping out of red plush; a ditto, ditto, green plush; eleventh and lastly, a combined clock, calendar and barometer—no doubt it tells fortunes as well and gives nightly talks to the cultivation of mangel-wurzels. Well I never did. And do all these clocks belong to Mr. Sorn?"

"Oh, no, sir," said Mrs. Bolster. "They're faather's."

"A collector, is he?"

"No, sir. Faather's religious, you see. He had a vision that the Zecond Coming was to be at midnight on April 3rd laast year; and wanting to be punctual and readee like, you see, he used to go round they auctions buying up clocks. He set them all up in yurr, so that if one or two went out of order sudden-lee, he'd still know when to have his loins girded up notwithstanding. Then, when the Zecond Coming didn't happen, he hadn't the heart to get rid of them. It'd got to be a habit, you see, winding them up every day. But he wouldn't live in this room any more, being a disappointed man, as you might say, so we let it to Mr. Zorn."

"I see," said Nigel.

Mrs. Bolster curtsied, to the extent that her figure allowed it, and retired. Nigel prowled about the room. The chairs and sofas were of a startling variety of shape but looked all uniformly uncomfortable. The book-case contained a most extraordinary con-glomeration of books: the plays of Shakespeare rub-bed shoulders with an earnest work on *How to De-velop Self-Confidence;* next to them came *Freud's Introductory Lectures,* a complete Ella Wheeler Wil-cox, bound—apparently—in sponge, a manual on cy-cling, *From Powder Monkey to Admiral,* the Sermons of the Rev. Spurgeon, *The Care of Mules, The Divine Comedy, The Letters of Sacco and Vanzetti, Rovering to Success.* The pictures represented, in the main, courting scenes of the eighteenth century; consump-tive blondes, splayed out on rustic benches or posed before marble urns, received the addresses of im-probable-looking young men in three-cornered hats, riding-boots and skintight breeches. The insipidity of these pictures was relieved by a bloater hung from the frame of one, and a pair of braces festooned over another.

"You know," said Nigel with awe, "this chap Sorn

really is admirably consistent. What with the cattle bellowing outside, the clocks clacking away inside, the books, the pictures and all, he has created a perfect surrealist environment."

"I'll surrealist him," growled the inspector. "Where did he take his walk on Thursday night, eh? Filling up Mrs. Bolster with that stuff about fetching a book!"

"Did you observe, though, the *time* when——?"

Nigel's point, whatever it might be, was drowned by an outburst of hellish din. The metallic torrent of ticking dwindled: a cuckoo shot out of the cuckoo clock and gave an excellent imitation of an owl hooting on a gallows tree; then there was a general wheezing, rumbling, hawking, belching, twanging and tittuping as the remaining ten clocks cleared their throats preparatory to striking four.

"Really," shouted Nigel, "I think it was just as well the Second Coming didn't happen. Father Bolster'd have to have a remarkably sharp ear to catch the Last Trump in the middle of all this shindy." As the hullabaloo died away, the door opened and Gabriel Sorn came in. When he saw them, his mobile, weak mouth involuntarily was drawn into a stubborn pout and his whole face seemed to close up. Nigel snapped his fingers: at last he had discovered who it was that Sorn resembled.

"I'm surprised to see you indoors on a fine afternoon like this, Inspector," said Sorn with rather ghastly levity. "May I sit down? Do you wish me to face the light, or anything fancy like that?"

The inspector brushed all this aside. His huge face rose up horrifically out of his uniform, pallid and somehow amorphous, like a giant ray, thought Nigel.

"Now, sir, there are one or two questions I have

to ask you. First, how long have you been aware of the contents of the late Mr. Bunnett's will?"

"That's easy. I don't know anything about it yet."

"You were not aware, then, that he left the greater part of his estate to"—the inspector paused a second, scrutinising Sorn carefully—"to your mother, Mrs. Annabel Sorn?"

The young man's face took on an expression of almost theatrical surprise and consternation.

"My mother?" he gasped. "But that's—I mean, why should he?"

"That's what I was hoping you'd tell me."

"Oh, I see," said Sorn, recovering himself. "Motive. But you can't put anything on my mother: she's in France, you know. Or is it me you're after? Of course: Son kills Employer to save Widowed Mother from Destitution. How vulgar of you!"

Sorn spoke through his nose in the snuffling voice that once was associated with Puritans and now, by some curious freak of succession, has been inherited by the aesthetic.

"We shall be going into all that," said the inspector, no more disturbed by all this than was Carson by the barbed witticisms of Oscar Wilde. "Will you please tell me what was your association with the deceased, how it arose, etc.?"

"He was an old friend of my mother's. Soon after I left the university, he offered to take me into the brewery as a pupil; I believe there was some idea of my becoming a partner, if I 'made good'—as you'd probably express it."

"I see. Salary?"

"Oh, I got a little. It doesn't amount to more than pocket money: and I have a small allowance from my mother. As you imply, I had every incentive to murder the old ruffian."

"So you *did* know about the will, eh?"

"No, I didn't, I'm not admitting anything. If you can't understand——"

"You know, Sorn," Nigel interposed, "I should lay off the irony. The inspector understands facts, but not figures of speech."

"Where were you on the night of the murder?"

"In bed."

"That's funny. Your landlady says she heard you creeping downstairs again not long after you'd come in from the party."

"Oh, yes," said sorn, a little too quickly. "I came down to fetch a book."

"What book?"

"*The Great Wall of China,* by Kafka, 7s. 6d. net." It all came very pat.

"Then how do you account for the fact that you were seen near the brewery gates not very long after midnight?"

Nigel sat up abruptly. The first he'd heard—oh, no, it was a long shot of the inspector's, and very definitely below the belt, too. Of course, Tyler could always say it was a case of mistaken identity if Sorn tried to make a fuss about it. But there was no need. Sorn's bravado collapsed. He hadn't the nerve to carry through his own deception: his mouth twitched and saliva appeared at the corners of it.

"I don't—I suppose I can go for a walk, damn your eyes, if I want to."

"A curious time to choose for a walk, eh?"

"Poets have curious habits, my good Inspector."

"Such as—working in the dark, eh?"

"Yes, if you like." Then Sorn perceived the double-entendre. "I wasn't in the brewery, I had nothing to do with it, how dare you bully me like this!" His snuffling voice rose into a dismal falsetto: Nigel felt hot and embarrassed.

"No one is accusing you of anything—yet," said the inspector. "Why did you prime Mrs. Bolster with this tale of going downstairs to fetch a book?"

"Because, if you must know, when we found Bunnett in that copper and they said he must have been killed the night before, I knew you'd be coming nosing round asking where I'd been."

"I think," Nigel pointed out in his most dispassionate voice, "that is actually in Mr. Sorn's favour. If he'd committed the murder, he'd have attempted to establish his alibi as soon as possible. As it was, he didn't do so until the evening after—at supper, Mrs. Bolster said."

"H'm. That is as may be, but——"

"Stop it!" cried Sorn. "Will you stop it! I tell you I didn't do it!—talking about me as if I was something under a microscope! Don't you see—it's silly, I mean—I couldn't—this sort of thing can't happen to me! And now you've made me feel very ill: I've got a headache: I wish you'd go away," he added, snuffling ridiculously.

"Control yourself, sir. Will you kindly tell me exactly where you went for your walk, with approximate times?"

After a good deal of trouble, this was elicited. Sorn claimed to have gone out again between 11.30 and 11.45, to have walked down Long Acre, over the railway bridge at the south end of the town, then turned right along the outskirts of Honeycombe Park, and so down Honeycombe Hill into the town again. He had passed the brewery gates, he supposed, about twenty to one.

"Your statement is that you didn't enter the brewery, then?"

"Of course I didn't. How many more times do I have to——? And if——"

"You saw or heard nothing suspicious? No lights on the premises?"

"No. Unless you call a man on a motor-bike suspicious."

"Oh, dear, dear," thought Nigel. "Guilty or innocent, the young fool is now going to be too clever." With ponderous and quite transparent geniality, as though he might be saying to an errant motorist, "Oh, you were driving at twenty-five miles an hour, were you?" the inspector took up this point.

"A motor-bicyclist, eh? And where might you happen to have seen him?"

"When I'd got—oh, almost fifty yards beyond the brewery, I heard a motor-bike being started up somewhere behind me and ridden away in the opposite direction."

"And this cyclist of yours came out of the brewery yard, did he?"

"He's not a cyclist of mine. And I don't know where he came from—or even if it was a man: it was far too dark. He might have been visiting at one of the houses opposite. All I know is that he hadn't passed me as I came into the town. I'm surprised," Sorn added with an accent of suspicion, "that whoever it was saw me passing the brewery didn't see this cyclist."

"Very surprising, I'm sure, sir, *very* surprising," replied the inspector, heavily sarcastic.

"But I tell you——" wailed Gabriel Sorn.

"Oh, forget it!" Nigel said impatiently: "it can be verified easily enough, one way or the other. There *is* a question I should like to ask you, though, Sorn."

"Go ahead. Don't mind me. Only please don't ask me again if I committed the murder. I do find repetition tedious," said Sorn, something like his old self again.

"No, it's not that. I just wanted to ask how long it is that you've known Eustace Bunnett to be your father."

Gabriel Sorn's whole head jerked back, as though a fist had been aimed at it. Then his face was suffused with blood and he sprang at Nigel viciously. The inspector had quite a job pulling him off and dumping him down in his own chair again. After a little the glare went out of his eyes; he smiled a wry smile and panted:

"I apologise—how primitive one's reactions are—devoted son defends mother's honour—I'll thrash the cad who calls my mother a—too terribly Victorian and feuilleton-ish."

"So you did *know*?" said Nigel gently.

"I didn't know. Suspected, if you like. A certain unfortunate resemblance in feature did begin to obtrude. Really, too humiliating. I wonder nobody else noticed it."

"It's very slight. It didn't occur to me—except that you vaguely resembled someone I'd met—till I heard that clause in the will. That explains the bequest, I suppose."

"I suppose so. But there's something else—something I can't explain anyhow," said Gabriel Sorn in a voice they had not heard before.

"What's that?"

The young man's voice was almost inaudible; he wasn't really talking to them at all.

"Why my mother ever—how could she go with that swine, Eustace?"

# VII
## July 18, 9–10.15 p.m.

*It was a maxim with Foxey—our revered father,*
*gentlemen—'Always suspect everybody!'*
DICKENS, *Old Curiosity Shop*

"I NEVER thought I could fancy a drop of beer again,"
said Sergeant Tollworthy. "But you never knows till
you tries, do you?"

Herbert Cammison and Nigel applauded this neat
statement of empirical philosophy, the sergeant took
a hearty draught and wrung the moisture from his
moustache back into the tankard. It was nine o'clock
on the same evening. The sergeant seemed to be
enjoying a brief respite from his labours, sitting with
his collar unfastened and a pint of beer at his side
in Herbert's most comfortable arm-chair. Sophie had
gone up to bed early: a bad headache.

"Suppose I really oughtn't to be accepting your
hospitality, seeing as I'm here partly on a matter
of business, doctor," said the sergeant. "Still, I never
did hold with red tape, and there's a bleeding sight
too much of it in the Force."

He took another and more contemplative draught.

"I thought it was only suspects you weren't allowed to drink with," said Dr. Cammison, eyeing
the sergeant keenly. "Got me on the list, too, Jim?"

"In a manner of speaking, sir, yes. Of course, you

and I know one another. You knows I've got my duty to do, and I knows you're O.K., so what I says is—why shouldn't we have a friendly drink on it? Combine business with pleasure like?"

"A very sound sentiment, nobly conceived and nobly expressed," said Nigel. "Well, here's wishing."

"You see, doctor," Tollworthy explained, "it's this way. I wouldn't've come bothering you myself, but that Tyler—he's a fair terror, he is, and no lie. No respecter of persons, Tyler isn't; and seeing as how certain information had come to his ears, he sent me up here—just as a matter of routine, sir, I need hardly say—well, the fact of the matter is he wants to know where you was on the night of the murder, the silly chump."

Sergeant Tollworthy, having got this out of his system, broke into a profuse perspiration, sighed with relief, produced a red and white handkerchief the size of a medium bath-towel and mopped himself.

"The night before last?" said Cammison. "We had a party. The guests were all gone by 11.30. Strangeways and I had a last drink. Went up to bed about quarter to twelve. In bed the rest of the night. No witnesses, I'm afraid. I sleep in a different room from my wife, and the maid was presumably snoring in the attic."

"That's good enough for me, sir," said the sergeant, raising his hand in a point-duty gesture. "You was in bed, and we'll leave it at that—inspector or no inspector. Mind you, sir, I didn't want to come up here—official, I mean. It's that Tyler. Suspicious, he is. Ar, a very suspicious man, Tyler. He'd suspect the backside off Hare Tiler, Tyler would. Give him half a chance, and he'd suspect the Archbishop of Canterbury."

"Well, it's his job after all, isn't it?" said Herbert.

"Job be blowed! There's no sense I can see in stirring up trouble. But Tyler's suspicious, y'see. A very low view of human nature that man has."

"Have some more beer?"

"Thank you, I won't say no. . . . Here's your very good health, sir, and yours, sir."

"Didn't you say some special information had come to Tyler's ears, though?" pursued Dr. Cammison.

Sergeant Tollworthy looked exceedingly embarrassed. He fingered his neck-band, shifted his feet, breathed heavily; then blurted out:

"It's that bastard, Feather, been making trouble."

"Feather? You mean——?"

"Ar. Him that works in the brewery. Came along to the station this evening and said he had some information to lay, the shifty little——, if you'll pardon the expression, gentlemen. If I had that Feather standing up at the wicket, just for one over, I'd bowl him some information: just one over, and there'd be nothing left of him barring what they scraped off the sight-screen. Information? Pah!"

"But what did he say?"

"Says he overheard a quarrel between you and Mr. Bunnett down at the brewery a while back. Says he heard you say you'd see Bunnett dead before you left him get away with something or other; so when Mr. Bunnett is murdered, he puts two and two together—this Feather does—and comes along to Tyler with the answer. That's *his* story. Had quite a bit of trouble to keep my hands off the ruddy little liar, I did."

"Unfortunately it's quite true—the quarrel part, I mean. We had a row about the conditions in the brewery, and no doubt Bunnett saw to it that this spy of his was listening in somewhere."

"Is that so, sir? That's bad, isn't it? Awkward like for you, I mean. Of course I know very well you didn't do it. But that Tyler, being a suspicious chap—Oh, well, least said, soonest mended. But that's not the worst of it. Tyler says to me, 'What for does the murderer put the body in that there copper?' he says, 'Why,' he says, 'to destroy evidence of how the crime was committed. Which suggests that the murder was done in such a manner as to give away the murderer supposing there was remains. Now,' says Tyler, 'who's more likely to be able to kill someone in a specialised sort of way than a doctor—drugs, poison, or a neat bit o' work with a knife'—begging your pardon, sir. But there it is, you see. Quite bright for Tyler, really."

"Alas," said Nigel. "I'm afraid *I* fathered that sinister idea on him. Still, there are other ways of looking at it. The night-watchman, according to this schedule, was due to visit the platform where the coppers are at about ten minutes before midnight. The murderer might have killed Bunnett up there, then heard the watchman coming or known that he was due, and chucked the body into the copper in a hurry, just to get rid of it."

"You're not in your best form, Nigel; I could puncture that in about twelve places. As for instance: whoever did the job must have been familiar with the workings and geography of the brewery; therefore he would have taken care to do it when and where the night-watchman was certain not to be coming."

"Yes," said Nigel abstractedly. "What's worrying me is why he put old Bunnett into the copper at all. It was either part of the murderer's plan, or it was done on the spur of the moment. Your argument, Herbert, seems to dispose of the second alternative. Why was it part of his plan, then?"

"Sort of poetic justice, sir," said Tollworthy, "chucking him into his own beer?"

"*Poetic* justice? I wonder. Gabriel Sorn, of course. That is a possibility."

"Just a blind fit of rage?" suggested Cammison.

"But that would imply the whole crime was unpremeditated, and the anonymous letter contradicts that."

"Not necessarily," said Cammison. "A certain type of character—the moral weakling, sensitive, neurotic type, to put it roughly—would be apt to see red *after* the first blow was struck. You know, the sort of chap that would run over a cat in his car, and then get out and pretty well beat it to a jelly; it's fear, really; a combination of fear and sadism."

"Yes, there was a lad like that at my school. Timid, bullied, solitary. One day another boy was ragging him, and this lad turned on him and knocked him down with a lucky blow, and then he damned nearly beat out his brains on the floor. It took three of us to pull him off, and the other chap was in the san' for a fortnight. But would that type ever work out a murder and screw himself up to striking a first blow? That's what I doubt."

"I should say it was unlikely, but not impossible," Cammison replied. "The type we have in mind is probably a phantasy-builder. He would work out the execution of the murder in phantasy; he would be quite capable of sending the anonymous letter and even going to the brewery himself. In the ordinary course of events he would stop there. But, supposing he was discovered by Bunnett lurking about the place, supposing there was any sort of a row, his phantasy murder might actually be committed in real fact—in self-defence, almost. Once he'd knocked him silly, he might quite well taste blood—so to speak—and do the thing properly."

"Yes, that's reasonable, I think. Again, the cap seems to fit that wretched Sorn most accurately. One can't call the head brewer, for instance, or Miss Mellors a phantasy-building neurotic."

Nigel was wondering, though, who it was who had been recently described to him as "a bit of a moral weakling!" Not Gabriel Sorn, surely. No, Sophie had used the phrase about Joe Bunnett.

"Then again, there's the possibility of dementia praecox. What they call 'dual personality,' Jim," Dr. Cammison said. "The mind becomes split and its two parts work alternately. It's what's behind those cases of clergymen and schoolmasters of the most exemplary character suddenly committing indecent assaults in trains. Your murderer may be some normally harmless chap—and quite unaware of what he's done. Jekyll and Hyde, you know."

"Give us a chance, doctor," protested the sergeant. "You'll be telling me next it was Tyler, or your own missus, who did it."

Nigel said, "I wonder whether a deliberate, conscious splitting of the personality can make the subject specially prone to the morbid condition. Sorn, for instance, seems to keep himself pretty successfully in two separate compartments. He's quite a different person in the brewery from what he is chez Bolster."

"That I'm afraid I can't tell you."

"Anyway, it's all very abstract. What we want is some more facts. How about that anonymous letter, Sergeant? Is anything being done about that?"

"We've had a man on it, sir. The afternoon collections in Weston Priors are taken at 2.20 and 7.20. The letter must have been put in the box between those times, so I've been inquiring about people's movements on the afternoon of the 15th as well as the night of the 16th and 17th. Here's a list of people Tyler gave me, with their statements filled in. Care to have a look?"

"My hat!" exclaimed Nigel, glancing at the sheet of paper, "your inspector certainly is pretty broadminded in his choice of suspects." He read it out to himself.

| Name | 2.20–7.30 (July 15) | 11.30 onwards (July 16–17) |
|------|--------------------|-----------------------------|
| G. Sorn | In brewery till 5.30 p.m. (corroborated by H. Barnes and others). In lodgings 5.35–7.30 (Corroborated by Mrs. Bolster). | Out walking from 11.40 to 12.45 approx. (no corroboration yet). |
| H. Barnes | In brewery till 5.30 p.m. (corroborated by G. Sorn, etc.). Arr. at Stag's Head 7.5 and remained there till 8.15 (corroborated by barman, etc.). On own statement motoring in country between 5.30 and 7.5: route given (no corroboration given yet). | In bed (corroborated by wife). |

| | | |
|---|---|---|
| Mrs. Bunnett | 2.20–4.0 p.m. resting (partially corroborated by maid). Tea-party 4.15–5.30 (corroborated by Mrs. Amberley). 5.30–7.30, in garden and dressing for dinner (corroborated by maid). | Inbed (no corroboration yet). |
| J. Bunnett | Arr. Royal Lion, Poolhampton, 3 p.m. (corr. by porter, etc.). Movements during rest of day corr. by Elias Faulkes—in charge of Bunnett's boat, *The Gannet*—Hotel staff, etc. | No evidence. Presumably at sea. *The Gannett* put out from harbour 7.45 p.m. (corr. Elias Faulkes, etc.). |
| E. Parsons | In brewery till 5.10 p.m. (corr. by J. Stokes, etc.). Took Lily Barnes for ride on motor-bicycle—route given; did not go within 10 miles of Weston Priors (no corr. yet except by L. Barnes). Ret. 7.20 (corr. H. Barnes). | At dance till 11.30 p.m. Left with Lily Barnes—joy ride in country. (corr. by L. Barnes). L.B. ret. to her house, 12.30, (corr. H. Barnes). E.P. ret. to lodgings 12.15 approx. (corr. by landlady). |

| A. Mellors | Refuses to state whereabouts from 2.20–3.30 3.30–4.30 making jam (corr. by maid). 4.30–6.30 committee meeting (corr. by Rev. Summers). 6.30–7.30 gardening (corr. by neighbours). | In bed (no corr.—lives alone in house). |
| --- | --- | --- |
| H. Cammison | ? ? | ? ? |

"Um. I doubt if the July 15th column is much help. There are so many more ways of getting a letter posted than dropping it into the box oneself. Barnes, Mrs. Bunnett, Joe Bunnett, Parsons and Miss Mellors all might have done it, as far as we know at present."

"What's all this about?" asked Herbert.

"Question of who posted the anonymous letter, at Weston Priors between 2.20 and 7.20 on the 15th. You'd better fill up your little space· while we're about it."

"The 15th? Dear me, I was over at the Eglinton's that afternoon. Passed within a couple of miles of Weston Priors on the way back—you know, Jim, the road-fork at Aldminster. I seem to be qualifying rapidly for the rôle of first murderer."

Sergeant Tollworthy laughed heartily.. "Well, sir, you will have your little joke. If you'll just let me have the details——I expect Tyler'll want me to go routing after the A.A. man at Aldminster and such like."

Cammison gave them. Nigel was studying the list.

"I see you've got Ariadne down. Why wouldn't she tell you where she was that afternoon?"

"Search me, sir. Blew up very strong about it, she did; said her private affairs were nothing to do with a bunch of nosey-parker policemen. I felt like a house of cards in an earthquake, and no error. We'll have to look into it, I suppose. If Miss Mellors was anywhere on the blinking landscape, somebody couldn't have helped spotting her."

"I see this Ed Parsons has got a motor-bike," said Nigel. "I suppose the inspector told you Sorn's story to us about the masked raider and all."

"Masked? Cor! I never heard he was masked."

"Figuratively speaking. By blackest midnight masked from human view. Blank verse."

"Ar. Tyler's going after Parsons himself. His landlady might have made a little mistake about when he got in, and that Lily Barnes—a saucy bit—she *said* she was joy-riding with him, but——"

"But why should Ed Parsons do in Bunnett? Had he a motive, too? Is there anyone in the whole town and county who hadn't got a motive?"

"Knowing Bunnett, I should be inclined to doubt it," said Cammison grimly.

"Ed Parsons'd had a bit of trouble with Mr. Bunnett. About the lorry-loading. Case of some of the lorries being overloaded. We brought it into court. Young Ed said he had only acted on instructions from Mr. Bunnett, which Mr. Bunnett denies very vigorous. Ever since then, according to my Gertie who used to be regular thick with Lily Barnes—Lily being sweet on young Ed—Mr. Bunnett made his life a fair hell for him—always chivvying him about and finding fault and that. Got on his nerves, you might say. And that's not the whole of it. My Gertie told mother that Lily's been put in trouble and blames it on Mr. Bunnett, though you needn't let that go beyond you for the present, seeing as Gert told mother confidential."

"Yes, that's motive enough, I suppose. But I can't see that, if Parsons had murdered Bunnett, he'd advertise his presence by roaring out of the brewery gates on a motor-bike at midnight."

"That's right, sir. And Parsons is a decent, straight youngster too—a sight too good for that Lily, if you ask me."

"I wonder did Mr. Barnes know about his daughter being in trouble."

"That's what Tyler would ask, too. Only I've not told him about Lily yet." The sergeant shifted his feet and tugged his moustache uneasily. "I was just thinking, sir—if I might be so bold—would you have a word with Lily first yourself. You being unofficial like, she might be more willing to talk to you than to us."

"Mm. I don't know that I fancy myself as a squire of errant dames. Still. Yes, I'll do it. I've got to talk to her anyway about this Truffles business. What's the news from the Poolhampton front, by the way?"

"Mr. Joe Bunnett arrived there in his car about 3 o'clock. Spent the rest of that afternoon getting in stores, petrol for his engine and that——"

"Petrol for his engine?" said Nigel. "Didn't—surely Sophie told me that he despised engines, wouldn't have anything but sail?"

Herbert Cammison said, "Yes, he's a regular old shellback. But he told me he was putting in an auxiliary engine this cruise as he hadn't found anyone else to go with him and didn't care for the idea of managing the boat single-handed at his time of life, with nothing but sail. Very sensible. He's getting on for fifty, you know, and he's no Viking in physique."

"I see. And since, what is it—7.45 p.m. on Thursday, he's been sailing westward, has he?"

"Yes, sir. We've warned all the places he may put in—Lyme Regis, Exmouth, Plymouth and the rest—to be on the look-out for his boat, but he's not put in anywhere yet."

"Nor will he, I don't expect," said Cammison: "he's got enough stores for a whole trip and a good big keg of water. I went on a cruise with him last year and he kept at sea the whole of the first four days on end. Hove-to at night and sailed all day. A storm'd be the only thing that'd drive him into port."

"Seems as if we'd better warn shipping to keep a look-out for him. Still, there's no immediate hurry about that, I reckon. The brewery can get on without him for a day or two longer. Seems a pity to spoil his holiday."

After which lamentably unofficial statement, the sergeant sucked his teeth and gazed abstractedly into his tankard. Herbert interpreted these signs correctly; the tankard was refilled.

"This is a lousy case," said Nigel. "No corpse—to speak of. Everyone's got a motive. No one seems to have an alibi except Barnes and Parsons—and their alibis are only supplied by their women, which means they're worth damn all to us. The whole thing is really most unorthodox. The textbooks aren't going to help us. We shall have to take to a planchette board or a divining-rod or something. What candidates is Tyler backing—or is the old fox keeping an open mind?"

"He fancies Mr. Sorn at present, I'd say, sir. The

*118*

young gentleman stood to gain most by Mr. Bunnett's death. The inspector's asked the French police to get in touch with Mrs. Sorn, but there won't be anything in that quarter. The lady's never visited this town—that we *do* know, so she couldn't've known enough about the brewery to do what was done."

"You know," said Nigel, "I feel there's something we've missed. There's something sort of ringing in my head, connected vaguely with that party after the literary society meeting. Now what the devil is it?"

Nigel went over in his mind what had happened in this room two nights ago. Mrs. Bunnett had taken a firm line about having some sherry. Eustace had said, "Are you sure you wouldn't rather have a glass of water, my dear?" or words to that effect. The precise, crackling voice echoed in Nigel's head; but there was something missing; another sound ought to accompany it. Another sound——

"Ha!" he exclaimed. "Keys! Bunnett jingled a bunch of keys that night. Where are they? Why did the murderer leave everything in Bunnett's pockets except the bunch of keys?"

"Oh, but we *did* find them, sir. I made a second search in the hop-back that night, Mr. Barnes having stated that the deceased always carried a bunch of keys—and there they was, sure enough. Easy enough to miss them the first time in that lucky dip: filtered it all the second time: found some more teeth too."

"Gone!" declaimed Nigel tragically; "all, all my little ones! That's the very last idea I had left. Now I shall resign."

Sergeant Tollworthy rose, not without difficulty. "Well, gentlemen, I must be getting along. Now don't you worry, doctor: we'll get the chap before long. And if that Feather starts talking any more, I'll knock his block off."

"A friend at court," Nigel said when the sergeant had gone.

"Yes. He's a good sort. I pulled his boy, Ned, out of a nasty attack of pneumonia last year, and old Tollworthy's been almost embarrassingly grateful ever since."

"It certainly is quite a nice change to find a bobby who doesn't suspect everybody on principle. That's one of the two bright spots in this stygian case."

"And the other?"

"Whoever slew Bunnett had his heart in the right place, so we needn't anticipate any more murders. The *fons et origo mali* has been—shall we say, choked off? So everyone should be quite happy."

"Let's hope you're right," said Cammison equably.

# VIII
## July 19, 8.20–11.30 a.m.

*Surely the continual habit of dissimulation is but a*
*weak and sluggish cunning, and not greatly politic.*
BACON, *Advancement of Learning*

SUNDAY morning. Maiden Astbury hangs in a state
of suspended animation. The Prior chimes have rung
out cheerfully for the early service, and ceased ringing: the five-minutes' bell has played its game of
cat-and-mouse with belated worshippers; sounding
with quickening impatience, then falling ominously
silent so that old ladies lifted their black-satin skirts
and took to their heels, then striking up again in
leisurely fashion—putting out its iron tongue, no
doubt, at the panting old things; then repeating the
process all over again. Now the mischievous five-
minutes' bell is silent too, and the streets settle down
to doze and enjoy the mild sunlight. Even the pieces
of tinfoil and paper, with which a roaring charabanc
party littered them yesterday evening, look peculiarly smug and lifeless. The only sound that breaks
this Sabbath calm proceeds from the bathroom of
Dr. Cammison's house, where Nigel is favouring the
chromium-plated taps with a selection from his rep-
ertoire. Even the politest Wykehamist would have
had some difficulty in expressing an admiration for
Nigel's singing voice: his own friends compared it

to the barking of a sea-lion, to the sound of one of
the earliest tractors surmounting a particularly steep
gradient of ploughed land, to the hoarse shouts of
a brutal soldiery mopping up some devoted outpost,
to a road-drill, to the croaking of ravens on a wild
and rock-bound coast—according to their natural
bent and powers of invention. On one thing everyone would agree, and that is the really shattering
volume of sound which Nigel, when warmed up,
can emit.

> "*I met with Napper Tandy,*
> *And I took him by the hand,*"

he roared, beating time with a defeated-looking loo-
fah. Instead, however, of proceeding to inquire how
poor old Ireland was and where did she stand, Nigel
fell suddenly silent. "I met with Napper Tandy and
I took him by the hand," he said to himself. "Now
that's a point that might have struck me before. Did
the murderer meet Bunnett at the brewery entrance
and say, 'Fancy seeing you here at this time of night!
Well, as you're here, just come into the office a minute, will you; I want to slit your throat with this
decent little knife I have in my pocket.' Because,
if he didn't, how could he be sure that Bunnett would
ever be in a vulnerable position to be murdered?
After all, Bunnett had gone there to catch out the
watchman in his alleged pilfering: he would keep
near Lock, wherever Lock went, so Lock would be
a sort of unconscious bodyguard. Of course, the murderer could lie in wait for Bunnett somewhere *en
route* between the brewery gates and—and where,
though? Bunnett might decide to go straight to the
storeroom, or the place where the bottled beer was

kept, or Lock's cubby-hole. How could the murderer know which route Bunnett was going to take? Of course, he might lurk in the brewery yard and cut his victim off before he entered the actual premises. But the yard was overlooked by the row of houses opposite, and there would be just a chance of someone seeing him in the act. Apart from that, if he killed Bunnett in the yard, why go to all the trouble and danger of dragging him into the brewery and up the steps of the copper platform? Why not leave him weltering in his gore? Which, of course, brought one back to the original teaser—why was Bunnett put in the copper at all?

"Leaving that aside," thought Nigel, "perhaps my first idea is not so crazy as it sounded. It is quite conceivable that the murderer—call him X—should have met Bunnett at the brewery entrance. What excuse could he have for being there? Holed out in one!—say he had received an anonymous letter; produce it, in fact—he could easily have posted himself one at the same time that Bunnett's was posted. After that, it should be easy enough to manoeuvre Bunnett into some secluded corner where the blunt instrument or whatnot could be wielded with maximum impunity. But not, surely, the copper-room? There could be no possible excuse for dragging Bunnett up there when the two of them were supposed to be padding on the trail of the errant Lock. Bunnett *must* have been murdered somewhere else—in some room where X could plausibly take him in the process of catching out the night watchman. Where? Well, why not one of the offices—Bunnett's own room or Joe Bunnett's, or the clerk's office? None of these was visited by the night watchman, which would make it easier still. X might say—*par exem-*

*ple*—'Look here, this chap Lock may cut up nasty; there's a jolly little life-preserver (revolver, loaded stick) in so and so's office: let's go and fetch it first.' Or—but there were dozens of pretexts for getting Bunnett up there. There ought to have been some signs left, though, if any of the private rooms or offices was used. I must ask the office staff about that: or whoever cleans them out in the morning. I wonder if Joe Bunnett's room is locked up in his absence. That would have been a good place.

"And then there is another thing. If my theorising is correct, it eliminates Mrs. Bunnett, Miss Mellors and Herbert Cammison from the list of suspects: because none of them could conceivably have claimed that "Well-wisher" had sent them a letter telling them how to catch out the night watchman. Joe Bunnett might also be eliminated: he couldn't plausibly assert that he'd returned from his cruise on the strength of an anonymous letter. No, not plausibly to anyone but a semi-maniac like his brother. Eustace Bunnett, in his horrible zeal to catch out his employees anywhere and anyhow, might overlook a consideration like that. Joe cannot be absolutely eliminated. That leaves me with Gabriel Sorn, the head brewer, Ed Parsons, and—more doubtfully—Joe Bunnett as starters in the suspicion stakes." Nigel was aroused from his reverie by a banging on the door.

"Hoy!" a voice cried. "Have you had a syncope? Or are you carrying out experiments with boiling water? I want a bath."

"Sorry, Herbert. I was just thinking."

"Well, your thinking is less offensive than your singing, I'll admit, but equally inconvenient for your fellow men."

Nigel made some lurid observations on the verbiage of pedants, and prepared to get out. . . .

Two hours later he was entering the neat and unassuming residence of Mr. H. Barnes. He was shown into a parlour which, for sheer heat and luxuriance of fern-growth, fell little short of a tropical forest. The head brewer shortly appeared, in his shirtsleeves. He greeted Nigel with one eyebrow lifted and the other depressed.

"Well, sir, and what brings you to my humble abode so early in the morning?" he asked jocularly.

"I wanted a word with your daughter, Lily. I'm supposed to be running the Truffles angle of this case, and I thought I'd make a beginning with the office staff."

Mr. Barnes scratched his bristly chin. "Well, I suppose that's all right," he said dubiously. "If you like wasting your time, it's none of my affair. Don't worry Lil, will you sir? She's not been herself lately. Don't know what's up with her: but tell her old dad about it—not she. Shouldn't wonder if it wasn't nothing but them daft film magazines she spends her money on," he added darkly.

"No, I'll not worry her. Just a few harmless questions I want to ask. But, look here, there are one or two things perhaps you could tell me first."

Nigel elicited the information that *(a)* Joe Bunnett's room was locked in his absence, but there was a master-key in the office which would open it; *(b)* the private rooms and offices had not been cleaned the morning of the murder, but the police had been through them since; *(c)* that Eustace Bunnett was no loss to the world, and the brewery would be a different place with Mr. Joe in command.

"Yes, put it on its legs again, he will," said Mr. Barnes.

"That reminds me. Didn't you say, that afternoon in your office when Mr. Sorn and I were there, that there were rumours about Bunnett selling the brewery?"

Mr. Barnes tapped the side of his nose. "Don't ask no questions, and you'll be told no lies."

"But surely it can't make any difference now. Eustace is dead, so presumably the thing'll fall through."

"Yes, there's something in that," said the head brewer, who clearly liked confidences to be extorted from him with due deliberation and ceremonial. "Mind you, Mr. Strangeways, I'm not saying it's gospel. It may have been a canard. Yes, a canard," he repeated with relish: "but it did come to my ears, through channels which I will not specify, that Roxby's—that big Midland firm—were in negotiation with Mr. Bunnett to buy him out."

"Why should he—I mean, it seems odd that Bunnett should have contemplated selling the business when he got so much kick out of bossing it."

"Put that way, it does. But that's only half the matter," said Mr. Barnes magisterially, "you see—mind you, I'm making no assertions—there's such a thing as selling out *and* there's such a thing as being sold up."

"You mean the brewery was bankrupt?"

The head brewer's eyebrows nearly shot off the top of his head with horror.

"Now, please, Mr. Strangeways," he protested, "really, you mustn't leap to conclusions like that. The truth of it is this. The guv'nor was hidebound; he didn't like newfangled ways and he didn't like spending money—and there's no use shutting our eyes to it. Consequentially, the brewery was having a hard time to compete with firms that've got better methods and newer equipment. Bunnett's wasn't bankrupt, but I doubt we'd not have stood the racket another ten years—or even five, may be."

"Have you any idea how long these negotiations had been going on?"

"With Roxby's? Couldn't say for certain. Quite recently, I should guess."

"Oh, well, we'll get in touch with Roxby's about that."

"That's all right. But don't forget"—Mr. Barnes did complicated things with his eyebrows—"I told you nothing."

"You——? Oh, of course. No, we'll call it 'information received.' Tell me one thing more. If Roxby's had taken over Bunnett's, would it have meant big changes in the staff?"

Mr. Barnes gave Nigel one of his unexpected shrewd glances. "I see what you're getting at." He was silent a moment. "No, you're barking up the wrong tree, Mr. Strangeways. I don't reckon the transfer would've affected our staff—they're good lads, worth their money, all of 'em. They'd not be turned off."

"And what about Joe Bunnett, yourself and Mr. Sorn?" said Nigel, meeting frankness with frankness.

"What? The key men in the place? Now you're joking, sir."

Mr. Barnes laughed heartily.

"Too heartily?" thought Nigel: "mightn't Roxby's have made a clean sweep? Of course, Joe has a share in the brewery; they couldn't do anything about that: but they could install a new manager in his place. And surely Sorn, a pupil brewer, couldn't be called a key man."

"Well, many thanks," said Nigel. "Can I have a word with your daughter now?"

"Righty-ho. I'll call her."

Mr. Barnes ambled to the door, his long arms swinging loosely.

"Hey, Lil!" he called up the stairs.

"Yes, Dad?"

"Gentleman wants to see you."

This announcement was received with an audible giggle, and "Tell Ed not to be so fresh! I'm all in my best Sunday undies. He'd better try!"

"It's not Ed. It's a gentleman—he's staying with Dr. Cammison. Look sharp and get dressed, my girl!"

There was a stifled shriek. Then silence. Mr. Barnes put his head in at the door of the parlour and said—with that air of deep significance which his lugubrious face contrived to impart to the most ordinary statements:

"Two's company, Mr. Strangeways. I'll get along. Lil will be down in a minute."

Whatever Nigel was expecting—and certainly, after the exchanges he had just heard, he expected the worst—he could not have anticipated the apparition that entered the room five minutes later. Lily Barnes inherited her long face, long arms and lanky body from her father; on this groundwork she had built up a remarkably accurate representation of Greta Garbo. Her coiffure evidently dated from "Christina of Sweden," a sort of tawny mane flopping along her shoulders: she had powdered her face till it was stark-white as any film close-up of the great original: she had used no make-up, except for the subdued red on her long, drooping mouth. Lily Barnes wore an old raincoat—and nothing between it and the "best Sunday undies," Nigel suspected. She slouched into the room, her hands in the pockets of the raincoat, leaning her back against the door and mooed huskily at Nigel.

"You want to see me?"

Nigel, with superhuman efforts, restrained himself from replying, "No, I tank I go 'oame," and said:

"Er—yes, just for a few minutes. I want—I say, won't you sit down?"

"I like to stand."

"Oh—er—well, you please yourself." He pulled himself together. Shock tactics might be best for this Garbo. "I want to talk to you about Mr. Bunnett's dog, Truffles."

One of Lil's hands came out and began stroking the woodwork of the door. That was foolish of her, thought Nigel, noticing how the hand shook. She kept up her end, however.

"Truffles? Yes. Poor little dog," she mooed wearily.

"Now, I have good reason to believe that, when Truffles—er—met his end, everyone in the brewery was satisfactorily accounted for except the office staff," said Nigel briskly. "I have also reason to believe that the killing of the dog may be connected with the killing of Mr. Bunnett."

"So what?" asked Lily sharply, with a temporary lapse into Jean Harlow.

"So, as I'm sitting in on this case, I thought I'd come to one of the office staff and see what she had to say about it."

"Oh, a detective, yes? You accuse me of killing the poor little dog?"

Nigel changed direction with fluency and astuteness. He gazed at Lily admiringly, as though he had not noticed her properly before.

"You know," he said, "when you came into the room, I couldn't think for a moment who you reminded me of. Really, it's an extraordinary resemblance. I should say you had a real film personality:

and it's personality that does count on the screen nowadays."

Miss Barnes swallowed the bait voraciously. She beamed in a most un-Garboesque manner and said:

"That's what I'm always telling Ed."

"Ed?"

"Ed Parsons—he's my bo—one of my admirers, I mean," Lily amended hastily.

"Well, whaddya-know-about-that?" exclaimed Nigel, desperately ransacking his memory for film vocabulary. "Ed Parsons? Well, isn't that just too bad now?"

"What do you mean?" asked Lily sharply.

"Well, I'll say that boy is in one tough spot just now with the bulls."

"Oh, come off it!" said Lily, dropping Greta Garbo with a thump onto the floor. "Talk English! My Ed's not done anything, and if anyone says——"

"Half a minute," interrupted Nigel gratefully, resuming his own personality. "Let's get the Truffles business straight first. Either his death is connected with Bunnett's or not."

"Go on!" Lily said derisively.

"I will. If it was connected, it implies that the murderer wished to make an experiment in the sarcophagous qualities——"

"The *what* qualities?"

"Sorry, the flesh-devouring qualities of the pressure copper. In other words, whoever killed Truffles killed Bunnett too. So naturally a certain amount of suspicion falls on the office staff."

The dawning consternation in Lily's eyes did not escape Nigel. But he continued glibly, looking down his nose now, "Of course, the whole thing may have been a practical joke that went wrong—or explainable in some innocent way; in fact it would be very much more comfortable for everyone concerned if it was. But I'm afraid——"

Lily Barnes was beside him, clutching his shoulders. "Look here, if I tell you, will you promise not to spill it to Mr. Joe or Dad. They'd be ever so angry, and it was all an accident, I swear it was."

Nigel's sighting shot had hit the bull. He tried to look as omniscient as Lily evidently believed him to be, sat the girl down in a chair and made her tell her story. Briefly, it was this. Eustace Bunnett had been raising hell in the office the day before. Lily and the two clerks, rabid with indignation, had planned to kidnap Truffles. This was partly to spite its owner and partly because they were genuinely sorry for the animal—Truffles had not escaped his master's ill-temper that morning; they had heard Bunnett thrashing him in his room. The plan was that when Bunnett went out for his morning tour of inspection the next day, Lily should take the dog, hide him under her coat, walk into the brewery yard with him and hand him over to her friend, Gertie Tollworthy, who would be waiting just outside the yard gates with a hamper. Gertie would take a bus and hand over the dog to some friends of hers who lived in a small village twenty miles away. There he would be kept till a permanent home was found for him. All had gone swimmingly, up to a point. But just as Lily was about to walk out of the premises, she heard Bunnett talking to the clerk in the entrance office. So, unfortunately, did Truffles. He began to yelp under her coat. Lily lost her head and rushed through the door and up the ladder into the copper-room. Luckily there was no one there at the moment. Lily stood behind the wall of the open copper, ready to duck down if Bunnett should come that way. Truffles was now thoroughly restive. He had heard his master's voice; and, with that perverse and horrible instinct that drives a dog to come cowering up to the hand that will beat him (his instinct told him he was doing wrong not to be sitting tamely in his basket in Bunnett's room), Truffles squirmed and wriggled, and before Lily could get a proper grip on him, he had squirmed out of her arms and fallen straight into the open copper.

That was that. Lily knew he would be dead in a second after dropping into that seething brew. She hurried back to the office and told her fellow conspirators what had happened. When Bunnett made his inquiries into the dog's disappearance, both the clerks swore black and blue that Lily had been in the office all the time that he was out of his room; and, if any of the other employees had seen her elsewhere on the premises, they liked her too much to rush off to Bunnett with the information.

This tale was at the same time so odd and so circumstantial that Nigel had no difficulty in believing it, apart from it's teller's obvious sincerity. But there was one point.

"I'm sure that is the truth," he said: "don't get the idea that I'm doubting it, because I'm not. But from all I've heard of the late E. Bunnett, I'm rather surprised he didn't bully the truth out of you himself."

Lily blushed and twisted her fingers round one of the raincoat buttons.

"He didn't try very hard. You see—well, it does seem silly, him being as old as the hills and past that sort of thing, you'd think—but he was a bit sweet on me and I suppose that's why."

132

This was going to be a ticklish operation, thought Nigel. Well, he might as well have a go at it.

"I suppose Ed was pretty jealous—if he knew that, I mean."

Lily's face grew hard and sullen. "Here," she said, "are you trying to put anything on Ed, because, if you are, I'll thank you to keep your nose out of it."

"It's not what *I* am trying to put on him. It's the police—and their noses are a sight sharper than mine."

The girl's long mouth began to quiver. She burst out:

"But Ed wouldn't—anyhow, he didn't know—and I was with him that night, out in Honeycombe Wood, we were, we went out there on his motor-bike after the dance—we didn't get back till half-past twelve—so he couldn't have done the murder, that proves it, doesn't it?"

Nigel claimed no infallibility as a lie-detector. Indeed, he might easily have accepted all this if he hadn't just before heard Lily telling what was almost certainly the truth about Truffles. There was such an obvious divergence between her ways of telling the two different stories. Ed's alibi came too readily, too mechanically to her tongue in spite of the emotional strain which made the actual wording of it a little incoherent: and she gave the impression—an impression that all unpractised liars give—of listening to her own words and listening for their effect on the audience.

Nigel said, in his gentle but detached voice, not looking at Lily:

"You know, I've been mixed up in several crimes, and there's one thing I've always noticed. It does pay to tell the truth. I remember a case not long ago when several witnesses—from the best and most unselfish motives—withheld certain bits of information and distorted others. It was an awful mistake on their part. They wanted to shield someone; and, of course, we soon tumbled to who that someone was, and it merely had the effect of making us suspect him far more seriously than we should have done if his friends had told the truth all along. That's all rather complicated: but you see what I mean? If you really believe someone is innocent, then much the best thing is to tell the truth about him. To tell the truth is really a test of how strong your belief is. If *you*, for instance, love Ed Parsons enough to believe absolutely in his innocence, then——"

Nigel was interrupted by a subdued sob from the girl. She mastered herself and said:

"You really mean that? Honest? You're not trying to trap me into——?"

"I don't look like a grizzled trapper, do I?"

"I'll trust you, then. I've been ever so miserable, wondering if I oughtn't to. You see, Mr. Strangeways, it was like this——"

Then Lily Barnes began to tell her tale—a different tale. She and Ed had left the dance at 11.30, as she had originally said, and gone up to Honeycombe Wood. There a quarrel had flared up. Ed had started throwing his weight about on the subject of Eustace Bunnett. Lily had replied spiritedly that she was not married to Ed yet, and if he didn't like her gentlemen friends, he knew what he could do about it. Ed replied darkly that he did know, and Bunnett'd better watch his step and so had Lily—if it wasn't too late already. Just what exactly did he mean by that? Well, he said, it wouldn't've been the first time

134

that a girl had been got into trouble by her employer. Lily had been furious at this totally false (she assured Nigel) insinuation: so furious, indeed, that she hadn't even bothered to deny its truth. If Ed believed she was that sort, he was welcome to and she wouldn't take him back, not if he went down on his knees to her. Nigel asked how the young man could have got such an idea into his head, and Lily replied that that dirty little cat, Gertie Tollworthy, who apparently nourished a hopeless passion for Ed, must have been telling stories. Remembering the sergeant's statement, Nigel could verify this. But, he said, he thought Lily and Gertie were bosom friends. Lily made some forceful comments on the subject of vipers in bosoms, and told him that she had quarrelled with Gertie soon after the Truffles episode and not been on speaking terms since. Nigel led her tactfully back to the dust-up with Ed. After raving for a bit, Ed had asked her point-blank whether she was with child by Bunnett. Lily had said if he liked to believe that, then she was not going to stop him; and added some excusable but ill-advised remarks on the comparative potentiality of Ed and Mr. Bunnett for fatherhood. That, as she said, tore it properly. Ed had taken her refusal to deny his accusation as a confession of guilt, jumped on his motor-bike and ridden off at breakneck speed, leaving Lily to walk back by herself into Maiden Astbury. The evening after, Ed had come round in a fair panic. Eustace Bunnett had been murdered and the police would be bound to suspect him of the murder. Lily herself was terrified that he might have done it, though he swore that, after leaving her the night before, he'd ridden about the country lanes half-trying to break his neck and not gone near the brewery. So she had made it up with him and agreed to say that she had been with him all the time that night.

"What time did Ed leave you, actually?" asked Nigel.

"I heard the Priory clock strike midnight just before he went off. You don't think he——?"

"No, I don't. And it just shows you how very much more satisfactory it'd have been if you'd told the truth at the beginning. You see, it's not likely that Ed would've made plans to kill Bunnett until he had heard from your own mouth that the old satyr had done you wrong. But the anonymous letter that got Bunnett into the brewery was written on the 15th, the day before your quarrel. Mind you, that doesn't clear Ed absolutely; but it will make things look a good deal better for him."

Lily smiled at Nigel. She had recovered her spirits and a certain measure of her Garbo personality as well.

"You know, you're a nice boy. A very nice boy, you are, really," she said.

"Yes," said Nigel, backing hastily towards the door, "so my wife tells me. I'll be seeing you."

# IX
## July 19, 11.30 a.m.–1.20 p.m.

*I'll example you with thievery.*
SHAKESPEARE, *Timon of Athens*

*Frost and fraud have dirty ends.*
WILLIAM GURNALL,
*Christian in Complete Armour*

ON his way to the police station, Nigel called in at Ed Parsons' lodgings. Ed was a tall young man, with a mop of stubborn red hair and a rather delicate, pallid complexion. He was inclined to be truculent at first; but, on hearing that Lily had told Nigel the real story, he calmed down and admitted its truth. He had left Lily in a towering rage and ridden madly around the deserted lanes for nearly half an hour before returning home. He was ashamed now of ever having suspected her of relations with Bunnett; but he'd been ragged about it a bit at the brewery, and when Gertie Tollworthy told him Lily was going to have a baby and Lily led him on to thinking it must be true, what could you expect?

"When did Gertie tell you that?" Nigel asked.

"Oh—let me see now, it was during the dance— on Thursday night, that was."

"Good. If she corroborates that, you're out," thought Nigel to himself. "The letter was posted on Wednesday afternoon. Unless, of course, there's a conspiracy between Ed and Gertie, and that doesn't seem likely. Anyway, if Gertie had told Ed her story *before* Thursday night he would have already determined to kill Bunnett and written the anonymous letter—in which case it would obviously not be safe to let Lily know that he believed her guilty."

However, to make sure certain, Nigel obtained the Tollworthy's address from Parsons, found Gertie in, and soon reduced her to a proper state of tears and repentance. Yes, she agreed that she had come to Ed with that tale about Lily and Mr. Bunnett on Thursday night: she couldn't help it; seeing Ed dancing with Lil made her feel so jealous of a sudden, it all slipped out: and of course, Mr. Bunnett *had* been carrying on a bit with Lil—at least, that's what people in the brewery were saying; so really it was only right for someone to warn Ed.

Nigel cut short this casuistry, and walked the thirty yards farther to the police station. There he found Sergeant Tollworthy, positively bursting his buttons with suppressed excitement.

"Mr. Bunnett's house burgled last night," he said.

"Eustace Bunnett's?"

"Yes, sir."

"What was taken?"

"That we don't rightly know yet. No silver or nothing like that. The chap seems to have been after higher game."

"Cool! You interest me strangely, Watson. Not private papers, by any chance?"

The sergeant leant back, put his head on one side, and gazed at Nigel admiringly.

"I told that Tyler only this morning that you'd got a head on your shoulders," he said. "It never does to judge by appearances, does it, sir?" he added enthusiastically.

"No, I suppose it doesn't," replied Nigel, with less enthusiasm.

"Papers—that's what it was, sir. Properly rifled, Mr. Bunnett's study was. Drawers opened—everything all over the shop. Inspector's going through them now with Mrs. Bunnett, though I don't reckon she knows much about her husband's private affairs."

"Did he break in—the burglar, I mean."

"No, sir, just walked, seemingly. You was right about them keys, after all, sir."

"Right about the keys?" said Nigel, mystified.

"Ar. It's like this. When, in the course of our investigations upon the scene of the crime, we found no traces of breaking and entering," the sergeant declaimed sonorously, "we deduced that the burglar must have been in possession of keys. The front door was bolted as well as locked at night, of course: but there's a side door with a Yale lock, unbolted, and it was through the same that the criminal must have effected his entry. Similarly, the drawers of Mr. Bunnett's buroo had not been forced, which pointed to the presence of a desk-key in the possession of the miscreant."

"Quite so," said Nigel, his head reeling a little from the solid impact of this jargon. "But how did the keys come into the possession of the—er—miscreant?"

"Ah," said the sergeant rather gratuitously, "now you've laid your finger on the vital spot. Tyler had an idea—a bit overdue, I reckon, but he does his best with the brains God gave him. He showed Mr. Bunnett's key-ring, what was found in the hop-back, to Mrs. Bunnett, thinking as how the murderer might have slipped a couple of 'em off before he pushed the deceased into the copper. 'Nothing doin',' says the lady: 'all present and correct.' Tyler was looking fair disheartened, when Mrs. Bunnett pipes up, 'But what about the duplicates? Where are they? So it transpires as Mr. Bunnett used to keep duplicates of his door keys, and the keys of the desks in his home and in the brewery, in his waistcoat pocket; so as, if he lost one set, he'd still have another—if you take my meaning.'

"In fact, it's dollars to doughnuts that the bloke who was making merry with Bunnett's papers last night was the bloke who murdered Bunnett."

"That's right, sir. But there ain't no fingerprints, none that haven't a business to be there. So I can't see as it helps us much."

"Oh, come now, I don't agree with that. However, did Mrs. Bunnett take the point? I mean, how did she react to the idea of having had a midnight visit from the murderer?"

"Oh, she's a regular caution, the old girl is. Murderer in the house? Husband's study burgled? Did that worry her? Not a bit of it! Kept nagging at Tyler to arrest Alice—that's her servant—for eating a cake and a couple of loaves she'd baked the day before. In a fair taking over it, the old girl was. Tyler had to dry her up pretty sharp in the end."

At this point the inspector came in, carrying a file and a sheaf of papers under his arm. He nodded curtly to Nigel and sat down at his table.

"Find anything missing, sir?" asked Tollworthy.

"All in good time, me lad," said Tyler, spreading the papers out in front of him and perusing them. Then he added, over his shoulder, "Can't tell what was missing because we don't know what was there originally."

The sergeant subsided. After a minute or two,

Tyler pushed the papers away impatiently.

"Nothing there that I can see. That leaves us with this file. New file marked 'Roxby's,' Mr. Strangeways, found it empty, and no papers in Mr. Bunnett's study connected with it. Roxby's? Now where the devil have I heard that name?"

"The night watchman was in their employment before he came to Bunnett's," said Nigel demurely.

The inspector frowned. "Yes, of course. Had it on the tip of my tongue. I always thought there might be something fishy about that man Lock."

"Not fish, beer," said Nigel, succumbing, as usual, to his weakness for exhibitionism. "Roxby's is a big brewery firm in the Midlands. The missing papers contain preliminary negotiations between Roxby's and Mr. Bunnett for the sale of Bunnett's controlling interest in the brewery to Roxby's."

Nigel looked down his nose and waited for the storm to break. The sergeant's eyes appeared to be coming out on stalks. Tyler was sitting quite rigid, his big white face motionless as a frozen moon: then he burst out:

"Look here, sir. Have you been withholding this information?"

"No, no! Certainly not. Never withhold information—at least, scarcely ever. Most irregular. Very bad form. I only heard the—er—details this morning."

Nigel proceeded to recount his interview with the head brewer. Tyler told the sergeant to get a trunk-call through to someone in authority at Roxby's.

"Pity Barnes didn't tell me all this before. Obstructive that man's been all along. Still, it pretty well lets him out, I suppose."

"Lets him out? Why?"

"Well, sir," explained the inspector, his small eyes

narrowed superciliously, "that's surely quite obvious. If Barnes had gone to all that trouble last night to destroy the evidence of this forthcoming deal with Roxby's, he'd not be likely to tell you all about the deal this morning."

"I don't know about that. It would be an excellent way of diverting suspicion from himself."

"Oh, come now, Mr. Strangeways. That's much too subtle for me. People don't behave like that, outside of books."

"Well, then, why didn't the thief take the file away? And why did he leave the room in such disorder?"

"Lost his head, I expect. The servant, Alice, says she got up and went out of her bedroom about one o'clock in the morning. No doubt the thief heard her moving about and did a bunk."

"That's very theoretical. If it was of such vital importance to him to keep the Roxby's affair quiet by stealing the papers, why on earth didn't he take the file too?"

"I suppose he didn't see the name. 'Roxby's' written on it. It's on the underside of the cover-flap where he could easily miss it."

"Well, I still think the whole thing suggests the murderer's deliberately drawing our attention to the Roxby's transactions; which would imply that his real motive for the murder was quite a different one."

The inspector laughed. "With your imagination, sir, you ought to write a book."

"I have," replied Nigel sourly. "I have also eliminated another of your suspects."

"Is that so, sir?" said Tyler in a humouring voice.

"Is it so. Ed Parsons."

Nigel gave the gist of his interviews with Lily, Ed, and Gertie Tollworthy.

"Humph! So them two were telling us lies all the time, were they? They'll hear some more from me about that."

"No doubt. But in the meantime we've got this little affair of a murder on our hands. I——"

Nigel was interrupted by the tinkle of the desk telephone. The inspector took off the receiver.

"Hallo! This is Inspector Tyler, speaking from Maiden Astbury, Dorset. . . . A round of golf? Yes, sir, it must have been inconvenient for you: but I happen to be investigating a murder. . . . Yes, Mr. Eustace Bunnett. . . . Yes, sir, very sad. . . . Now I just want to know the details of the negotiations between him and your people for the sale of Bunnett's. . . . Yes, sir, of course it shall remain confidential. . . ."

The metallic gabble from the other end proceeded. At one point the inspector's eyes grew round and he whistled under his breath. "Closing the place down, you say? . . . Yes, of course. . . . And was there anyone else, at your end or over here, who'd be likely to know of these negotiations? . . . I see. Thank you very much, sir. I think that will be all for the present."

Tyler turned to Nigel with a triumphant look.

"I wonder how your Mr. Barnes is going to explain that."

"You speak in riddles. Elucidate, I pray you."

"Roxby's were planning to extend their trade down this way. They're building a new works near Bath, and they proposed to buy up Bunnett's and close it down, so as to remove the competition. Said it'd pay them better than to modernise the place. And there was that Barnes stuffing you up with stories about how no one at the brewery'd be affected by the change! Played you up for a sucker properly, didn't he?"

"Well, he who sucks last sucks worst. We shall see. And are you rushing round to Mr. Barnes with a nice bright pair of handcuffs on the strength of that?"

"You bet I'm not. Plenty o' routine work to be done before that. But you amateurs aren't interested in that, are you? Too much like hard work, eh?" the inspector said, with the heavy jocularity of a giant squid that has digested a hundredweight of fresh fish and it now telling a baby cuttle where it gets off. "I'm not saying that Barnes is our man. But I reckon I've narrowed it down to him, Mr. Joe Bunnett and that Mr. Sorn. They're the only ones who'd be interested in those negotiations with Roxby's not going through—and the only ones likely to know about them, too."

"Well, I'm still inclined to think that this Roxby's business is a smoke-cloud put up by the murderer. Still, supposing you're right: what about Joe Bunnett? He'd be the one most likely to know the details of the negotiations. Closing down the brewery would be a bad show for him financially; whereas Bunnett's death gives him absolute control over it; and he does seem to have been really interested in the place— as a human being, I mean—the idea of all those chaps being turned off——"

"Ah, very likely. But where is he? He's so well known in this town and the villages around, because of his travelling round the pubs owned by the firm. Somebody'd be bound to have seen and recognised him by now. If it was him that entered Bunnett's study last night, he can't be very far away; he hasn't been seen at the railway station here, and his car is in garage down in Poolhampton. But it'd be madness for him to stay anywhere near the town if he did the murder and this cruise of his was intended for an alibi."

"No news about *The Gannet* yet?"

"No. Funny, that. Shipping's been warned, as well as the coastguards and harbour authorities. Fairly easy for a man to disappear, but how you make a decent-size cabin-cruiser vanish, I just don't know."

"Some bird got a magic wand, I expect. Or alternatively, it might have sunk."

"In this weather?"

"Yes, it's a brute, isn't it? I suppose Joe Bunnet hasn't been buying a motor-cycle lately?"

The inspector's moon-white face assumed a positively Machiavellian expression.

"Aha!" he said. "I wondered would you think of that. I'm making inquiries. Still an' all, he's not the only pebble on the beach. This young Mr. Sorn now—very suspicious his behaviour's been. Said he was out for a walk that night, but——"

"Somehow I doubt if we'd have got him to admit that so easily if he had done the murder. I dunno, though."

"And look at his motive. Fifty thousand quid to share with his mother—she's O.K., by the way: heard from the French police. She was sitting quiet in her villa over there when this happened."

"You're not committing yourself to the Roxby's motive, then?"

"Not altogether. It doesn't do to be bigoted, sir. Keep an open mind and study the facts is what I say."

The sergeant entered and informed Tyler that there was a man wanting to see him outside. The inspector went out. Nigel lit a cigarette, laid the cigarette-card on his thumb and flicked it neatly into the waste-paper basket at the other side of the room.

"Aha," he said to himself, "the old hand has not lost its cunning: which is more than can be said for the old brain, it seems. I just don't begin to have an idea who killed Bunnett. Gabriel Sorn, now. He seemed so obviously the villain of the piece that maybe I didn't think about him hard enough. He had opportunity and motive for the murder. On the other hand, he seems to have an alibi for the posting of the anonymous letter. Still, he could have got someone else to post it. Must find out if he knows anyone in Weston Priors. Motive, though. Somehow I can't quite see that young man killing anyone for money: he's not the calculating, cold-blooded type; and he did seem to be telling the truth when he said he knew nothing about Bunnett's will. What he really seemed upset about at that interview was that his mother should have had relations with Bunnett. Yes: the idea of that and of Bunnett being his father, might well push a neurotic sort of chap like him over the border-line. And Bunnett had been wounding him in another vital spot too: he'd been making him write doggerel advertisements for Bunnett's beers; remember how worked up he was about it on the night of the party. He'd resent that humiliation more than anything else almost. H'm. Gabriel Sorn. Yes. And the way, as I believe, the murderer's been drawing our attention to this Roxby's business; that points to Sorn too: he would be diverting our attention from himself and his own motives, because he actually stood to lose least by Bunnett's being closed down. Yes, Gabriel Sorn will bear looking into.

I wonder was he taking another of his nocturnal outings last night."

At this point the inspector entered with a puzzled look on his face.

"Chap called Carruthers outside," he said. "Just like someone to turn up with fresh complications when I thought I was beginning to get things straight."

"These things are sent to try us," said Nigel.

"Dunno what to make of it. This chap looks after the refrigerating-room in the brewery, he says. Apparently, on the morning after the crime, Friday morning—that is, he found some emergency bell connected with this room out of order."

"The devil he did! This is great news. Now we're getting somewhere at last. Why on earth didn't he say something about it before?"

"Afraid of getting into hot water. It was his business to look after the refrigerators, you see. So he put the bell right and said nothing. Now, as you know, on Friday night we made a thorough search of the premises looking for anything that'd give us a line on the exact spot where the crime was committed. We found nothing. So next morning we typed out an appeal, which Mr. Barnes posted up in various parts of the brewery, asking anyone who had noticed anything unusual or amiss the day before to come forward. So this Carruthers sleeps on it and to-day he decides it's his duty to bring the information. I don't see, though, as——"

But Nigel was already out of the room and beginning to question Carruthers.

"The bell was out of order. You mean it had been disconnected, switched off—whatever the word is, or deliberately damaged?"

Carruthers began to be exceedingly technical.

"Hoy! Stop!" said Nigel. "I was suckled on irregular verbs, not high-frequency coils. Tell me in words of one syllable. Uncle Percy's first lessons in electricity to the tots."

Carruthers grinned and did his best. Nigel gathered that the bell had been put out of order, in such a way that it might well seem the result of an accidental breakdown: Carruthers, however, knew that this type of bell was most reliable, and was strongly of the opinion that it must have been tampered with.

"Come along!" Nigel exclaimed. "We must visit the scene of the crime. This is big stuff. Noted amateur bloodhound follows up the Clue of the Sabotaged Bell."

He led the way to the brewery, Tyler and Carruthers vainly attempting to match his long, loping strides. Soon they were standing outside the solid door of the refrigerating-room. Carruthers gave a short lecture-demonstration.

"And this bell was in working order on Thursday?"

"Oh, yes, sir. Tested it on Thursday afternoon myself."

"Let us explore, then," said Nigel.

"You're wasting time, sir," said the inspector. "We've been over that room already."

"Never mind."

The heavy door was swung open and they entered. They searched for a quarter of an hour. The refrigerating-room was cold, clean, blanched and empty as a winter sky.

"There you are, sir," said the inspector.

"Yes. There—it seems—I am." Nigel was standing near the door, his back to one of the refrigerators. "Doesn't seem so cold as when I was here last."

"No, sir," said Carruthers. "We're defrosting now."

148

Nigel stiffened. Then his mouth fell open and his face took on the blank, staring expression of one who has been shot and is just on the point of toppling over.

"Defrosting!" he yelled. "God, what a fool I am! Good old Jack Frost! Where's that blasted coat got to, I wonder?"

He took to his heels and ran like a mad dog out of the room. The inspector, pounding after him, arrived a very bad second at the head brewer's signal-box of an office. Nigel was already rummaging in the pockets of several long white coats that hung on the wall. Now he held out his hand to Tyler. On the palm lay a fragment of some dark green substance, about the size of a third of his little finger-nail.

"There you are," he said breathlessly: "the missing clue. Feast your eyes on it, old boy. Now we're off."

He hurried back to the refrigerating-room, the inspector rumbling ominously at his side. When they had returned, Tyler burst out, "Now, then, sir. What *is* all this about? What's the idea concealing evidence like——?"

"Concealing my backside! I only just remembered it. When I was being shown over this room on Friday morning, I picked up that little slip of stuff—without thinking—you know—and put it in the pocket of the white coat I was wearing. Carruthers mentioning defrosting touched the spring in my memory. You see, this object was lying on a pocket of frost at the bottom of that groove there."

"Well, but——"

"Don't you see? Lying *on* a pocket of frost. It caught my eye. That means it must have dropped there quite recently, otherwise the frosting would have covered it. When did you defrost last—before the night of the murder, I mean, Carruthers?"

"Temperature was raised on Wednesday evening, lowered again on Thursday morning."

"So frost would be forming all Thursday?"

"That's right, sir."

"Q.E.D.," said Nigel triumphantly. "If this little object had been dropped there *before* Thursday night, by Friday morning it would have been covered over with frost. But it was *not* covered with frost. Ergo, it was dropped some time *during* Thursday night or Friday morning."

"But that don't lead anywhere necessarily. One of the employees might have dropped it there on Friday before you came in."

"Just have a look at it, will you? It's a fragment chipped off something. Off what?"

Inspector Tyler scrutinised it closely. There were fine lines, part of some pattern, indented on the solid dark-green surface. The inspector breathed heavily over it for a minute.

"I've got it!" he said; "it's a fragment off the seal of a signet-ring. But——"

"Exactly. And it could only have been splintered off by violence: its owner taking a swipe at that refrigerator, for instance, and cracking it hard with his fist, so that the seal is chipped and that fragment falls on to the pocket of frost underneath."

"But, damn it, sir, people don't go about taking swipes at refrigerators."

"No. Certainly not. Deuced bad taste, knocking refrigerators about. That's just the point. But a bloke might easily take a swipe at another bloke, *in a struggle, in the dark*, miss him, and crack his fist up against the frige, by mistake."

"M'm. Something in that. I'd better take charge of that bit of seal. Shouldn't be difficult to find out who owns a seal ring, though I expect he'll have got rid of it when he found it was splintered. It's not a piece of Mr. Eustace Bunnett's, anyway: his was intact."

"I should say the College of Heralds might be able to reconstruct the whole crest from that bit there, and once you knew the crest you'd be as near as nothing to the murderer."

"We'll take a look at it under the microscope first, sir." The inspector was peering closely at the side of the refrigerator. "Ah, here's a little chip here, straight above where you found that bit of seal, looks as if it'd been freshly made. H'm. Four foot six from the ground. That's about the height you'd strike it with a fist if you were aiming at the jaw of a chap Bunnett's height."

Nigel was staring abstractedly at his feet. "I wonder why it was that the murderer's plans went wrong," he said.

# X
# July 19, 1.30–5.30 p.m.

*The lips that touch liquor shall never touch mine.*
TEMPERANCE BALLAD *(nineteenth century)*

NIGEL was still somewhat abstracted when he returned to the police station after lunch. This might
have been ascribed to the two helpings of roast beef,
three helpings of plum-tart, and plateful of cheese
and biscuits which the Cammisons had, with growing
apprehension, watched him eat.

"You know," Herbert said, "you'll do yourself an
injury if you persist in eating like this. I had a case
not long ago——"

"I don't mind about that," said Sophie. "It's my
larder I'm worrying about. We shall have to build
an annexe on to it before Nigel's next visit."

"Mphm. Jolly good cheese this. Could I have some
more?"

"It'd be interesting to test your blood-pressure at
this stage."

"I'm sure there'll be nothing left for supper," said
Sophie.

"Oh, I say. Won't there really? Look here, let me
take you both out to the hotel then," said Nigel,
genuinely moved.

Sophie laughed. "No, it's all right. We'll scrape

something together. You *are* funny, you know. But nice."

"Thank you."

"Are you stoking up for something definite, or just on general principles?" Dr. Cammison asked.

"Well, both. Men of genius have commonly been notoriously large eaters. Also, I'm going to interview Miss Mellors. What do *you* think of her?" he shot point-blank at Sophie.

"Me? Oh, I don't know about people." Sophie looked solemn and a little harassed behind her horn-rim spectacles, like an owl mobbed by tits. "She's quite nice really, though she *is* bossy. I think she's probably a sentimental old thing and ashamed of it, and that's why she puts on that sort of sergeant-major manner. I shouldn't be surprised if she had a secret sorrow."

"Darling, and you talk about *her* being sentimental!" said Herbert.

"Well, I do then. She's very kind-hearted, and it's always those gruff, kindly souls who have secret sorrows—in books, anyway."

"Oh, books!"

"Books are all right," said Nigel; "if you don't let them get a hold over you. Would you say, now, that Joe Bunnett was Miss Mellors' secret sorrow, by any chance?"

Sophie burst out laughing. "Joe! Oh dear!" Then, in a soberer voice, "Joe Bunnett? Well it might be, 's matter of of fact. She does look at him in rather a doggish sort of way sometimes—faithful, I mean, not playful. And she does mother him a bit too; like going round and seeing his house is clean and warm just before he comes back from his holidays. They live nearly next door to each other, you know."

"Do they now?"

"Look here, young Nigel," said Cammison, "just what are you up to?"

"I don't quite know. Really I don't. Waiting for the dawn. Does Joe Bunnett wear a signet-ring?"

"No. Never seen him, at least. Have you, Sophie?"

"No."

Herbert Cammison regarded Nigel impassively. He said:

"Are you suspecting Joe of killing his brother, by any chance?"

"Things don't look too good for him."

Sophie gave a little gasp. "Nigel! you can't—Joe isn't—you wouldn't think that if you knew him."

"But he's on a cruise. How could he possibly——"

"Unfortunately, Herbert, he doesn't seem to be on this cruise. His boat has disappeared, anyway."

"But whatever reason would he have?"

"You must keep this under your hat for the present, you two: the brewery was in danger of being closed down." Nigel told them about Eustace's negotiations with Roxby's. "So there it is. With his brother alive, Joe would have seen Bunnett's closed down and all those chaps you admit he was fond of and popular with thrown out of work. With Eustace dead, Joe would inherit the controlling interest, and be able to break off negotiations with Roxby's, and modernise the brewery in the way you and he wanted to."

"Yes, there's a lot in that, I suppose," said Cammison. "But honestly, though Joe is a very good chap and all that, I can't somehow see him committing murder for such an altruistic motive. He's too fond of comfort and *bonhomie* to be one of those it-is-meet-that-one-man-die-for-the-people fanatics."

"Agreed. But supposing he had a strong personal motive for getting rid of his brother? You say Eustace always had Joe under his thumb—and obviously Eustace's thumb was a pretty galling one to be under. Well, when the Roxby's affair happens along, that provides Joe with a rationalisation of his own personal motive and a justification for acting on it."

"Possibly. Joe was certainly thwarted and repressed by his brother all along the line. The Roxby's affair might have turned on the extra bit of heat that made him boil over. But, mind you, Eustace didn't have it all his own way. Joe hadn't the guts to stand up to him openly, I admit: but he got a good deal past him in more devious ways. Eustace could be managed up to a point, if you took the line of least resistance with him: kow-tow to him a bit, give him the feeling that you thought him the Lord's anointed, never oppose him openly—and while he was lapping up that kind of flattery, the mice could play: up to a point, as I say. Joe knew that all right."

Sophie looked bewildered and indignant. "Herbert, how can you? It's different for Nigel: he doesn't know Joe like we do. But talking about him as though he was one of your patients' insides or something— it's so heartless. Why, think of all the times he's sat where Nigel is sitting now, enjoying himself; and those comic little men he makes out of fruit and matchsticks, and pretending his teeth had fallen into the soup. It's——"

"Diagnosis must precede a cure," said Herbert rather stiffly. "We're not going to help Joe by pretending he's someone quite different from what he really is." . . .

When Nigel got to the police station he found the inspector engrossed over a microscope.

"Here, sir, take a look. What do you make of this?"

The fragment of seal from the ring was lying on the slide. Nigel looked long and hard.

"Seems like an animal's bim, with tail attached. What are those vertical lines on either side? A tropical rainstorm?"

"Might be the stems of flowers, or corn, or something."

"M'm. Gryphon couchant on field of blé. Or perhaps it's a dog. Too many dogs in this case. Well, that ought to be some help. By the way, the Cammisons say they've never seen Joe Bunnett wearing a signet-ring."

"They're friends of his, though."

"Well?"

"It's obvious."

"H'm. 'Foxey—our revered father, gentlemen.'"

"What's that?"

"Nothing. A Fragrant Moment from Charles Dickens. Have you bent your mind to the great problem that I proposed you?"

"Meaning?"

"Why did our murderer alter his plans? Obviously he had everything rigged up to make it look like an accident. He had tampered with that emergency bell. Bunnett was to have been induced to enter the refrigerator-room and then the door would have been shut on him. He could have banged away and yelled himself hoarse, but the watchman wouldn't have heard: the room is sound-proof: that's why the bell was installed. Bunnett would have been frozen to a chip by next morning; hadn't the stamina to keep moving all' night, like the last bloke who got shut in. Anonymous note found later, to explain his presence in the brewery: or maybe destroyed—yes, it'd have been safer for the murderer to have destroyed the note; Bunnett was always snooping around the brewery, after all. Emergency bell found broken down. It would have been almost impossible to prove it hadn't been an accident. So why, when he had a ripping little scheme like that all taped out, did he put Bunnett on to boil instead."

"That's easy, sir. The reason must have been that he failed to get his victim into the refrigerator-room without a struggle. Bunnett may have pulled the murderer in with him: or he may have opened his mouth to yell and the murderer decided to drag him inside before the watchman heard. Anyway, there was a struggle and the murderer knocked Bunnett out in some way that left a mark on him. That ruined his idea of making the whole thing look like an accident. What's more, I still believe that something was done to Bunnett then that would have given away the identity of the murderer, and that's why the body was put into the copper."

"Yes, that all seems plausible enough. Though, mind you, marks found on Bunnett's body could easily have been attributed to his beating himself in frenzy against the locked door of the refrigerator-room. Still, the murderer might quite likely overlook that, being all of a dither with his original plan going wrong. But what *could be* these tell-tale marks on Bunnett?"

"Well, sir, the murderer might've brought some acid, vitriol say, to throw at Bunnett, supposing his plan went wrong. What sort of person would that suggest?"

"A woman, I suppose."

"Or a doctor?" asked Tyler, a sly and dangerous look in his eyes.

"Possibly."

"Well, then, there might have been marks of acid-burning on Bunnett's face. Or supposing the murderer was left-handed. Medical evidence can generally show when a blow has been struck by a left-handed person. That'd be a give-away all right, eh?"

"Ingenious. Um. I prefer the left-handed idea. Vitriol's a bit too melodramatic. Are any of our troops left-handed?"

"Afraid I haven't noticed, sir. The idea only came to me to-day. We'll find out soon enough, though."

"Well, I'm going along to see Miss Mellors, I think. Get some more dope on Joe Bunnett. Have you any affectionate messages for her?"

"You can ask her what she was doing that afternoon the anonymous letter was posted, and what the devil she means by refusing to give Tollworthy the information."

"O.K. I'll turn on the heat. What's her number? I'd better ring up and see if she's in."

Nigel put through the call and was informed by a maid that Miss Mellors was expected back to tea at four o'clock. He filled in the time walking about the town, drinking in the sunlight and the fragrance of limes and wallflowers. As the Priory clock boomed the hour, Nigel was strolling up Acacia Road, looking for *Le Nid*, as Miss Mellors' house was rather unsuitably named. Ah, there it was. And two doors away stood a neat stone house, the ground-floor shutters closed and the blinds drawn upstairs, presumably Joe Bunnett's. On an impulse, Nigel walked up its stone-flagged path round to the back, and peeked in through the kitchen window. Everything looked tidy, spick-and-span, and deserted.

He turned away and entered the gate of *Le Nid*. There was a witch-ball hanging outside its front door, and on the lintel a rune of welcome done in poker-work and rather indifferent verse. This prepared Nigel for the array of arts and crafts that awaited him within: the drawing-room was full of papier-mâché articles, amateur leatherwork, insipid statuettes, home-made mats and the like. A reproduction of a Van Gogh's flower-painting was the most daring exhibit on view. Apart from this, there was nothing but objects of far too easy virtue. Oh, no; Nigel perceived a small table tucked away behind a screen at the other side of the room, with a few pieces of silver standing upon it. He walked over. Very nice too: heirlooms, presumably: two snuff-boxes, a crucifix, a coffee-pot, a card-case and one of those miniature ivory hands on long, slim handles employed by elegant eighteenth-century ladies when they wished to delouse themselves in public. Nigel was never backward about prying into other people's possessions. He took up a snuff-box and clicked it open: then he fiddled with the lid of the coffee-pot; then he suddenly picked up the snuff-box again and peered at it closely. Stamped on it there was a crest— a dog of dubious ancestry and truculent appearance sitting in a field of corn, with the legend beneath— *Semper Fidelis*. Nigel bent over quickly, and saw the same crest engraved on the coffee-pot and the card-case. Quite absent-mindedly, he slipped the snuff-box into his pocket: and at that moment the voice of Miss Mellors boomed behind him, "Do you make a habit of pocketing the silver, young man?"

Nigel was covered with confusion.

"R-really," he stammered, "I'm t-terribly sorry. No, I don't. I was just thinking of something else at the moment, and it sort of——"

"Conveyed itself into your pocket. I know. And what is this something else you were thinking of?"

"Well," thought Nigel, "two can play at shock tactics." He said:

"I was just wondering whether you have a signet-ring with the same crest on it."

Now it was Miss Mellor's turn to be confounded; and confounded she certainly was. A painful blush spread over her face and neck; her heavy features seemed to dissolve and set again in a queerly lop-sided expression.

"A ring? No, I haven't. I mean, I had; but I gave it away. Quite a long time ago."

Nigel was almost as much taken aback by the success of his question as Miss Mellors had been by the question itself. However, drawing a bow at a venture, he said:

"To Joe Bunnett, you mean?"

"Joe—yes—how did you know that? He promised never to——" She broke off, eyeing Nigel suspiciously.

"Never to wear it in public?" he asked.

She nodded silently. Nigel felt a bit ashamed of himself; a bit embarrassed, too, by the utter self-betrayal of her expression when Joe's name was mentioned. Miss Mellors took a grip on herself and said, with something of her old, hearty manner:

"You're a very inquisitive young man, you know. Steal my silver first and then start worming secrets out of me. Are you collecting material for a novel?"

"God forbid!" exclaimed Nigel fervently. "I may be a thief, but at least I'm not a novelist."

Miss Mellors grinned at him, and gave a sharp bark of laughter.

"Well, that's something to be thankful for. All filth and fornication. However, I don't suppose you've come here to discuss the modern novel. What do you want to know? And what's all this about my— Mr. Bunnett's ring? Has it been found somewhere?"

"Well, yes and no. In a sense—er—that is."

"Fiddlesticks! The ring has been found or it hasn't. Make up your mind, young man."

"No, really. I mean, a piece of it has been found— a piece of the seal."

Nigel tried to keep his tones smooth and ingenuous; but Miss Mellors was not buying it. Her face took on that lopsided appearance again. She asked sharply:

"Found? Where?"

"I'm afraid I can't tell you that, yet. I should be very grateful, though, if you would tell me more about the ring—and about Joe Bunnett. It's impertinent of me, I know, but——"

"You mean Joe Bunnett is suspected of murdering his brother, and the police want you to do their dirty work for them?"

"Joe is only one of several suspects. You yourself are another——"

"Me? Oh, really, Mr. Strangeways——"

"And as for 'dirty work,' you'd probably find that the inspector was a very much better hand at it than myself."

"All right, young man, don't lose your wool. If you're afraid of a little plain speaking, you've come to the wrong shop."

"I'd welcome a little plain speaking. That's why I'm asking you about Joe Bunnett."

"Good. Now we know where we stand. But let me tell you, if you've got it into your head that Joe killed that unspeakable little swine of a brother of his—though God knows Eustace richly deserved it— you're making the biggest mistake of your young life."

"I sincerely hope so. Well, now, you were going to tell me——"

"When Joe came back from the war, he and I struck up a friendship. We became attached to one another. I had looks in those days—yes, yes, yes, there's no need for you to be polite, I know I'm a battered old war-horse now, though I *am* on the right side of fifty still. An attachment, yes. No sentimental rubbish——" Miss Mellors glared truculently at Nigel—"I never thought Joe was a Greek god or a pantechnicon of all the virtues and I never shall; but we got on all right, and after a bit I popped the question—or he did—I've forgotten which, and we decided to get spliced up. But I made one condition. Joe had got to cut adrift from that blasted brewery. I'm not more bigoted than the next man, but my father drank himself to death and I had to nurse him during the last stages—and if you've ever seen the sodden, snivelling, maudlin wreck that drink can make out of a good man, you'd understand well enough why I wouldn't marry Joe as long as he had anything to do with the liquor trade. Well, Joe started to argue; but I soon shut him up—he'd got to take it or leave it. In the end, he decided to leave it— the brewery, I mean. But he'd reckoned without that ruffian, Eustace. God knows what hold Eustace had over him? Joe always had been under his thumb, but I thought he'd have the guts to break away for my sake. Well, he hadn't. So that was that. I'll never forget that afternoon Joe came to me and said he couldn't do it; white and trembling, and darned ashamed of himself—as well he might be. How I came to fall in l——, to get fond of a weak-willed little whipper-snapper like him, the Creator alone knows. But there it is. Well, I'd given Joe that ring of mine, and when he begged me to let him keep it still—I suppose I was a bit sentimental in those days—I hadn't the heart to take it back. But I wasn't going to have him wearing it in public, and I told him so; there are limits beyond which I won't go as laughing-stock of Maiden Astbury, and that was one of them. Of course, Joe said we'd only got to wait and everything would come out all right. A touch of Mr. Micawber, Joe's always had. I knew better. We've remained the best of friends; but I reconciled myself to dying an old maid, however much poor Joe might blather about silver linings and Came the Dawn. I suppose you're wondering why I tell you all this? Girlish confidences of a decayed gentlewoman, hey?"

"Well, I——"

"You've a sympathetic face, young man, even though you are no Clark Gable. But it's not that— don't flatter yourself. I suppose you've found Joe's ring, or whatever it is, on the scene of the crime. Believe me, you're chasing the wrong hare. If Joe was going to murder that brother of his, he'd have done it when Eustace first came between us. He wouldn't wait the best part of fifteen years to do it. Stands to reason, doesn't it? If he hadn't the sense to cut that little rotter's throat fifteen years ago, he'd certainly not do it last week. I might have been worth doing murder for in those days, but I'm no prize now and I know it. Why doesn't that blasted girl bring in the tea?"

Miss Mellors rang the bell-cord violently. It was an outlet for her emotion and gave her an opportunity to turn away and hide it. When the maid had gone out again, Nigel said:

"Thank you for telling me all this. I agree with what you say: but unfortunately Joe seems to have had other possible motives besides that."

Miss Mellors broke a shortbread biscuit with unnatural deliberation.

"Other motives? I don't believe it. What are they?"

"Well, he inherits his brother's share of the business."

"Yes. . . . Yes, I suppose he does. I hadn't thought of that. But, damn it, Mr. Strangeways, Joe has his faults, but he'd not commit murder for gain."

"N-no. I dare say he wouldn't." Nigel did not feel justified in telling Miss Mellors about Roxby's. She must have sensed that he was keeping something back, for she said:

"What's on your mind, young man?"

"I'm wondering," Nigel prevaricated, "whether it would help Joe at all if you gave me the information you refused to give Sergeant Tollworthy."

"Vacuum-cleaners," said Miss Mellors decisively, after a short pause.

"I beg your pardon?"

"That's what you ought to be doing. Selling them. You've missed your vocation. Just the right combination of plausibility, low cunning and ruthless sales-talk."

"And, like a vacuum-cleaner, I go around picking up the dirt?"

"Why should it help Joe? Eustace wasn't murdered that afternoon."

"No; but, for reasons I can't tell you, we want to know what Joe was doing between the time he left here and the time he reached Poolhampton."

"Driving to Poolhampton, presumably."

"Agreed. But what was his state of mind? Was he just happy and carefree, going off for a holiday? Or was he agitated, moody, taciturn—like someone who's planned to commit a murder the next night?"

"No, not a bit of it: he was quite normal, I can ass——"

"You were with him, then?"

"All right, young man, all right. You needn't be so cockahoop. Don't imagine you've caught me out. I'd every intention of telling you. Joe asked me to drive a bit of the way with him. Actually I went as far as Aldminster and then took the bus back. The conductor will tell you, if you don't believe me."

"You didn't pass through Weston Priors, did you?"

"Weston——? No, that's off the main road. Besides, it's beyond Aldminster."

"Joe picked you up here, and you went with him to Aldminster."

"No, not here, I met him on Honeycombe Hill."

"Accidentally?"

"No, I'm telling you, we'd arranged to drive together."

"Was Joe wearing the ring during this drive?"

"Yes."

"Why didn't you give this information to Tollworthy?"

"The man's a gossip. I don't want my private affairs blabbed about all over the town."

"But surely there's no reason why you shouldn't go for a drive with an old friend?"

"Don't be a fool. Of course there isn't. But Maiden Astbury doesn't need reasons for gossiping; all it needs is an excuse."

"How long had you to wait for the bus at Aldminster?"

"About quarter of an hour. We got in at about two-forty-five and the bus leaves at three."

"And Joe picked you up when?"

"Two-fifteen sharp."

"You took half an hour to cover the ten miles odd to Aldminster?"

"There was no hurry. We had plenty to talk about."

"And Joe seemed to you quite normal?"

"Of course he did. I've told you that once. Perfectly normal he was, talking about the cruise and so on." Miss Mellors got quite angry over it.

Nigel did his best to pacify her. Then, thanking her very much for the tea and the information, he returned to the Cammisons. While the interview was fresh in his mind, he wanted to test its bearings on the case. He took out a large sheet of paper, and wrote rapidly in his small, scholarly hand:

*Joe Bunnett.*
(i) Additional motive for killing Eustace—Eustace's interference between him and Miss Mellors. His hatred of E. for this should have cooled in fifteen years: depends on character—some people break out at once, others smoulder. The Roxby's affair might well have fanned the more personal motive into flame: brought to a head J.'s life-long repression by his brother.

(ii) It was a piece of Joe's ring I found in the refrigerator-room. This is damning evidence that he was there on the night of the murder. Unless Mellors is lying about J.'s being in possession of the ring when he went off for his holiday. And why should she lie? (Echo answers, why?)

(iii) The anonymous letter. If Mellors' evidence is correct, Joe had quarter of an hour to get from Aldminster to Poolhampton, which is a distance of five and a half miles. (c.f. Tollworthy's time-chart.) This would give him time, if he hurried, to make the four miles detour by Weston Priors and post the letter. Arrivals and departures will have to be verified by Tyler.

(iv) J.'s state of mind. Mellors insisted (with perhaps too much vigour?) that he was perfectly normal. Wasn't the whole business of this drive rather odd, though? M. and J. (according to M.) didn't want to be gossiped about: yet what more fruitful source of gossip could there be than M. going off with J. at the beginning of his holiday?—the fact that M. returned soon afterwards would be no obstacle to scandal-mongers, merely an additional juicy fact to speculate about. True, steps were taken to avoid discovery—M.'s meeting J. outside the town: but J. was well known in the county—M., too, probably— and they might easily have been seen driving together. Rather risky for them, surely? Which suggests that it was worth their taking this risk. Why? Obvious answers: either *(a)* Joe had planned to kill E., and was taking a sort of nerve-tonic, plus a farewell in case he got caught; *(b)* All this, and in addition M. was to give him, unwillingly, an alibi for the posting of the letter (if so, this must have failed somehow); *(c)* Joe and Mellors were in collaboration over the crime, and took this opportunity of talking over the details. But if *(b)* or *(c)*, why has not J. a better alibi over the anonymous letter?

Nigel sat back and read his notes over again. Several points began to stand out and suggest a quite different pattern—a most unexpected and sinister pattern, too. He took another sheet of paper and wrote:

*Ariadne Mellors.*

(i) No alibi for night of murder. Maid sleeps out. Suggests innocence, but might be double bluff.

(ii) Has physical strength to have laid out Bunnett and conveyed him into the copper.

(iii) Might conceivably have gained enough knowledge from Joe to write the anonymous letter and be familiar with geography of brewery. Is she expert enough to have tampered with the emergency bell in that way? (Good with her hands, c.f. the art-and-craft stuff in her house.) Main difficulty here—how could she explain her presence in the brewery to Eustace? Almost insuperable, this. Pass on. Joe might have told her about Roxby's; so she might have stolen the Roxby's correspondence to divert suspicion. But suspicion thus diverted on to Joe. Surely she wouldn't want this?—but see (v).

(iv) Motives. Very strong. *(a)* Her horror of drink—father drank himself to death—effect on daughter incalculable. By killing Eustace she would kill two brewers with one stone—Joe would be free from brother's influence and thus enabled to give up the trade. *(b)* Personal hatred of E. for his influence over J., all the stronger in a woman of her domineering character. *(c)* Death of Eustace would free Joe to marry her. . . .

(v) Is it possible that she murdered E. and is trying to incriminate Joe? Latter, *either* because she's lost her nerve, *or* from a subconscious hatred of J. for having through moral weakness deprived her of wifehood and motherhood in the past. Sounds a bit fantastic, but would explain several points—*(a)* Her comparative readiness to tell me about the ring. N. B., I have nothing but her word to support J.'s ownership of ring. Her confusion when I first mentioned it may have been due, not to coyness about Joe, but to her being made suddenly aware that we had found a clue to *her own* presence in the refrig.-room. Whole story of giving ring to J. may thus be result of Mellors' losing her head. (*Note:* Ask hotel servants, etc., at Poolhampton if J. was wearing ring.) *(b)* Mellors admitted to animus against Eustace—innocence or cunning? *(c)* She also manifested a certain degree of contempt for Joe. *(d)* "I shall never forget that afternoon Joe came to me and said he couldn't do it; white and trembling"—was this a subtle way of impressing me with the idea of Joe as a potential murderer? *(e)* At one point she said, "What's all this about my—Mr. Bunnett's ring?" If ring had been in Joe's possession all those years, would she have begun to say *"my ring"*? Possibly. A negligible point, this. *(f)* Her protestations that Joe seemed perfectly normal during the drive may have been *deliberately* over-emphasised in order to make me suspect her of concealing the fact that J. was not normal.

(vi) The anonymous letter. It is noticeable that Mellors gives herself something very like an alibi for this. She got out of J.'s car at Aldminster at two-forty-five: this wouldn't have given her time to get to Weston Priors and back before the bus started unless she hired another car—which would obviously be too dangerous. If she wrote the letter, it must have been posted in one of two ways—*(a)* she asked J. to post it at Weston Priors *en route* for Poolhampton (but W. P. isn't *en route*: therefore, unless M. and J. were in collusion, M. could surely give him no plausible reason why she wouldn't post it herself in Aldminster. Anyway, he'd almost certainly see Eustace's name on the envelope, which would be fatal for M.) *(b)* J. and M. made a detour and posted it before they got to Aldminster: this would account for the unusual length of time they took over the journey.

Nigel studied all this with an expression of distaste. It struck him as rather ponderous and much too theoretical. The only thing in its favour was that it would give some direction to the police inquiries in the Aldminster district. After another twenty minutes, he took a third sheet of notepaper, and slowly wrote:

(i) Joe Bunnett. Best tip so far.

(ii) Collusion between Joe and Miss Mellors. Promising; but, if there was collusion, surely they could have thought up a more definite alibi for the anonymous letter. Only two explanations so far: either the alibi has been deliberately made rather weak, or M. has lost her head.

(iii) Miss Mellors. The most likely outsider at long odds.

# XI
## July 20, 8–11.30 a.m.

*He that gropes in the dark finds that he would not.*
**ENGLISH PROVERB**

"No," thought Nigel, sipping his early morning tea, "this case is not really my dish at all. Its grotesque apparatus flattered but to deceive. Eustace Bunnett, thy bones are marrowless. From fair beginnings the case is falling away to foul routine. The police will take reams more of evidence, they will test every alibi, they will indulge in orgies of deduction—and, at the end of it all, someone will come forward and state that they saw X emerging from the brewery on the fatal night dripping with gore. That's the way murder cases are solved. Or else, in a couple of days' time, the chief constable will arise from his dreams of foxes and five-barred gates and call in the Yard, and some bright spark will be sent down and maybe discover the criminal's identity, but there won't be enough evidence to justify a prosecution, and one more will be added to the number of suspected murderers tripping it with light fantastic toe over the bodies of baffled policemen. And I must say I shan't be wild with regrets. Eustace Bunnett was a crook, a menace, and a stunger. We can get along very well without him. And the case can get along very well without me."

No doubt things would have turned out this way. A long, tedious investigation, with the police doing their best to give the murderer enough rope to hang himself with. But for one fact: the fact, which in an hour's time Nigel would be compelled to realise, that the criminal was in a hurry. Unlike most murderers, whose trump card—if they have the nerve to play it—is to sit tight and say next to nothing, this one had a crying need for haste. Every minute was precious to him, and no one could deny afterwards that he had acted with skill and despatch. Nor could one deny that it was the very conditions of the crime itself that inexorably laid the toils into which the criminal fell. A very neat—in fact, an almost classic—performance by Nemesis, but reflecting little credit, Nigel considered, on himself and the other mortal agents of that unchancy goddess. All he could take credit for was that he tumbled to the murderer's identity at nine-ten this Monday night: but it was a purely academic success on his part; for the murderer was destined to be caught anyway only a few hours later.

Nigel's first indication that the march of events was accelerating into a double came at exactly 8.27 a.m. The telephone bell rang, Nigel was summoned, and the inspector's voice barked from the other end:

"Mr. Strangeways? Tyler speaking. From the brewery. Been trouble here last night. Night-watchman caught someone on the premises. The fellow got away. Rang us up at once—Lock, I mean—and we made a search immediately. Couldn't find anything. Making a more thorough search now. If you'd care to give me the benefit of your co-operation—"

Tyler was in the habit of coming out unexpectedly with stilted phrases like this, otherwise Nigel might have suspected a latent sarcasm. But the inspector's voice sounded edgy and irritable: probably furious with himself for not keeping an adequate watch over the brewery, and taking it out on some wretched subordinate, thought Nigel; though no one could have expected——"

"O.K.," he said, "I'll be along in quarter of an hour."

Ten minutes of that was spent in breakfast; and, as Herbert Cammison said, if any two other men could put down as much breakfast in the time, he'd like to know their names. The remaining five minutes brought Nigel to the brewery. Tyler was certainly doing himself proud; there seemed to be policemen everywhere, poking about, asking questions, or just standing still and radiating suspicion. The employees, too, were obviously affected by the excitement in the atmosphere; they worked spasmodically, outbreaks of furious energy followed by pauses for muttered talk and covert glances. Only the girls employed in the bottling processes tended their levers and conveyors without a break in their mechanical, jerky, marionette-like ritual.

"Quite like old times," said Mr. Barnes coming across Nigel on his way through the bottling-room: "Never seen 'em working like this since the guv'nor popped it. Eh, well, it's an ill wind—as the saying goes. And to what do we owe the pleasure of this visit from you, sir?"

"The murderer."

Mr. Barnes' eyebrows shot up and remained levitated, as it were, against the white expanse of his brow.

"Meaning, if I take you rightly, that the bloke Lock surprised in here last night is His Nibs in person.

He must have a nerve. Well, they say the murderer always returns to the scene of his crime, don't they?"

"Um. Of course, if the murderer is an employee here, he couldn't very well help returning to the scene of the crime, could he? Darned disturbing for the chap having that copper staring him in the face all day, don't you think?"

"Copper? Oh, I get you. I thought for a moment you was referring to our Boy Blue, our esteemed Inspector Tyler." The head brewer's lugubrious countenance performed the unnerving contortions that represented his idea of a smile. "Which reminds me. Don't bandy any witticisms with Tyler this morning, if you take my advice. Fair raging he is. Swallowed a fish-bone he has, proper. Badgering me about that pressure-copper again just now, so I said— humorous-like, but quite friendly—'there's a ruddy sight too many coppers in the brewery this morning,' I said. My word, that didn't half set him off. Somebody ought to design a safety-valve for that man or he'll blow his lid off one of these days."

"Dear me, that would never do. Where is he now, by the way?"

"Up in the guv'nor's room."

As Nigel arrived outside Eustace Bunnett's door, he heard the voice of the inspector raised in querulous indignation.

"What the hell do you think I put you at the brewery gate for? First you let the fellow get in and then you let him walk out again."

"I can't be in two places at once, sir," a sullen voice replied.

"And none of your lip, my lad, either! I suppose you went to sleep, eh?"

"No, sir."

Nigel thought it was time for someone to pour a

little oil on these troubled waters. He entered.

"Oh, there you are," said Tyler ungraciously. "This damned fool"—he jerked his head towards the red-faced and sweating young constable who stood at attention beside the desk—"has let the murderer slip through his fingers."

Nigel gathered that the constable had been on guard at the main gates, had heard shouts from within the brewery at about ten to one that morning, had rushed inside and met the night-watchman in full career after the intruder. Only the intruder somehow had got lost. The constable swore he had not passed by *him,* while Lock swore with equal vehemence that he had been escaping in the direction of the main entrance.

"How did the chap get in, anyway?" asked Nigel.

This turned out to be a somewhat tactless question. For it had been made apparent that, unless the intruder had climbed over the high wall—and there was not a trace of his having done so—he must have entered by the side door in Ledgett's Lane; and that side door had not been guarded.

"How should I know he'd be likely to return to the brewery?" complained the inspector. "Why, it was only a formality stationing Palmer at the main gate."

"Who has keys of the side entrance?"

"There was one on Mr. Bunnett's ring. Joe Bunnett has one, and Mr. Barnes and Ed Parsons. Anyone could have taken an impression, of course, and had a key made."

"Or anyone might have stayed behind in the brewery and hidden after the day's work was over. Then he could have stolen the master-key out of the office."

"The master-key hasn't been stolen," replied Tyler

sourly. "Besides, if the chap had stayed behind, why did he wait so long to do whatever he wanted to do?"

"Yes. That's so. But what *did* he want to do? Destroy evidence?"

"I suppose so. It was in this corridor outside here that Lock found the fellow. But there's no sign of anything having been taken out of this room. Or from Mr. Joe Bunnett's. Lock seems to think he surprised the chap before he'd got properly to work, and I'd say that's quite likely. What worries me more is that I can't think of anything in the nature of evidence which the murderer'd want to destroy. We went through these rooms and the office very carefully a couple of days ago; we'd have found it then, if——"

"It must be something which doesn't appear incriminating on the face of it, but the murderer knows to be a danger to him." Nigel snapped his fingers and went on excitedly. "Look here, this must link up with the burglary of Eustace's house. Suppose Eustace had something in his possession—letters, say—that would point to the murderer's identity. Murderer ransacks his study, fails to find them, and steals the Roxby's correspondence in order to confuse the trail. The next night he comes to the brewery, hoping to find what he's looking for in Eustace's room here."

"Yes, that's all very well; but what *is* this piece of evidence? There was nothing in here with the remotest bearing on the murder; just business documents."

"Perhaps there's a secret drawer, or an oubliette, or something jolly of that sort."

"I've told you. We've searched this room, sir. And

when we search a room, we do it properly," said Tyler, visibly aggrieved.

"Yes, I'm sure you do. Oh, well, I'd fancy a talk with Lock. Is he here still?"

"I'll send for him."

A few minutes later, Lock entered with his stiff, military stride. Nigel asked him to repeat his story of what had happened last night.

"It was like this, sir. I'd finished the midnight round of inspection and was sitting in that little room near the main entrance, taking a breather. After a bit, somehow—you know how it is—I seemed to remember hearing a sound I didn't ought to have heard."

"What sort of a sound?"

"I didn't connect it with anything just then. You see, I didn't hear it, in a manner of speaking. I remembered that there'd been a sound, that's all— like when you're busy on something, you don't hear the traffic outside, and yet you do hear it——"

"Subconsciously?"

"That'd be it, sir, no doubt. I've thought about it since, and—as I told Mr. Tyler here—I'd make a guess it was the noise a swing door makes closing; you know, the kind that work by air-compression. Anyway, I goes along—it was just after quarter to one—the way where I remembered the sound to have come from."

"Turn on any lights?"

"Bless you, no sir. I knows my way about here in the dark like a mole. I'd a torch, of course; but I didn't want to use it in case it should give away my position to the enemy. A proper night-attack— that's what I wanted to spring on the blighter, see? Well, I came upstairs quiet, and just as I rounded the corner at the other end of this passage, I saw someone outside the door of Mr. Bunnett's room. There's a bit of light comes in through the skylight just above; not what you'd call light, but not as dark as the stairs; just enough for me to see a sort of figure. So I clicked on my torch; only, me standing close against the wall, the movement hit the torch against it about a second before the light went on—the button's a bit stiff, you see. The blighter heard the sound and it gave him time to nip round the corner and be off; moved like a bleeding streak of lightning, he did, if you'll pardon the expression: just saw his tail-light whisking off, as you might say. I goes after him, thinking he'd be bound to run out by the front entrance, but seems like he didn't."

"You didn't hear him running away?"

"No. It's a long passage, you see; by the time I'd got to the other end, he could have been half-way to Margate. He must've had rubber-soled shoes, though, or I'd've heard him clattering down the stairs."

"This figure you saw standing by the door—which Mr. Bunnett's door, by the way?"

"Couldn't say for sure. Mr. Eustace's, I presumed. I dunno."

"We'll come back to that. The figure. Could you say anything more about it? Height? Bulk? Sex?"

"No, sir. It was quite still a second, and I stood quite still. I got an impression that it was bending forward, as it might be to feel for the keyhole. Reckon I thought it was a ghost for a second."

"Perhaps it was," said Tyler irritably. "I'm half-inclined to think you imagined the whole thing."

"Not me, sir. No. It was a bloke all right. But more than that I can't tell you—unless you'd like me to imagine a lot o' details as I never saw," he added with heavy humour.

"Get that torch, will you?" Nigel asked.

"What's all this?" said the inspector suspiciously, when Lock had departed on his errand.

"An experiment in optics—if that's the word I'm groping for."

Lock returned. Nigel inspected the torch and noted that the button was still stiff. He stationed Lock at the end of the corridor where he had been the night before, and himself stood outside the door of Eustace Bunnett's room.

"Now," he said, "shut your eyes tight. Count ten. Then click on the torch; try and hit the end of it against the wall first, like you did last night. When you know the torch is lit, open your eyes."

Nigel leant forward to the door. When he heard the tap of the torch against the wall, he paused a fraction of a second, then raced for the corner.

"No good, sir! I seen you!" Lock called out. He had grasped the point of the experiment now. They repeated it several times, Lock deliberately taking longer to switch on the torch before he opened his eyes. But every time he saw Nigel before he could get round the corner.

"It's proved then, that the chap was not trying to get into Eustace's room. Now we'll try Joe's."

Joe Bunnett's door was only a yard from the end of the corridor, nearer to it than Eustace's though on the same side. This second set of experiments had a very different result. The first time, Lock saw Nigel just before he turned the corner, the second time he only saw the tail of his coat, the third time he saw nothing at all.

"That's that, then," said Nigel. "There's reasonable

evidence that the person you saw was trying to get into Joe Bunnett's room."

"Or just coming out," said the inspector, who had been looking on.

"Now we've got to turn Joe's room upside down. There's just *got* to be something there. I don't believe the murderer would have had time to remove it. A trained watchman like Lock would become conscious of that sound—the swing-door or whatever it was—very soon after his subconscious mind had noted it. A reaction of ten to thirty seconds, I'd say. But even supposing it was a minute, or two or three minutes—even that would hardly give the intruder time to open the drawers, perhaps the safe, and get what he had come to get. Obviously he didn't know exactly where the thing was to be found, or he wouldn't have wasted time burgling Eustace's house the night before."

The inspector looked cunning. "Suppose the intruder was Joe Bunnett himself. Suppose the burglary at his brother's house was simply to get hold of those Roxby's papers, and there was something else in his room here he had to have too. *He'd* be able to find it quickly enough. *And* he's the most likely person to have a key to his own room, what's more."

"Yes. That's true. Though I can't understand why he shouldn't have burgled Eustace's study and his own room on the same night. Does he ration himself to one deed of darkness per twenty-four hours? Seems rather whimsical. Well, let's make a last attempt to crack this nut."

They entered Joe Bunnett's room. A safe, a desk, a filing cupboard, a threadbare carpet, a photograph of an outing of the brewery employees, a pencil drawing of *The Gannett,* and a few chairs, formed the bulk of the furniture.

"You searched the room this morning?' Nigel asked.

"Yes."

"Dust?"

"No good, sir. We left too many marks in the dust during our first search to be able to pick out any fresh ones. There are no new fingerprints."

Nigel opened a drawer in the desk at random. It contained nothing but copies of *Razzle* and *Film Fun.* He closed it hastily, murmuring:

"Tut-tut. A harem. Revealing, but not pertinent."

He poked his fingers into one of the pigeonholes. "He put in his thumb and pulled out a plum—no, not a plum, a passport."

He flipped over the pages idly. The usual debauched-looking photograph. "Joseph Bunnett. Age forty-eight. Height, five feet eight inches. Fair hair. Moustache. The usual stuff. Visaed for France and Switzerland last year." Nigel starting rummaging again. Then he stiffened suddenly and let out a wild whoop.

"Eureka!"

"How much? Wasp stung you, sir?"

"Not wasp. Idea. Yes, why not? Joe wants to get out of country. Wants his passport. All quite regular. What about it?"

Tyler scratched his chin. "Um. There's something in that. Yes. But, look here, if he'd planned to kill Eustace and clear out of the country, surely he wouldn't forget to have his passport with him?"

"No. But supposing all that cruise business was meant for an alibi, and something went radically wrong with it. Suppose he intended to turn up in

Maiden Astbury after a decent interval and say, 'Well, boys, I only heard about my brother being dead when I put in at Falmouth,' or words to that effect; and suppose for some reason that plan got scuppered, and he realised that Fortune (fickle jade) had given him a kick in the pants, then what's more likely than that he should lose his head and make a bolt for it—calling in for his passport *en route?*"

"I dare say. Well, that may give us something to work on."

"Something to work on? That's meiosis. Don't you see—he's in a tearing hurry now. *He'll be coming back for his passport again.* He's got to have it, and then we have him."

"Optimistic, aren't you? You must know by now that we could have him arrested wherever he lands in France."

"No; because he doesn't know that *we* know that it's the passport he's after. He has no reason to believe that we suspect him yet to the extent of warning the French police. He imagines that we're still swimming round in circles looking for *The Gannet.*"

"Something in that. Where's he hiding, though? That's what I'd like to know. Can't be far away if it's him that's been doing these burglaries."

"Maybe he's staying at the Royal Hotel, disguised as the Archdeacon of Wessex."

"And maybe my name is Winston Churchill," retorted the inspector ferociously.

Nigel stared at his shoe-laces. He went to stub out his cigarette in an ash-tray on the mantelpiece. The ash-tray, he noticed, was one of those advertising ones; "Castle Brand Mineral Waters" was stamped on it.

"An Englishman's home is his castle," murmured

Nigel. Then, pianissimo, "I suppose Joe Bunnett is not hiding in his own house, Tyler?"

"His own!—what?—Do you think he's crazy?" the inspector almost shouted.

"No. Perhaps just cleverer than we thought. Have you searched the house?"

The inspector's eyes swivelled away from Nigel. He looked uncomfortable. "Searched the house? Well, no, sir. We had no call to; I mean, we couldn't possibly suppose—it's ridiculous," he blustered—"of course, we've been through his study and bedroom—on Saturday morning it was—to see if there was anything that'd give a clue to his present whereabouts. But we've not been all through the house, not torn up the floors, and tapped the walls and all that hokey-pokey. When the search was made, there was no reason to suppose he was the murderer."

"Shades of the Bow Street Runners!" Nigel ejaculated to himself. Aloud he said, "Well, I should think a careful search ought to be made now, don't you?"

The inspector conceded this, somewhat grudgingly. He did not enjoy being caught out in an error. To hide his feelings and reassure himself, he proceeded first with a meticulous examination of the room. Every paper was taken out, perused and tossed over to Nigel. It was thus that the second discovery of the morning took place. In a drawer, mixed up with a number of personal letters, several ancient dance programmes, the menu of a regimental dinner, and some extra-strong peppermints, they found a document, duly signed and witnessed, by which Joe Bunnett bequeathed everything of which he should die possessed—to Ariadne Mellors.

"Well, for crying aloud!" exclaimed Nigel. "This really is a most ill-regulated case. First we don't get a sniff of a clue, and now they're raining down on us like autumn leaves—and all pointing different ways—more like the Sibyl's leaves, I should say."

"May be significant, after what you told me about your interview with Miss Mellors yesterday."

"Um. Opens up all sorts of avenues. As for instance, Mellors may have planned to murder Joe as well as Eustace; motive, to get the brewery into her own hands and close it down—staggering blow to the liquor trade; then lost her nerve and decided to get hold of this compromising will and destroy it—or keep it till things had blown over. Or she may have been in collusion with Joe, may even have been hiding him in her own house: one or other of them kills Eustace; then Joe loses his nerve, and Mellors has to silence him—I never could imagine why Lady Macbeth didn't put something in her husband's coffee when he started making embarrassing remarks at the dinner-table. Come to think of it, there's a good deal of superficial resemblance between the Macbeths and Joe and Miss Mellors. Well, she kills Joe to safeguard herself, and comes after the will for the same reason. There are any number of possible permutations and combinations of this situation."

"No doubt," said the inspector dryly. "I'm not interested in sums just at the moment, though. We'll find out where Miss Mellors was last night, and then look over Joe Bunnett's house."

Miss Mellors was not in. The maid had not seen her that morning, but Miss Mellors always cooked and washed up her own breakfast, and was often out before the maid arrived. They were on the point of taking their leave when the girl exploded a bombshell. Nigel had remarked aside to Tyler that, as she went home after dinner every night, she could know nothing about her mistress's movements. The girl overheard this: a sly look came into her eyes: she said she had been talking over the garden fence that morning with her friend, Iris, who worked next door; Iris told her that last night she had been saying good-night to her boy inside the gate just before twelve o'clock, and they'd seen Miss Mellors come out of her house ever so stealthy and hurry down the road. In which direction? The maid pointed. Ah, thought Nigel, past Joe Bunnett's house towards the brewery. This was a push-over. The inspector knew that Joe Bunnett left the keys of his house in Miss Mellors' charge when he went off on holiday. He had borrowed them for his previous search. The maid was sent off to fetch them. After a few minutes she returned, looking bewildered, and said that the keys were gone from the hook they usually hung on; they'd been there yesterday evening, she'd happened to notice: funny goings-on, wasn't it?

The inspector thanked her brusquely, asked her to show him the telephone and rang up his headquarters. He arranged for several men to come up at once, two to cover the back of Joe Bunnett's house, another with a bunch of skeleton keys to open the doors and a fourth to guard the front gate. Meanwhile he and Nigel waited in the porch of *Le Nid*. In six minutes' time, a couple of plainclothes men walked past and gave an unobtrusive signal meaning that the rear of the house was now covered. The inspector and Nigel followed. One man stayed at Bunnett's gate, the other walked up the neat flagged path behind them. The house seemed preternaturally still: its closed shutters gave it a vacuous look: was there a madman's brain hidden behind that blind, vacant front? Nigel wondered; or the desperate frenzy of a murderer, nervous as a hair-trigger after three days of suspense, isolation and peril, cornered now, ready to break out? It was strange to think that he had never set eyes on this man whom they had now run to earth. Or had they? Was it conceivable that he would have the cold nerve to stay on in his own house all this time?

A key clicked and the door opened. The inspector shouldered his way past his subordinate into the dark hall. Nigel followed, instinctively putting out his hands as though to ward off the blow that might fall out of the shadows. But no blow came: no sound, except the harsh echoes of their own feet on the stone floor. Dining-room, empty. Lounge, empty. Furniture shrouded in white dust-covers. Tyler plucked these covers away one by one. Kitchen, empty. Cellar, empty. Every cupboard, every cranny was explored. Not a word had yet been spoken; that was odd, thought Nigel; there was something oppressive about the house that forbade them to talk, even in whispers. They filed upstairs. One, two, three bedrooms, all empty. At the end of the passage, a smaller room—Joe's sanctum; sporting prints on the walls; a bureau; fishing rod and golf clubs in a corner; a shove-halfpenny board; a deep arm-chair facing the fireplace, its back to them, shrouded, too, in a dust-cover. Automatically the inspector moved up to it and twitched off the cover. He gasped. The arm-chair was the one thing in the house that was not empty. Ariadne Mellors was sitting there, her head battered in.

For several seconds the three stood there, stunned by that discovery. Then Nigel said in a whisper:

"That's a steep price to pay for the proof of one's innocence."

As though this released him into activity, the inspector started furiously to work. It was almost unimaginable that the murderer could still be in the house, but Tyler sent his subordinate to search bathroom, lavatory, linen-cupboard and whatever else there might be, while he himself telephoned for assistance. Nigel glanced from the hideous thing slumped in the chair to the blood-stained poker that lay in the grate. A shattered electric torch on the floor, patches of blood between fireplace and desk. Miss Mellors must have entered the room, surprised the murderer (or had he been lying in wait for her?) and been killed without preamble or mercy. Had she had time even to scream once, it would surely have been heard next door and reported. Nigel felt sick. He was, he realised, indirectly responsible for this. Interviewing Miss Mellors yesterday evening, he had made it all too plain that Joe Bunnett was under grave suspicion; so she had come over last night, surely to find if he had left any incriminating evidence against himself and to destroy it if need be. *Semper Fidelis* was the family motto of that uncouth, comical, ill-starred woman; she had lived up to it and died by it. It was unthinkable that, if she had been Joe's accomplice in the murder of Eustace, Joe should have killed her: for, as an accomplice, she would have known of his hiding place and he would have expected her to visit him there; whereas, if Joe *was* the murderer at all, he had evidently struck out at his visitor of last night in the darkness and desperate panic, not realising who she was.

But there was still no definite proof that Joe had murdered Eustace, apart from the fragment of the signet-ring found in the refrigerator-room. It was possible that someone else, the real murderer, might have got possession of the ring or had a replica made, and left the clue behind to implicate Joe. On the other hand, if the murderer was not Joe, what was he doing in this house last night? Nigel clicked his fingers. Got it! Planting some more false evidence. Well then. Yes, it fits in. We thought that Joe killed his brother and hid himself here. But surely three nights in this house would be bound to leave some traces of occupation. Yet we've found none. This cuts both ways, though. If the murderer wants to make us believe that Joe has been skulking here and therefore is the killer, he'd surely have faked some evidence pointing to that. Perhaps Miss Mellors caught him out before he had time to do that. Yet he couldn't have known that the police would not make a detailed examination of the house till to-day. Perhaps there is some evidence, planted or genuine, which we've failed to discover. Damn! How could any evidence have been planted when Miss Mellors kept the only keys of the house. Had anyone else a set of keys? There must be a duplicate for the front door, at least. Only Joe Bunnett, surely. Still, I suppose somebody might have taken an impression of his key and had another made. More work for the inspector. Perhaps they'll feel inclined to call in the Yard after all this.

Nigel found that, lost in thought, he had wandered into the passage. He lit a cigarette and, in his absent way, dropped the match on the carpet. This reminded him of Sophie Cammison and her strictures about his untidiness. He bent down to pick it up; as he did so, he observed a faint round dent in the thick pile of the carpet; then another, then two more. Somebody, quite recently, had been standing on a chair just here—that was the obvious interpretation.

Nigel called to the policemen whom Tyler had sent to search the rest of the house.

"You been standing on a chair here?"

"Chair? No, sir. Not investigated this passage yet."

"Good. Must be the murderer. Get me one, will one—a chair, I mean, not a murderer. Don't leave your prints on it."

Nigel placed the chair-legs in the indentations. They fitted.

"Um. Must've been this one or another of similar pattern. Find all the chairs of this size and shape of leg in the house, and have 'em tried for finger-prints."

He took off his coat, spread it over the seat, and climbed gingerly upon it. The passage-ceiling was now only a foot above his head. It was papered in the same loud and riotous pattern as the walls. But from his vantage-point Nigel could see four sides of a square outlined against the pattern. A trap-door! Using his handkerchief, he pushed gently upwards. The trap yielded. Only when his head was through the opening did he realise that it might be, for him, a trap in more senses than one. The murderer might be up there, under the roof, nervous as a hair-trigger, cornered! In an involuntary spasm of fear, Nigel closed his eyes an instant. Then he opened them again and looked round. There was nobody there. He hauled himself through the opening. The joists were boarded over for half the length of the attic. Some oddments lay on the boards; a few boxes, an old tin of paint, a scrap-book. But he paid no attention to them. What held his gaze was the pile of rugs and the cushion spread out beside them. Here at least was proof that the murderer had been hiding out here: no, it wasn't proof, this might be the faked evidence—and faked with what fiendish ingenuity and self-confidence, too. Nigel inspected the pile of bedding closely. A faint odour hung about the cushion. Brilliantine. Nigel remembered the photo of Joe Bunnett in Eustace's house, the smarmed-down hair. Taking out a pocket magnifying-glass he studied the cushion. One or two hairs were clinging to it. He put them away in an envelope. Next he noticed some crumbs lying in the cracks between the boards; with tweezers and infinite delicacy he extracted them and dropped them into another envelope; taking them under the skylight he examined them; they were still soft, some of them, and some of them smelt— smelt—smelt—what was the smell?—Ah, carraway-seed.

Nigel proceeded to ransack the boxes. It was then that he made his last and most lurid discovery. Behind the torn lining of a suitcase he found a handkerchief, spattered with fresh bloodstains. There would be no fingerprints on that poker in the study; the murderer had held its handle in this handkerchief. Nigel unfolded the crumpled square of linen. At one corner were marked the initials, J. B.

# XII
# July 20, 11.30 a.m.–5.15 p.m.

*He holds him with his skinny hand,*
*"There was a ship," quoth he.*
                    COLERIDGE, *The Ancient Mariner*

THE medical examination bore out the self-evident fact that Miss Mellors had been killed somewhere about midnight with the poker that was lying in the grate. She had been struck down by somebody standing in front of her; which suggested, though it did not prove, that the murderer was already in the room before she entered. So, at least, the inspector read it. Nigel considered it interpretable in another way: it might mean that the murderer was known to Miss Mellors and trusted by her, otherwise he would not have risked letting her see him by getting in front of the beam of her torch. A more sinister feature of the crime was revealed when Herbert Cammison stated, with his usual objective and precise utterance, that—as far as he could tell on a cursory examination—the victim had been killed by the first blow—a right-handed one, and the murderer then must have continued wildly striking at her long after he'd known she was dead.

Panic or hatred? thought Nigel. If it was panic, then Joe Bunnett was most likely their man; if hatred, it could be that shadowy and abominably ingenious X who—they might yet prove—had been scattering false evidence against Joe with such a light touch, such masterly discrimination and lack of over-emphasis. Inspector Tyler, after being shown the contents of the attic, was in no two minds about it. Nothing remained, as far as he was concerned, but to get a warrant for Joe Bunnet's arrest and find him. His description would now be broadcast all over England; police at every port would be warned to prevent him embarking for a foreign country: it could only be a matter of days. Hours, more probably; for he could not move out of England till he had regained possession of his passport.

Three different sets of fingerprints were exposed in the house. One belonged to Miss Mellors, the second to the woman who "did for" Joe Bunnett and had cleaned up the house on the afternoon of his departure: the third, presumably, was Joe's, though that could not be proved till they had caught him. No fingerprints, however, were found on the few possible surfaces in the attic. This was a point slightly in favour of the hypothetical X being a reality, Nigel considered. All the other fingerprints might have been made by Joe before he went on his holiday; whereas it was unlikely—though not impossible—that, if he had been living in the attic for three days and nights, he would have left no prints. The inspector, anyway, was far too busy to listen to any such wild hypothesis from Nigel. Before the routine work in Joe Bunnett's house was finished, Tyler received a message which made him busier still.

The Poolhampton police were on the phone—straining at the wire, in fact. They asked Tyler to come down at once. *The Gannet* had been located, and they also had information about the motor-bicycle over which he had asked them to make inquiries. The inspector jerked out orders all round, put Sergeant Tollworthy in charge on the spot, and was soon racing the twenty miles to the coast, sitting in the back of the police car with Nigel.

They were greeted at the station by Superintendent Flaxenham, a tall, red-faced man, slow of speech but evidently capable. With little preamble he pointed to a large-scale ordnance map lying upon the table.

"See that indentation there?" he said. "That's a small cove, used by smugglers once, they say: deep water entrance, even at low tide—the shore shelves sharply there, you see; high cliffs on either side; and inland"—the superintendent stabbed a large forefinger at the map and tapped it several times—"inland is Basket Down, a lonely expanse of upland uninhabited save for a few farms situated in the deep combes, typical of this countryside." Flaxenham was evidently deriving his inspiration at this point from the local guide-book, Nigel noted. "For reasons, which will transpire in due course," Flaxenham continued meatily, "this area has lately been rendered ever more desolate than heretofore. Since receiving your message, we have been making inquiries along the coast—in the villages, camping grounds, farms and so on—relative to *The Gannet*. No one had seen her, nor at first did we find anyone who had noticed anything untoward on Thursday night. Yesterday afternoon, however, we received a report from Constable Harker. Harker is stationed in the hamlet of Biddle Monachorum, which—you will observe—is five miles west of Basket Cove. Harker reported that the proprietor of the Jolly Monk had laid the following information before him. On Saturday night a tramp, name of Ezekiel Penny, came into his pub and in the course of conversation commented upon a fire he had seen on Basket Down early on Friday morning. The proprietor, Harry Bean, said he'd heard nothing of any fire and hinted that Penny must've been properly boozed up or maybe dreamed it all. Whereupon the man Penny grew very heated, swore he was sober as a judge and had been an abstemious man all his life, and as for dreaming it—it couldn't be that because he'd been asleep and only seen the fire when he woke up. Penny came in for a good deal of chaffing from the fellows in the bar, of course. One chap asked him had the fire taken the shape of a flaming serpent, and so on: but Penny stuck to it that he'd seen a glow in the sky, seaward in the direction of Basket Cove. Thought maybe it was some boat had caught fire: but it wasn't his business, he said, so he turned over and went to sleep again.

"Well, gentlemen, Harry Bean thinks this story over that night and he puts two and two together and the next morning—that's yesterday—he decides to pass it on to Constable Harker. Harker acted very promptly. He communicated with us, and on our instructions found this Penny and pulled him in. I questioned Penny, and some further interesting facts were divulged. It'd be simplest if I read out the interview as taken down verbatim by Constable Oak."

The superintendent took up a sheet of paper, cleared his throat remorselessly, and read:

"Q.—Name?

"A.—Ezekiel Penny.

"Q.—Address?

"A.—God's great open spaces.

"Q.—No fixed habitation. Will you describe in your own words what happened on Thursday night?

"A.—I had been walking from Poolhampton. Very nice little town. Salubrious resort——

"Q.—Keep to the point please.

"A.—O.K., General. As the shades of night fell, I found myself on the Basket Down you call it, don't you? I looks for a place to doss down, and I sees a ruined cottage a hundred yards off the track, to my left. So I takes up occupation of same and has a bit of shut-eye. After a while I wakes up——

"Q.—What time would that be?

"A.—Unfortunately I'd mislaid my gold bleeding wristwatch, so I can't tell you exactly. Was still dark. Maybe two o'clock in the morning. Maybe three. Well, I wakes up——

"Q.—Any particular reason? Some sound wake you up?

"A.—Ah! What it is to have a brain! I'd forgotten all about it. That's right, General: must've been that perishing motor-bike what woke me up.

"Q.—Motor-bike?

"A.—Yes. I heard the sound of a motor-bike receding inland. Must've passed along into the lane that leads to the main road up along.

"Q.—Did it sound like a powerful engine?

"A.—Couldn't say, General. I was never in the motor trade. Must've been pretty asterisk powerful to wake me up.

"Q.—What happened then?

"A.—I gets up and goes to the door of my temporary mansion, and I has a bit of a look around and I sees a sort of glow in the sky, just about where this Basket Cove would be. So I says to myself, 'Something's on fire over there,' and I lies down and goes to sleep again.

"Q.—You did nothing about it? Why didn't you report this?

"A.—I ain't a ruddy fire brigade, am I? And there wasn't a telephone in this here cottage. Nor I don't carry a portable wireless about with me.

"Q.—That's enough. You saw no suspicious person that night, while you were walking over the downs? Heard nothing apart from the motor-bicycle?

"A.—Not a soul, General. I was monarch of all I bleeding well surveyed."

"That," said Superintendent Flaxenham, with a subdued twinkle in his eye, "was all we could get out of Ezekiel Penny."

"It's queer, isn't it, nobody else seeing anything of this fire," said Tyler. "Weren't there any campers about?"

"That's just it. As I hinted before, this particular part of Basket Down is specially deserted just now. You see, the Air Ministry has bought it for bombing practice."

"Ah!" murmured Nigel, *"Solitudinem faciunt; pacem appellant."*

"Well, gentlemen, on receiving this information, we made further investigations. The upshot of which was the discovery yesterday evening of a sunken wreck lying near the mouth of the cove. We're having it raised and beached now, and I'll lay long odds on it's being the boat you're looking for. We'll go over there at once, if it suits you. I've got hold of Elias Faulkes, the man who looked after *The Gannet,* and he'll come with us. No news of Mr. Joseph Bunnett your end?"

"We've not found him yet. We've heard from him all right though," said the inspector morosely. He gave Flaxenham a brief account of their discovery in Joe's house.

"Well, now! He must be a tough customer!" exclaimed the superintendent. "Bad, that: very bad:

dear, dear, dear. And I was thinking we should find Mr. Bunnett and Bloxam on *The Gannet.*"

"What's this?" asked Nigel sharply. "Bloxam?"

"Ay. The man he took with him. Fisherman here— or used to when there was some fishing. Took him on board at the last moment."

"Forgot to tell you, Mr. Strangeways," said Tyler.

"But damn it, this alters the whole complexion of the case. Don't you see——"

"Doesn't alter my theory of the crime, sir. All fits in perfectly," replied the inspector in his most irritatingly superior manner.

"Oh, you have a theory, have you? And when does the unveiling ceremony take place?"

"Wait till I've had a look at *The Gannet,* sir."

"Hmm. Well, I hope your theory explains the two extraordinary and blatant contradictions that this cruise of Bunnett's presents us with."

"Contradictions, eh?" said Tyler, trying to look as though he knew all about it. "Yes, contradictions. And what would *you* say the contradictions were, sir?"

"Ha! Trying to pump me! Well, then, here you are. First we know Joe Bunnett was a hardened shellback; had no use for engines; born with a sheet in his mouth."

"You hold the sheet in your hand, sir," said Flaxenham, "not your mouth."

"Of course. Stupid of me. Well, here's this fellow, a devotee of sail, suddenly for no apparent reason installing an auxiliary engine in his boat. Contradiction number one."

"But we were told that he did this because he felt he was getting beyond sailing the boat singlehanded."

"Exactly. But if the reason for installing the engine

was that he should be able to run the boat single-handed, why did he then take on a paid hand at the last minute? Contradiction number two."

Inspector Tyler scratched his chin meditatively. "Ah. Clever of you seeing that, sir. But I think—yes, it all fits in. It doesn't invalidate my theory."

"The sphinx of Maiden Astbury, on being questioned, declared that he had nothing to say. The oracles are dumb, no voice nor hideous hum runs through the arched roof in words deceiving. Except perhaps, the hideous hum of a motor-bike."

"Yes," said Tyler. "The motor-bike. That just about proves it, I think."

"Well, if you gentlemen have finished telling riddles, we'd best be getting along," Flaxenham said slowly.

Elias Faulkes, a bronzed, taciturn man, was introduced to them, and the four bundled into a police car and set off. On their way to Basket Cove, Tyler plied Faulkes with questions. This auxiliary engine, now—when had Mr. Bunnett decided to install it? Faulkes did not know when he had *decided;* all he knew was that Bunnett had advised him of his intention about three weeks ago and had come down to supervise the fitting of the engine shortly afterwards. Faulkes himself knew a fair bit about marine engines and had lent a hand. Tyler appeared to be very interested by this. He asked for the exact date when the engine was installed. The third and fourth of July. Had Joe stayed in town on the night of the third or returned to Maiden Astbury? Stayed: the same hotel as usual. What sort of a man was this Bloxam? Reliable? He was all right: a good fisherman: a bit lazy. Was he accustomed to marine engines? No. But anyone could pick up the hang of them things in ten minutes. Why had Mr. Bunnett chosen him, and why had he left it so late to engage him? Faulkes didn't know why it had been left so late; but Mr. Bunnett could always be pretty sure of getting Bloxam to sail with him, because Bloxam made a living now hiring out rowing boats to visitors, and his lad, Bert, could do that while he himself was away earning good extra money on *The Gannet;* besides, Bloxam would do anything for Mr. Bunnett—Bunnett had rescued young Bert from drowning a few years ago when his sailing-dinghy had capsized in a squall.

"Dinghy!" exclaimed Nigel, awaking apparently out of a deep slumber. "Where's *The Gannet's* dinghy? Joe must have had one, didn't he?"

"He had one in tow when he started, he did all right," affirmed Elias Faulkes.

"I've no information about any dinghy," said Flaxenham.

"Well, if that *is The Gannet* sunk in the cove, the dinghy must be somewhere about. There'd be no point in Bunnett swimming ashore."

Nigel looked questioningly at Elias Faulkes, but the man remained silent as a bronze image.

"Smugglers!" Nigel said, after a short and frenzied groping in his memory. "Basket Cove was used by smugglers. Maybe there is a cave there?"

"There might be," replied Faulkes cautiously. Then, turning his head and gazing at Nigel as though he was a ship hull-down on the horizon, "But what'd he go for to put his dinghy in a cave, mister? It isn't sense."

In a little over thirty minutes they turned off the Poolhampton-Bridmouth road into a lane whose offshoots seemed to multiply and run riot like bindweed. Approached the sea thus deviously, the lane soon degenerated into a rough track climbing on to the bleak solitude of Basket Down. They passed a number of notices warning in official language whomsoever it might concern that this land was the property of the Air Ministry and trespassers would only have themselves to blame if they got their heads blown off. The tang of salt and thyme was in the air, and the ghostly cries of gulls. Bright sunlight turned the cliff-faces to an almost dazzling gold on either side of the cove; the water was green as crème de menthe. The track along which they had been driving became a bridle-path, trodden once no doubt by the ponies of smugglers, leading down the cliff in great loops. On the little sandy beach at its foot a blackened hulk was resting, guarded by two police-men. The salvage gang was there, too, and several small boys who had sprung up in their mushroom manner as it were out of the ground. A number of sightseers sprawled along the top of the cliff, throwing banana-skins and cartons negligently down into the cove. Someone was playing "I'm in heaven" on a mouth organ; the last perfect touch of the macabre, Nigel reflected, that the scene de-manded.

The task of salvage, it appeared, had been unusu-ally easy because of the sandy bottom of the cove. Divers had gone down and fastened grapnels to the wreck, which had then been dragged in by powerful winches set up on the shore. *The Gannet* was a mel-ancholy sight now, lying wearily over on one side, her hull charred, her upper-works black and blis-tered, the engine a tortured corpse of metal.

"Gives you a shock, doesn't it?" Flaxenham said rather unexpectedly to Nigel. "Like human beings, boats are. All alive and kicking when they're on the water, and now she looks like a dead body. A cruel shame it is."

"Mr. Bunnett was real fond of her," said Faulkes, staring at *The Gannet* with those long-distance eyes of his.

The foreman of the gang came up to them, and said:

"There's a stiff in the cabin, sir."

The sound of the mouth organ floated down to them, like the fluting of an irresponsible cherub—

*"I went to sea to see the sea——"*

Nigel felt an almost irresistible impulse to burst into tears.

The smell of charred wood and burned metal lay heavy on the summer air. Well, there was no use getting worked up about it. *The Gannet* had been burned alive and there was a stiff in the cabin. Let Tyler see to it.

Already the inspector was clambering up the boat's sloping side. A timeless silence, a hush only emphasised by the hushed and rhythmic plashing of the waves. The mouth-organ player was silent. The knot of men stood about silently, as if waiting for a funeral. After what seemed a very long time the inspector reappeared and beckoned to Elias Faulkes: the two of them went into the cabin. Another long pause. The small boys began to get restive and started clambering over the rocks on the western side of the cove.

Inspector Tyler was standing on the deck, bending down to Flaxenham. He looked oddly like an actor on the stage conferring with the producer during a rehearsal, Nigel thought. He could hear him say quietly:

"Bloxam is there. Burnt to death. Not much left of him. Faulkes recognises his ear-rings, and he's got one of those bracelets with his name on it. Looks as if the fire started in there—paraffin lamp all buckled up. We'll have to get an expert in on this, sir."

"I've sent for one. Expecting him along any time. Shall we get the body out now?"

Nigel wandered away. He felt dazed. So many questions to find an answer to. It all seemed trivial, compared with the fact of Miss Mellors dead and Bloxam dead—two people who had done no one any great harm, killed because they didn't fit in somehow with a murderer's plans. Or was that true of Bloxam? No reason why the fire on *The Gannet* should not have been accidental. A murderer would not want to set fire to his alibi, after all. After two murders one was apt to get morbidly suspicious.

"Hoy, mister, there's a boot in yurr!"

Nigel looked up, startled. The voice appeared to proceed, like an oracle, out of solid rock. Then, staring in its direction, he saw a boy's head growing—it seemed—from a heap of sea weed. Approaching nearer, he perceived that the piled-up drift half concealed the entrance of a cave at the foot of the cliff.

"A boot?" he said, somewhat bemused. "A football-boot, sea-boot, elastic-sided boot, surgical boot, or what?"

"Naw, mister, a boot."

This conversation was evidently not going to get Nigel much further, so he bent his head, entered the narrow opening and found himself in a cave whose floor sloped upwards and whose roof was invisible. Inside the cave was another small boy jumping excitedly up and down on the seat of the "boot." It was *The Gannet*'s dinghy. Another piece of the puzzle fitted into its place.

"Give over, Buffy!" yelled the first small boy, "yurr's one of the gents come aafter they smugglers."

The dancing one gave over, and Nigel fixed with an unrelenting stare.

"What smugglers?" asked Nigel.

"The smugglers as came in that thurr boot."

"But they—it wasn't a smuggler."

"Gourrn! 'Course they was. What'd they be doing in the Smugglers' Cave else? What'd they pile the drift against the mouth of the cave for, like Gran says her father toold her the smugglers used to do, if they wurrn't?"

Nigel had an inspiration. He addressed the boy gravely.

"Well, it mightn't have been a smuggler. In fact— can you keep a secret?"

"Slit my throat!"

"Maybe he will if you don't," Nigel said, with blood-curdling emphasis on the *"he."* The boy received this with keen relish. Nigel went on, "Now here's this smuggler. He comes ashore with the stuff. It's not hidden in here, is it? No. Very well. He must have taken it inland. Now, how did he do that? Had he a car or a motor-bike waiting for him? We're pretty sure he had no accomplice on land—which means there must have been a motor-bike hidden somewhere up on the cliff ready for him to ride off on. Do you know anywhere a motor-bike could be hidden, near here?"

"Ah, that's right," said the boy. "He'd have a motor-bike hidden. No, he wouldn't, though; he'd have a faast airyplane with a hollow propellor for to hide the jewels inside—or was it drugs, mister? Seen that on the flicks, I have."

"He might have had a fast aeroplane," rejoined Nigel with admirable patience: "or he might have had the Graf Zeppelin. But, as it happens, he didn't. It was a motor-bike. The question is, where was it hidden?"

"Hey, mister!" Buffy suddenly uncorked himself and yelled into Nigel's face. "Hey, mister! What about that motor-bike Fred seen laast week in th' shed up along?"

"Now you're talking. That might be it. Tell me all about it. What day was it, first?"

"Sunday before laast. Fred and Curly here and me comes up yurr, and me and Curly dares 'ee to go into that shed thurr the airyplanes be going to bomb. Fred, 'ee can't read, see, 'ee's daaft, see, so 'ee don't rightlee know this shed's a taarget for the airyplanes. So Fred 'ee creeps along on belly towards shed, and thurr was me and Curly fair splitting laarfing, see, 'cos we'm waiting for they airyplanes to come along and blow old Fred to bloody bits, see. Reckon 'ee had the laarf on us though, mister, 'cos they airyplanes never come aafter all," Buffy added with some chagrin.

"Too bad," said Nigel sympathetically. "What happened then?"

"Well, Fred, 'ee goes into shed and 'ee finds a motor-bike hidden beneath a crop of nettles and that. 'Ee beckons to we and aafter a bit us runs into shed and sees un, too. A Rudge motor-bike it wurr."

"A new one?"

"No. Reg'lar battered old thing."

"You didn't tell anyone about it?"

"No fear, mister. Dad 'ee'd take the skin off Curly and me if 'ee'd knowd we'd been in thurr, and Fred 'ee's daaft, see, 'ee caan't speak properlee, only bumble like."

"Notice the number plate on the bike?"

"No, mister."

By dint of distributing largesse and sinister threats in equal proportion, Nigel induced the boys to repeat their tale to Tyler. The shed was visited—it was a bare two hundred yards from the top of the cliff, lying in a fold of the down. Oil spots were discovered amongst the nettles and rubble where the motor-bicycle had lain. When the place had been thoroughly searched, without further result, they descended to the cove again. Nigel commented that it was a risky business for Bunnett to leave a bike in that shed for several days; if anyone had noticed it there, it would have been reported to the police in the course of their investigations, and the purchase of the bike might easily have been traced back to Joe. Anyhow, how could he know that the shed wouldn't be bombed in the interval. The local constable then volunteered that none of the people in the district would go near this shed because a labourer had hung himself in it a few years back; and visitors would be kept off by the Air Ministry notices. Flaxenham said that, as far as the bombing went, anyone could find out by a few tactful inquiries when bombing operations were due to commence. Tyler said there was very little danger of the bike being traced to Bunnett: he would presumably purchase it by some roundabout method, and remove all marks of identification from it; when he had finished with it, he had intended no doubt to take it aboard and pitch it off the boat into deep water.

Tyler's theory of the crime was now fairly clear to Nigel. However, they had no leisure to discuss it yet. There was the dinghy to be examined: a number of fingerprints were discovered on it and on the oars; the prints of the two boys were taken, much to their delight. The expert, Mr. Crankshaw, had by now arrived and was making his examination of *The Gannet.* He promised to telephone his report to Tyler as soon as the job was finished. He would not commit himself yet as to the origin of the fire. It was possible that it had started in the cabin, the result—say—of some carelessness by Bloxam in filling the paraffin lamp. Asked by Tyler whether it was possible for the lamp to have been upset by Bloxam getting out of his bunk in a sleepy, half-drugged state, Mr. Crankshaw replied that it was most unlikely; the lamp was swung from the cabin roof and designed to stand rough treatment. On the other hand, there was certain evidence to suggest that the fire, or another fire, had originated in or near the engine. This again could only be the result of carelessness or deliberate incendiarism; more minute examination might enable him to judge whether it was the former or the latter. Generally speaking, he would vote for deliberate incendiarism; but petrol-engines were notoriously tricky things in careless or inexperienced hands.

The inspector was in a hurry to get back to Maiden Astbury. Superintendent Flaxenham agreed to undertake the routine inquiries on the spot; to trace Joe Bunnett's movements on his previous visit to supervise the installing of the engine, to find out whether he had been seen at any time in the vicinity of Basket Cove, to inquire locally into the sales of second-hand Rudges, and so on. Tyler and Flaxenham put their heads together over the map and worked out the quickest route between the cove and Maiden Astbury; inquiries would be made all along this route to discover if anyone had heard a motor-bike passing north on the night of the murder or returning south before dawn. Allowing for the meanderings of the lane near the coast, they calculated that the route could be little over twenty miles. Tyler would check it by his speedometer on his return journey.

The police car started off. Tyler settled his huge bulk comfortably, turned to Nigel, and said:

"Now, sir. This is my case against Joe Bunnett"—

# XIII
## July 20, 7.30–9.17 p.m.

*And when I think upon a pot of beer.*
                                    BYRON, *Don Juan*

NIGEL was no subscriber to the theory that strong drink fuddles the intellect. Rather did he hold that, by taking off the censor and releasing the many sub-conscious influences which cloud, distort and inhibit the reason, strong drink gives the intellect free play and fair play. Thus it was not until seven-thirty that evening—the Cammisons had dined early and Nigel excused himself immediately after dinner—that he sat down alone to examine, aided by three bottles of beer, Inspector Tyler's theory of the crime. He poured out the first bottle into his tankard, balanced the tankard on his lap, lay back and shut his eyes.

Tyler's theory, he said to himself: let me first re-state it. The criminal is Joe Bunnett. His motive for murdering Eustace was his life-long oppression at Eustace's hands, in particular his brother's forbid-ding of the banns with Ariadne Mellors; all this brought to a head by Eustace's intention to sell the brewery and thus throw his employees out of work. There may have been some other recent quarrel of which we have not heard, as well. That is reason-able enough motive. One may add, too, that Joe—

humiliated by the way he had caved in to Eustace over Ariadne—was more or less consciously reasserting his manhood to her by killing Eustace; showing her in the most primitive, and therefore the most forceful way possible, that he was not the worm she and Eustace imagined him. Admittedly, it is on the face of it odd that he should have waited so many years to assert himself. But, as Herbert and Sophie have impressed upon me, Joe is a decent, ordinary fellow at heart—the sort that will contemplate violence only when it is justified by an altruistic motive, however deep the egoistic motives may be that in fact are drawing them towards this crisis of the will and explosion of violence.

Nigel took a deep draught, sighed and lit a cigarette. The motive, then, is more than adequate. Now for Tyler's reconstruction of the crime. According to him, Joe Bunnett prepared an almost perfect alibi, and an almost perfect crime, both of which failed through the interposition of Nemesis—or, as Tyler less classically puts it—damned bad luck. Joe had done a great deal of sailing off the Dorset coast. He knew the Basket Cove was a secluded spot, made doubly secluded recently by the purchase of the down behind it by the Air Ministry. Moreover, Joe was hail-fellow-well-met with all sorts of people; it would not be difficult for him to find out the periods when bombing practice would take place and the periods when he could leave the motor-bike in that shed with impunity. It is worth remarking that Basket Cove is almost the nearest point on the coast to Maiden Astbury. Up to this point—as far as he is concerned—every prospect pleases and only Eustace is vile.

Now the method of the crime. Roughly, Joe intends to lure his brother into the brewery with the bait of an anonymous letter. He intends to arrive at the brewery himself well before his brother, disconnect the emergency bell of the refrigerator-room and meet Eustace by the entrance of the brewery. At this point, either he will tell Eustace that he himself is here because of an anonymous letter he has received and in due course he will get him into the refrigerator-room; or he will stun Eustace at once in such a way that the injury may later look to have been sustained in the course of Eustace's struggles to get out of the room, and after stunning him will convey his body there. Joe's knowledge of the nightwatchman's schedule would enable him to do all this with absolute certainty of not being discovered in the act.

The murder was meant to look like an accident. Probably, if all had gone as Joe planned, he would have tried to get hold of the anonymous letter he had sent to his brother and destroy it; if found by the police, the letter might give rise to suspicion that the accident was not all it seemed. Accident, then, was to be Joe's first line of defence. But, in case that failed, he prepared an alibi; not too perfect or elaborate an alibi; just a nice, reasonable one. He had an auxiliary engine installed on *The Gannet*. For two obvious reasons. You cannot rely on steady winds in the middle of summer; it was essential that Joe should arrive at Basket Cove on schedule—in plenty of time to be able to climb the cliff, pick up his hidden motor-bike and get to Maiden Astbury by 11.30 p.m. at the latest. It was equally essential that, on his return to *The Gannett*, he should not find himself becalmed; he planned, no doubt, to put in at Lyme Regis, or whatever was to be his next port of call, at such an hour that he might reasonably seem to have been sailing all night.

How does Bloxam fit in with all this? On the whole I am inclined to agree with Tyler that Joe's taking-on of Bloxam was a last-minute strengthening of his alibi, and not a part of the original plan. Tyler's theory, sound enough surely, is that Joe told Bloxam he was going to stand the trick from 10 p.m., say, to 2 a.m. Before Bloxam turned in at 10 p.m., Joe prepared some coffee for them both, and put a sleeping powder into Bloxam's. While Bloxam was in a drugged slumber, Joe would change course, make all speed towards the land, creep into Basket Cove (*The Gannet* was equipped with a powerful acetylene headlight, Elias Faulkes had informed them), anchor, race to Maiden Astbury, shut Eustace in the refrigerator-room, race back, get rid of the motor-bike—probably by wheeling it down the bridle-path, taking it aboard and throwing it into deep water, and get *The Gannet* some way along on her original course before awakening Bloxam.

From the time *The Gannet* entered Basket Cove to the time she put out again there would be a minimum gap of two hours, Tyler calculated. Nigel took out the schedule of approximate times that Tyler had made up.

10 p.m. J.B. takes over wheel.

10.40 p.m. Anchors in Basket Cove; rows ashore; climbs cliff.

10.50 p.m. Sets off on motor-bike.

11.30 p.m. Arrives brewery; disconnects emergency bell; waits for Eustace.

Midnight. Meets Eustace near brewery entrance; gets him to refrigerator-room; shuts him in.

12.30 a.m. Rides out of Maiden Astbury.

1.10 a.m. Arrives on cliff above Basket Cove, wheels bike down bridle-path, puts it in dinghy, and weighs anchor by

1.20 a.m. *Gannet* puts out.

1.35 a.m. *Gannet* back on original course. J. B. throws motor-bike out of dinghy, and—

2.0 a.m. Awakens Bloxam.

How is that two hours to be accounted for to Bloxam? The man might easily notice, when it grew light, that *The Gannet* was not nearly as far on her course as she should be. Probable answer; *The Gannet* is proceeding under sail *only* during Bloxam's trick; Joe announces his intention of continuing under sail *only*; as soon as Bloxam is well asleep, Joe starts up the engine and uses the engine the whole time till just before he awakens Bloxam; this would make up most of the leeway, especially if the wind that night was light—as indeed it turned out to be. Bloxam, indirectly, would be able to confirm that the engine had not been used, for the unexpected sound and vibration of it would have awoken him out of any ordinary sleep, and he could have no reason to suppose that he had been drugged. In short, Joe had a witness who would be prepared to swear that he was sailing all night, and thus give him an excellent alibi for the crime—the more excellent for being apparently natural and not in the least elaborate.

It is quite possible, though we shall probably never have proof of it, that Joe strengthened this alibi by a little juggling with the petrol supply. It would be easy for him, just before he woke Bloxam, to fill up the tank from a tin he had secreted somewhere

on the boat—or better, had previously hidden somewhere on shore, in the cave for instance, and only
brought aboard on his return from Maiden Astbury.
He could then sink this tin, and call Bloxam's attention later in some unobtrusive way to the fact that
the tank was full. Thus, there would be apparently
incontrovertible evidence that the engine had not
been used at all that night.

One further point worth noticing. Joe had saved
Bloxam's son from drowning. If the worst came to
the worst, and the alibi started to leak, Bloxam would
probably perjure himself black and blue for Joe. On
the other hand, it would perhaps have been more
sensible of Joe to take aboard a man whom the police
could not possibly suspect of collusion with him.

Nigel took another deep draught and lit his second
cigarette.

Now for what really happened. Everything went
according to Cocker until he got to the brewery.
(It seems reasonable to suppose that, if Eustace failed
to be lured to the brewery by the anonymous letter,
Joe had some alternative plan of getting into his
house, waking him and bringing him there. He could
bank pretty confidently, though, on Eustace's passion
for catching out his employees in petty derelictions.)
We now come to the central problem of the case—
why was not the murder carried out as originally
planned? Tyler reconstructs it as follows. *Either*
there was a struggle when the pair entered the refrigerator-room, and some mark was left on Eustace
which necessitated the destruction of his body; *or*
Joe stunned Eustace near the entrance, but did not
stun him hard enough (through fear of leaving a suspicious wound), and Eustace recovered conscious-
ness when Joe was carrying him into the refrigerator-

room; a struggle took place, etc. The fragment of ring I discovered leaves pretty well no doubt that a struggle of some kind did take place.

For some reason, not yet demonstrable, the accident-plan goes wrong and Joe puts his brother into the copper. The idea that it was because of a wound inflicted by a left-handed person must be washed out; Herbert says that the blow which killed Miss Mellors was a right-handed one, and two murderers is more than one can stomach. Well now, according to Tyler, Joe put his brother in the copper and started back for Basket Cove. He was the man, probably, whom Gabriel Sorn heard riding away from the brewery on a motor-bike between 12.30 and 12.45.

Nigel jerked himself up straight, spilling some beer on his trousers.

Stop! Isn't there a discrepancy there? Sorn said he heard the motor-bike on his way home. From the brewery to his digs is about five minutes' walk. He got in at twelve-forty-five. Therefore he heard the cyclist at twelve-forty. Now, Eustace was due at the brewery at midnight. Speed was necessary to Joe's plan—he had to return to Basket Cove as quickly as possible, soon after one o'clock, if he was to get *The Gannet* back on her course by the time Bloxam was due to relieve him. That being so, why did he spend forty minutes in the brewery? Even allowing for a certain amount of delay in getting Eustace where he wanted him, and then in transferring the body to the copper, forty minutes seems an unconscionable time to have hung about. One can scarcely credit that, in the heat of the moment, he would notice that a piece had been chipped off his signet-ring and spend valuable time hunting for it. Yet what other explanation can there be?

Leave that aside. Joe returns to *The Gannet* and finds it in flames. That is the key of Tyler's case; it is the only theory by which he can explain Joe's extraordinary subsequent actions. Nemesis steps in and puts a match to Joe's alibi. What a headline it would make for the press! What a succulent text for the pulpit! What a subject for morbid clichés in suburban parlours. But is it true? Isn't it much, much too good to be true? Tyler's suggestion is that Bloxam, through waking up half-stupid from a drugged sleep, and/or through carelessness, and/or through his lack of experience with petrol engines, set the boat on fire. Of course, we can't say anything very positive about that till we receive the expert's report. But there are two minor, and one major negative point. The minor points are:—(i) if Bloxam started the fire, one would have expected him to have jumped overboard, not gone into the cabin where his body was found; (ii) even if he had not gone overboard at once, but fought the fire and got his clothes caught he would still naturally have jumped into the water then. By Jove though, there are two possible explanations for that. The fire-extinguisher was in the cabin; whether the fire started near the engine or in the cabin, Bloxam would go for the extinguisher, and he may quite possibly have been overcome before he could use it. Alternatively, he may have jumped overboard; Joe may then have found his body in the water and put it back into the cabin—in order that the body might be more completely burnt and thus there should be no danger of a post-mortem revealing that he had been drugged.

Both those, in our present state of ignorance about the source of the fire, are reasonable theories. But they both break down on my major negative point, which is this: the kingpin of Joe's plan was that Bloxam should be asleep while *The Gannet* was in Basket Cove. His alibi would be blown up with all hands if Bloxam should awake, find the boat lying in the cove and his employer disappeared. Therefore, the very last mistake Joe would be likely to make would be to give Bloxam an insufficient amount of the drug. Unless Bloxam had a freak resistance to whatever drug was administered, he could not possibly have woken up so soon, and therefore he could not have accidentally set the boat on fire. Therefore, the only solutions left are either that the boat caught fire of itself, or that some third party— neither Joe nor Bloxam—set it on fire deliberately.

"Eliminate the impossible; and whatever is left will be the truth." That's all very jolly; but I am faced with a whole set of impossibles. I'll have to pass that over for the present. Proceed with Tyler's reconstruction. Joe finds his alibi shot to pieces. He hides the dinghy in the cave, piling seaweed and drift against the cave-mouth; the idea being to conceal for as long as possible the whereabouts of *The Gannet* and so give him more time for escape. That fits the facts reasonably enough. He then puts his head in his hands and does a bit of thinking. This is to account for the time between his arrival at the cave—not later than one-thirty, and the time the tramp heard the motor-bike "receding inland," two or maybe three o'clock. Admittedly the tramp hadn't a watch; but these fellows develop a pretty accurate sense of time. Joe decided on the audacious stroke of hiding up for a day or two in his own house while destroying the evidence against him and getting hold of his passport.

He gets back to Maiden Astbury somewhere

around three o'clock, probably dumping his motor-bike somewhere outside the town; Honeycombe Wood would be a good place for concealing it; I wonder have the police searched it yet. He goes to ground in the attic. It is too late to get his passport from the brewery, for dawn will soon be breaking; anyway, he's had all the excitement his nerves can stand for one night. The next night, Friday, he lies low; he knows that Bunnett's body will only have been found that evening, and the brewery will be swarming with police. On Saturday night he makes his first move; he lets himself into Eustace's house with the duplicate keys he took off the body, removes the incriminating Roxby's papers, and—a point the inspector has overlooked—stole some food.

On Sunday morning, so Tollworthy told me, Mrs. Bunnett was in a tantrum because her maid—so she said—had eaten a cake and two loaves that had been baked the day before. Why did no one notice that point? Maids may steal a slice or two of cake from time to time; but they most certainly do *not* polish off a whole baking. This incidentally accounts for the crumbs in the attic.

Why did not Joe enter the brewery the same night and get hold of his passport? According to Tyler, because he was afraid the police might still be poking about in the brewery. That is plausible; but Tyler's theory at this point throws up several difficulties. First, if Joe intended to flee the country, thus inevitably drawing suspicion upon himself, why did he bother to destroy the evidence of the Roxby's trans-action? Second, was the destruction of *The Gannet* so disastrous that the only course open to him was this foolhardy one of returning to Maiden Astbury, getting his passport, going abroad and starting life

*217*

all over again? Surely the sensible thing to have done, when he found *The Gannet* in flames, was to have rowed the motor-bike out to deep water and dumped it, and then walked over Basket Down till he found a farmhouse. He could surely make up some plausible story to account for his having to put in at the Cove, the outbreak of the fire, and the death of Bloxam. Provided the bike had originally been obtained—as no doubt it had—in another part of the country and in such a way that the purchase could not be connected with him, and provided it was sunk deep, there was simply nothing to connect him with the murder. Still one must admit that murderers are apt to lose their heads, especially Joe's type; the natural impulse of his sort would be to run to mother when in trouble, and his return to Maiden Astbury can be explained by his desire to get in touch with Ariadne Mellors, whose relationship with him was clearly semi-maternal. The first objection, too, is not insuperable. It can be argued that he destroyed the Roxby's papers in order to give himself time; the longer the police believed that he was still cruising about on *The Gannet,* and the longer they had nothing like those papers to suggest his own motive for the crime, the longer it would be before they instituted a serious search for him. No doubt he had some bad moments on Saturday, when he heard them below examining his study and bedroom. But, when the search proceeded no further, he would assume that he was not yet suspected and could postpone going for his passport till a later night—when, with any luck, the brewery would be comparatively free of police.

Then, according to Tyler, Joe's hand was forced. On Sunday, about midnight, he was surprised in his study by an intruder; he struck out in panic, struck out again and again in the dark; then, all too late, found that he had killed the one person he could have trusted to back him through thick and thin. It was now imperative for him to clear out of the country at once, before the body was discovered. So he went over to the brewery after his passport, but was baulked by the night-watchman. Here again Tyler's theory fits the facts well enough; yet it doesn't seem to fit all the implications. For instance, is it conceivable that Joe could have struck down Miss Mellors? If she surprised him in the study, surely she would recognise and speak to him before he had time to deliver a blow; she had an electric torch, after all. If, on the other hand, he had heard someone moving about in the study, the natural thing would have been for him to sit tight in the attic; if there had been anything incriminating in the study, the police would have found it the day before. Finally, if it was Joe who visited the brewery on Sunday night, *where is he now?*

Arrived at this crux, Nigel swallowed the rest of his beer, walked slowly several times round the room, opened his second bottle, and sat down again.

Where is Joe Bunnett now? It is almost incredible, with the whole county police searching for him and considering how well known he is round here, that he has not been found. There seem two possible explanations. He is still in the brewery; there are probably a number of hiding places there that he would know of and the police would not guess. Alternatively, he may be dead. This fits best the uneasy conviction I've had all along that some unknown person has been trying to frame Joe. Let us predicate this X and see what follows. It follows, surely, that

X was in collusion with Joe over the murder of Eustace. Otherwise one would have to suppose that he happened to surprise Joe while he was killing Eustace, or immediately afterwards; but, if X was a bad lot, the result of this would be blackmail—the last thing X would want would be for anyone else to suspect Joe, and therefore he would not go around planting incriminating evidence against him. Alternatively, if X was the sole murderer, how on earth—without making Joe suspicious of him—could he arrange that Joe should put into Basket Cove that night and behave generally in such a dubious manner? And how did the burning of *The Gannet* fit in?

Suppose, then, that X and Joe are in collusion. Does that give me a line on X? There's no doubt that the people Joe would reasonably collude with are—in order of preference—Miss Mellors, Herbert Cammison, Gabriel Sorn, and Mr. Barnes. Cross out Miss Mellors. True, she was with Joe when he or she probably posted the anonymous letter; she might even have entered Joe's house to plant incriminating evidence against him, and been killed by him because he realised she was double-crossing him. But she is dead, and therefore it cannot be she who got rid of Joe. Anyway, she was surely too fond of Joe to double-cross him. Herbert Cammison? He and Joe were friends: they were the two people who had the strongest motives for killing Bunnett. How would it have worked out. Herbert would probably be the brain behind the whole plan. Also, he would post the anonymous letter. We know he was in the vicinity of Weston Priors that afternoon. Difficulty here, why hasn't Joe a better alibi for the posting of the letter? Answer: he probably had, and would have come out with it if asked by the police, only the burning of *The Gannet* upset the whole plan. Well then, Joe had the obvious alibi for the night of the murder; therefore it was he who did the actual killing.

Suppose all this is true, subsequent events admit of two different interpretations. *(a)* Herbert had planned all along to double-cross Joe. He went down to Basket Cove that night, presumably on a motorbike, possibly stopping Joe outside the town and riding pillion on his: knocked Joe on the head and disposed of his body somehow; set fire to the yacht; and he has since been dealing out this incriminating evidence against Joe; *(b)* Herbert had no intention of double-crossing his accomplice. Joe, finding the yacht burnt, returns to Maiden Astbury gibbering with panic and somehow gets in touch with Herbert. Herbert realises Joe's nerve has cracked; Joe may give the show away any minute and implicate Herbert. Therefore, Joe must be silenced. He kills Joe and disposes of the body—how, I do not yet know. How much of the evidence against Joe is genuine, so to speak, and how much Herbert faked, is for the moment irrelevant. This second interpretation is the more reasonable one in every way except that it assumes the fire in *The Gannet* to have been accidental. I don't believe Herbert is a villain; he would not have planned from the beginning to double-cross Joe; he is, on the other hand, a bit cold-blooded and ruthless; once he realised that his accomplice was breaking under the strain, he would be quite capable of sacrificing him. Herbert has a clear-headed idea of his own value to the world confused by no false modesty. He might easily say, in his dispassionate way, "The killing of Eustace was justified on social grounds; he was an enemy of society. Joe must be silenced now, too, because he is a danger to me and I am a valuable member of society."

There is no doubt that Herbert is the most likely candidate for the position of Joe's accomplice. He had both a social and a personal motive for getting rid of Eustace; he has an excellent brain and nerve; he is quite uncompromising; he might, under certain circumstances, be the most dangerous type of fanatic—the cool-headed one. At the same time, one must not pass over Gabriel Sorn or Mr. Barnes as possible accomplices. Gabriel was not, as far as I know, a close friend of Joe's. But he had those two very strong motives for killing Eustace—the money he would inherit (if indeed he knew about that), and his neurotic feelings towards Eustace as his father. The weak point about him or Mr. Barnes is that neither of them were in such a favourable position as Cammison to dispose of Joe's body. A doctor is expert at dissecting bodies; a doctor goes off on his rounds in the country, and has much more opportunity of getting rid of the remains than men who are pegged down all day in a brewery.

Nigel felt acutely uncomfortable about all this. He liked Herbert and he liked Sophie. In fact, he had only decided to stay on and help in the case because they seemed in obvious need of his help. Herbert had been absolutely open about his motives; moreover, Nigel had seen him examining the bodies of Eustace Bunnett and Miss Mellors; it was incredible that he should not have turned a hair, if he was responsible for the murder of them both, directly or indirectly. Alas, not quite incredible. Herbert was a man of steel, no getting away from it. However, might there not be some theory which would fit the facts and leave Herbert out of it?

Nigel took a deep breath, drained his tankard and poured out the third bottle—a signal, as it were, that the third phase of his battle of wits against this invisible enemy was beginning. He lay back in his chair, threw his long legs over the arm, and started a meticulous review of the case up to date.

The characters of the persons involved came first beneath his trained scrutiny. Then the events and material clues. Finally he exercised his astonishing verbal memory to recall everything he had heard said since his arrival in Maiden Astbury—not the evidence only, but also—and more important now— the apparently irrelevant remarks let drop from time to time. It was while he was engaged on this that the point came into his head which soon enabled him to work out a whole theory of the crime. It was a little remark made by Sophie Cammison, a remark of such seemingly grotesque irrelevance that there could be no possible excuse for lingering on it. Yet it teased him. It was like a small urchin making a long nose at the Nelson Column—absurdly impertinent, ludicrously disproportionate; yet somehow arresting. As Nigel rather irritably considered it, another point lit up in his mind, and then another. He jumped to his feet and began striding excitedly round the room. It was like watching those electric signs that light up letter by letter, gradually spelling out a name. And the name, Nigel knew as he watched with growing excitement these little points lighting up one by one—the name they unreeled was the name of the murderer.

He looked at his watch: 9.10 p.m. The question was, would the murderer put in another of his appearances tonight? The inspector was seeing to the brewery end of it all right; police would be watching from concealment every entrance; the murderer would be allowed to enter, but he would find it less easy to leave. If indeed, he wanted to enter; perhaps he was even now planning to strike somewhere else; perhaps his last visit to the brewery had only been a feint to conceal the direction of his next blow. Nigel stirred uneasily. It was an unpleasing thought that the next blow might be aimed at himself; the criminal was without mercy and had been a damned sight too efficient so far; maybe Nigel would be safest in the brewery to-night, with plenty of policemen on the spot. Oh, well, one could only die once. On with the dance.

Nigel went down to the hall telephone. There were two points still to be verified. He searched in the directory and dialled a number. Herbert Cammison, sitting in his study, heard him say—"Hallo. Is that Mr. Tripp? Oh, it's you speaking. This is Nigel Strangeways speaking from Dr. Cammison's. I'm helping the police in the Bunnett affair. . . . Yes. . . . Just one small point. That set of teeth you've been reconstructing. . . . Oh, you've finished . . . yes, it must have been a very delicate job. . . . Eustace Bunnett's, without any question? . . . Yes, I thought so. How did you identify them? . . . Of course, the plaster cast of the jaws: lucky you kept it . . . Joe's and Mrs. Bunnett's, too? Mm. You must have quite a nice little chamber of family horrors. No further identification necessary? . . . Quite so. Thanks very much. Good-night."

A faint look of perplexity appeared on Herbert Cammison's saturnine features. It deepened as he heard through the slightly open door another number being dialled and Nigel's voice saying, "Is Mrs. Bunnett in? . . . Thank you. . . . Mr. Strangeways speaking. Just a moment. Are you the——? . . . Oh, yes, Mrs. Bunnett's cook. Well, if you could just answer one or two questions, it would save troubling your mistress. . . . Yes, I am connected with the police. The night of the burglary, you remember; Saturday. Mrs. Bunnett said something about some food having disappeared. . . . Yes, of course, quite ridiculous. Some loaves and a seed-cake, wasn't it? . . . Yes, I expect the burglar took them, too. Hope he left you your Sunday joint. . . . He did. Oh well, it might have been worse, mightn't it? Thank you. Good-night."

As Nigel hung up the receiver, Dr. Cammison gently closed the door of his study. He stood quite still in the middle of the room, frowning a little. He was still standing there a minute later when the front-door bell rang. He went to the door. Gabriel Sorn was standing outside. "Could I see Strangeways for a minute," he said.

# XIV
## July 20, 9.20–11.20 p.m.

*Thy chase had a beast in view.*
**DRYDEN**

WITH Gabriel Sorn's arrival at the Cammisons', one may say that the last chapter of the Bunnett affair opened—the last chapter, for the murderer's confession can only be considered as an epilogue. This last chapter was a worthy climax to the events which had preceded, events so macabre, abominable and bewildering in themselves that one might well have supposed their conclusion could not fail to be anticlimax. This Monday night was distinguished for more than the catching of a cold-blooded and monstrously ingenious murderer. It was perhaps the first occasion on which a stolid policeman has nearly fainted, from something else than loss of blood; it was probably the first—and quite possibly the last—occasion on which Gabriel Sorn was to perform an act of indisputably the highest physical courage; and incidentally it came near to seeing the total destruction of Bunnett's brewery and of several estimable inhabitants of Maiden Astbury—not to mention Nigel himself.

At nine-twenty Gabriel Sorn, who had told Cammison that he wished to speak privately with Nigel, was shown by him into the bedroom. The young man, Nigel observed, was labouring under some strongly suppressed emotion; his left eyelid fluttered spasmodically with a nervous tic; the alternating prickliness and effusiveness of his manner were more strongly marked than before. He sat down in the basket-chair, clasping his hands so that the knuckles stood out white—as though nerving himself for a dentist's drill. Nigel, who at times could be as inhuman as Sophie had accused him of being, was far too interested in analysing Sorn's manner to feel pity or disgust for the rather lamentable figure he presented.

"Found your murderer yet?" said Sorn.

"The police, I understand, are confident of a speedy arrest," Nigel replied glibly.

"You 'understand'? That sounds as though you hadn't much confidence in them."

This remark was as good as a question; but Nigel made no answer. The best way to rattle anyone, he knew very well, was to remain silent, and compel the other chap to make the running. He stared noncommittally down his nose. After ten seconds Sorn blurted out:

"But what about you? Haven't you any theory who the murderer is?"

"I have no theory," Nigel replied softly: then, suddenly raising his pale blue eyes and staring fixedly at Sorn, he added.

"You see, I *know* who the murderer is."

Sorn's hands moved convulsively, a movement that he turned into a futile sort of gesture.

"You——? Oh, well. That's that, then, I suppose."

Nigel resumed his formidable silence.

"Well, damn it," jerked out Sorn after a little of this, "why haven't you arrested him?"

"I might not have enough evidence to convince

the police. Or again, I might not know exactly where he is."

Gabriel Sorn digested this. Then, visibly screwing himself up to make the effort, he said—feigned negligence and real anxiety as it were cancelling each other out in his voice and rendering it quite toneless—

"May I ask, am *I* the murderer?"

"You should know best, Mr. Sorn, you should know best."

Gabriel gave a funny little laugh, a laugh of almost genuine amusement.

"Because, if I *am,* and if—as you more or less imply—you haven't yet passed on your knowledge to the police, then it would be to my advantage to plant a knife in your manly bosom as soon as possible. Wouldn't you say so?"

"Scarcely. After all, Cammison knows you're in my room—and so presumably does the maid. No, I should call it a decidedly imprudent move on your part."

"Cammison. Yes." Sorn lay back a little in his chair. "I've been thinking about my mother. She's proud, you know. Proud and poor. The blood of earls, so I've been credibly informed, runs in the Sorn veins— pretty diluted, of course, I'm wondering will she be too proud to take Eustace's money."

"Tough on you, if she refuses it."

"Yes. You see, it would enable me to give up the brewery and devote myself to writing. No doubt you think that would be a major calamity," he added defensively.

"Oh, no. Not a bit. I'd say you could write good poetry. You've had the right stimuli. 'We learn in suffering,' and all that."

"Thanks very much," snapped Sorn ungraciously. "I didn't come here for emotional reassurance."

"Just what did you come here for? A small point, perhaps, but one worth making. Apart from planting a knife in my manly bosom, I mean."

Gabriel Sorn was silent for some time. Then, without looking up, he said:

"I came to tell you a story. But I don't know that you'll believe it."

"You can but try."

"I suppose this facetious manner is part of your stock-in-trade. Oh well, I will try then. It's quite a short story. Half an hour ago I was rung up by a certain person who asked me to be waiting with my car at midnight in that lane that leads through Honeycombe Wood into the London Road."

Nigel slapped his knee excitedly. "The devil you were!" he exclaimed. "Here, let's get this straight. What you mean is that the murderer asked you to help him make a get-away?"

"You've said it."

"And why should he appeal to you particularly? I mean, you're putting yourself in rather an awkward position by this statement. It sounds as if you had been his accomplice all along."

"Do you really think I'd be giving myself and him away like this, if I was his accomplice?" Sorn asked wearily.

"Well, why *are* you giving him away? Have you developed a sudden passion for bourgeois morality, *fiat Justitia,* and all that?"

"It doesn't matter much what we call it, does it? I suppose it's just that I don't fancy the idea of my father's murderer getting off scot-free."

"Very filial of you, to be sure."

229

"Oh, for God's sake, shut up this schoolmaster's sarcasm!" Sorn burst out. "Even bastards have feelings."

"Well, I'm sorry, but it really is rather a tall story."

"You don't believe me?"

"Oh, yes. *I* believe you," Nigel said unexpectedly, "but I doubt if Tyler will. Can't you supply any—er—additional confirmation? The name of the person who rang you up, for instance?"

"You say you know who the murderer is. Why should I tell you what you know already? I don't mind telling you, though, where he rang up from: the A.A. box at the crossroads at the top of Honeycombe Hill. He's been hiding in the woods since last night."

"He told you all this? Trusting sort of fellow, isn't he?"

Sorn stared at the carpet. "You needn't pile it on. I know I'm behaving like Judas. He's—he was a friend of mine, you see, and he trusts me. But he shouldn't have killed my father," he added in odd, childish, obstinate tones. He twisted his fingers together. "God! I hope I am doing right to tell you this. Is it right of me, or just contemptible?"

"Don't ask me. I'm an amateur detective, not a judge."

"Well," said Sorn, trying to recover himself, "what is the amateur detective going to do about it?"

"I'll convince Tyler somehow. We'll throw a cordon round the wood; you will keep the rendezvous in your car, and we'll have a bobby or two hidden in the back of it. That suit you?"

Sorn's face flushed; his voice rose up and broke into a falsetto. "No I'll not—damn it, you can't expect me to be there when he's caught. That's asking a bit too much. You can borrow my car, if you like, but count me out of it."

"Very well, then. I'll go along and tell Tyler at once. He'll need to get all the men he can spare round the wood. Here's a map. Just show me the exact place where you're supposed to be meeting our friend. . . . Right, and where do you keep your car? Tollworthy will probably be coming along for it."

"It's standing outside my digs."

Gabriel Sorn was dismissed. In five minutes' time Nigel was talking to Tyler in the police station. The inspector was, contrary to Nigel's prediction, keenly excited by Sorn's story.

"By Jove! sir, so that's where Joe Bunnett's been hiding all to-day. Well, we'd have found him to-morrow. I was going to have every inch of that wood searched. Sensible of him to try and clear out. We'll get him now, though."

"Just a minute. I had to pretend to Sorn that I was convinced by his tale, after registering a reasonable amount of suspicion at the beginning. But don't tell me you're taken in by it too."

The inspector's eyes narrowed to slits.

"Taken in? Are you suggesting——?"

"Yes, of course I am. It's an attempt, and not a very bright one, to draw our attention away from the real scene of action."

"I don't see that, sir."

"Look here, if the murderer was really hiding in Honeycombe Wood, he'd never be such a fool as to tell Sorn about it. Far too dangerous. He couldn't be certain that Sorn wouldn't split. Let us suppose, as Sorn's story implies, that the murderer has an A.A. key. The obvious thing would have been for him to ring up a garage—giving a false name, of course, ask for a car to meet him at such and such a place, conk the driver over the head, and make off in the car. He'd never trust himself to a chap who is obviously a suspect for the murder himself and therefore has every incentive to get the real murderer caught."

"But supposing Sorn was Joe's accomplice——"

"If Sorn was an accomplice, the last thing he'd want is for the murderer to be caught. Accomplices are apt to get hung. No. Either Sorn really believes that the murderer is in Honeycombe Wood or else he's helping him to escape for an altruistic motive. Whichever way it is, whether Sorn's an unconscious tool or a temporary ally of the murderer, the getaway is going to be in another direction. The idea behind all this is to distract our attention from the brewery."

"The brewery? But why should Bunnett want——?"

"Well, it's your own theory that he needs that passport of his. He would know, after his attempt last night, that the brewery would be more carefully watched. Therefore, he'd have to distract your attention from it."

"You may be right, sir. But I'm going to have Sorn's car waiting in Honeycombe Wood at midnight, for all that."

"Have a fleet of cars waiting if you like. Only don't relax your watch on Bunnett's."

"I'll put Tollworthy on to the car job. Then I'll be getting along to the brewery; it's dark enough now."

It was a little short of ten o'clock when Nigel and the inspector passed through the main entrance of the brewery. A plainclothes man started up out of the shadows and saluted. A whispered conversation was carried on. Then they walked softly through the yard to the side entrance; that too was unobtrusively guarded. If anyone entered the brewery, he was not to be challenged; nor was he to be allowed to get out again. The great brick wall soared up into the darkness above them, the smell of malt and hops was sour upon the night air. They entered the building. Tyler clicked on his electric torch, and made the round of his defences. A man in the clerk's office; the night-watchman, who was to make his tour of inspection at the usual times, but closely followed by a detective-constable; a fourth man in Eustace Bunnett's room, and another at the bottom of the staircase down which the murderer had fled the night before.

Nigel and Inspector Tyler finally settled down to wait in Joe Bunnett's room. So far the murderer had never moved till after midnight. They had nearly two hours' wait before them. Nigel enlivened the time by outlining his own theory of the crimes in a whisper to Tyler. The inspector was impressed but far from convinced.

"The proof of the pudding, sir——" he whispered hoarsely. "We shall know one way or another before the night's out."

"One way or another," thought Nigel. "Yes, no doubt. But it won't be much satisfaction to us if we have to hold a post-mortem on this case in the next world. He's entirely ruthless, probably quite insane by now. I wonder had Joe a revolver. All those passages and staircases—endless opportunities for ambush, and what a good target we should make. Let's hope he shoots at the uniform first. I must really get Georgia to buy me a nice bullet-proof waistcoat—

provided, of course, that I don't get a lead lining in the course of to-night's little spree. I should have tumbled to it before. Eliminate the impossible, and what you have left is—— After all, there was no one else who possessed the same qualification as ——. Why am I getting so worked up? Even if he does not turn up to-night, we can easily get proof to-morrow. Spades will be trumps and win us the rubber. I'd like to know what he's been doing all to-day. Must have been in the brewery. Quaint, the police searching the brewery this morning and him here all the time. This morning. It seems ages ago. Boom—boom—boom—boom: boom—boom—boom—boom: boom—boom—boom—boom: quarter to twelve. God! Who the devil's that moving about? Oh, Lock, of course; he's in the middle of his rounds now. Our friend won't move till he's finished."

Nigel automatically looked at his watch. He stiffened and looked at it again. It said quarter to eleven. It was hardly possible to believe that they'd not yet been in the brewery for the space of an hour. But—well, then, what was that noise he had heard? Who was moving about? The night-watchman should not yet have begun his round: the policemen had strict orders not to move from their posts—if they heard one blast of the whistle, the men inside the brewery were to run towards the sound; the watchers outside were not to move from their posts unless they heard three blasts.

So whose were the footsteps that Nigel could hear mounting the stairs and already moving along the passage towards their room? He clutched Tyler's arm, and croaked in a voice that he could not prevent from sounding a bit blood-curdled:

"Who's that?"

"Ah. That'll be him, I expect," replied Tyler stodgily. "You leave this to me, sir."

Nigel was quite content to do so.

Hands feeling along the wall, rustling against the door, feeling circumspectly for the lock. Hands, Nigel could not help reminding himself, that had already killed two people, perhaps three. A key turned gently in the lock. Yes, this is all as we arranged. We locked ourselves in here on purpose. We knew he had a key and would be expecting to find the door locked, but——

The door opened, inch by inch. It was too dark to see, but you could feel it opening. A gentle click. The beam of a torch sprang out, focused upon the centre of the floor. Instantaneously, as though it had been a challenge, Tyler put on his torch. For a second the two beams crossed, like swords: then Tyler's stabbed upwards to the face of the intruder.

The face of Gabriel Sorn!

"What the devil——!" exclaimed Tyler.

"Oh, my God!" cried Sorn.

Nigel said urgently: "The key. Where did you get the key?"

But already Sorn, with a little sound like the whimper of a dreaming dog, had flung his torch full at the inspector and bolted out of the room.

Roaring out an oath—he had been struck hard on the cheek-bone—Tyler rushed after him. Then he stopped and blew one blast on his whistle, remembering that the passage and the stairs were blocked.

"Phillips! Hempson! Look out!" he shouted. "Man escaping. Sorn! Stop him!"

Gabriel Sorn had evidently lost his nerve. They could hear him tumbling down the stairs, screaming at the top of his voice. Even after he had run straight into the stout arms of Constable Phillips he continued to struggle and yell. Thus it was that the police inside the brewery failed to hear the faint sound of a whistle from outside: but for the fact that Nigel had been half-expecting this move and had run in the opposite direction from Sorn, towards the entrance of the brewery, the murderer would have claimed another victim and perhaps escaped for good.

Constable Gurney, from his concealment near the side-door of the yard, had observed a figure moving stealthily through it and into the brewery some five minutes before. He had dutifully looked at the illuminated hands of his wrist-watch. Ten forty-four. He moved unobtrusively across to the door, locked it, and leant his solid figure against it. All was going according to plan. If the chap tried to get out this way again he'd get a bit of a shock. It was Gurney, however, who got the shock, as it happened. He was no less stolid, and no more superstitious, than most Dorset countrymen, which is saying a good deal—both ways. He heard the Priory Clock booming quarter to eleven. A few minutes after he heard Sorn screaming, his screams horribly deadened by the solid and invisible wall of the brewery. He heard a police whistle shrill once. "O.K.," he thought, "one blast, stay put!" He leant against the door, staring speculatively high up into the darkness whence this pandemonium had arisen.

Suddenly he heard a faint, scurrying patter of feet, coming in his direction. It all happened too quickly for his slow brain to catch up with. A small figure was scurrying along, almost noiselessly, like the shadow of smoke on a windy day, streaking towards him, moving in a horribly unerring arc from the brewery entrance to the side door. The figure was only eight paces from him when Gurney switched on his torch and focused. What he saw by its light was so unexpected, so appalling to his simple mind, that for a second he stood gaping, his heart stopped dead inside him, he felt he was going to faint. The figure, in its swerving course, ran at the beam of Gurney's torch; it was like a destroyer charging through searchlights. It leapt straight at Gurney. The constable was flung on his back against the door; fingers bit into his throat like wire. At least he knew now that he was fighting flesh and blood. His opponent was vicious and deadly as an imp of darkness; he was all over Gurney's unwieldy body, kicking, biting, his fingers tightening like wire. With a convulsive effort Gurney threw him off for a moment; it gave him time to blow one feeble blast on his whistle; then the imp was at him again.

Nigel heard the whistle as he ran out of the building. He shouted, "Stay where you are!" to the invisible watcher at the main entrance, and ran round the corner towards the side-door. Gurney's assailant heard the shout. He faded away like smoke into the darkness. Nigel rushed up to Gurney:

"You all right?"

"Yes, sir," he gasped. "God! he's a terror. Came at me like—took me all aback, see—why didn't they tell me it was——"

"You saw him?"

"Yessir. Or his ghost."

"It's no ghost. It's Eustace Bunnett all right. Where is he?"

"Made off when he heard you, sir. Looked as if he was running back into the brewery."

"Right. If he tries to get out this way again, use your stick on him."

237

"Don't you worry, sir. I'll fix the little——all right next time."

Nigel hurried back into the brewery and found the inspector and two constables in the bottling-room downstairs: Tyler was giving Sorn a piece of his mind. Nigel rapidly told him of the murderer's attempt to get out by the side door.

"So you were right, sir. Eustace Bunnett, eh? Well, he can't get away now."

Tyler leapt into action. Lock was sent to reinforce the outside guards. The detective-constable was stationed at the main-switch, to prevent any attempt by Bunnett to plunge the building into darkness during their search. Tyler phoned his headquarters to patrol the roads outside the brewery. While he was making his dispositions, Nigel drew Gabriel Sorn aside.

"Look here," he said, "I realise you put up your little performance to give the murderer a chance of getting away in the confusion. He told you he was Joe Bunnett over the phone, I suppose?"

"Yes."

"Well, it's Eustace. I haven't time to explain now. But this is going to get you into trouble, and the best thing you can do is to help us from now on: that is, provided your filial piety will allow it. Eustace killed Joe, by the way."

"Filial piety, my foot. I only talked like that to suck you in; but it doesn't seem to have worked. If I can help you to get that devil Eustace, count me in."

"Right. You know where the light switches are. You'd better come with us."

After some argument Tyler consented to this. He now had three constables at his disposal inside the brewery. One of them was told off to keep by Sorn's elbow in case he started any more funny stuff, and the party began their search. First the bottling-room, the head brewer's office and the store-room. In the latter they made their first discovery. Walking over the tops of the huge one and a half cwt. sacks that were stacked upright and close together, a constable noticed a small space between two full sacks, and an empty one lying there.

"That's where he's been hiding all to-day," said Nigel. "Last night, when he was surprised, he must have run in here, found an empty sack, got into it, and wedged himself upright into that space. I suppose these sacks weren't examined individually during your previous searches."

"It was Tollworthy's job, searching this room. I'll have something to say to him," replied the inspector grimly.

Systematically they worked through the ground floor of the brewery, Gabriel Sorn leading the way and snapping on the switches. After twenty-five minutes they passed through the boiler-room and entered the cellars. Their feet trod almost noiselessly on the sandy floor. The whitewashed walls glared back at them, and danced with monstrous shadows. Nigel noticed the rusty wrought-iron gate that guarded the well in its alcove on their right. They passed it, and made their way among the hundreds of barrels that lay like drunken men after an orgy, packed together in sodden immobility. Every corner of the cellars was searched. Suddenly the searchers grew tense; a strange, wheezing, ticking sound arose from the middle of the cellar.

"It's only one of the barrels," said Sorn; "they belch every now and then."

"Well, he doesn't seem to be in here. We'd better go back," Tyler said.

Nigel suddenly clicked his fingers. "The well," he said. It was hardly more than a whisper; but these long gallery-like cellars carried sound uncannily. They had scarcely begun to retrace their steps when they heard a rasping squeak. The iron gate that protected the well was being pushed open. They made a rush; but they were still thirty yards away when Eustace Bunnett stepped out from the alcove, a revolver in his hand. In a rasping, hoarse voice, like the sound of the gate hinges, he said:

"Stand back! Get back, I tell you! What are you doing in my brewery? I'll shoot the lot of you." Then he broke into a stream of foul language. His appearance was so unnerving that they all paused involuntarily for a few seconds. He was wearing a seaman's jersey and trousers, and black sand-shoes. There was a stubble of hair on his chin. His cold eyes glittered madly at them, steely-blue and dangerous as the points of bullets. Worse than that, his hair and clothes were matted with cobwebs, and his mouth was horribly sunken, like the mouth of a corpse. Tyler collected himself, and said:

"Now then, sir, put down that gun."

Nigel had hardly time to grin at the word "sir," when the inspector strode forward, Bunnett's gun roared out, and Tyler spun round clutching his arm and dropped behind one of the barrels.

"Get down, men!" he ordered, biting his lips with pain.

They all took cover. Tyler whispered to the constable next to him, "Broken my arm, I think. Draw his fire," and fainted.

The constable removed his helmet and pushed it slowly above the top of the barrel he lay behind. There was a bang, a plock, and a hiss, then a smell of beer incongruously spreading into the air. Bunnett had holed the barrel. He glared at them for a second: then rushed for the door, snapping out the switch as he went. Tripping over barrels in the pitch-darkness, it took them half a minute to reach the door and turn on the light again. The door was locked. Sorn fumbled for his master-key. As he did so, the air was shocked by a terrifying sound, a sound deafening and inhuman like some gigantic machine crying out in a nightmare. Whoo-ah! whoo-hooo-hoooo-ah! Above this whooping screech they could just hear Sorn yelling.

"My God! He's turned the cold water into the boiler! The whole place'll go sky high! Get out, all of you!"

He flung the door open. Two constables hoisted Tyler up and staggered with him towards the brewery entrance. Nigel ran in front, turning back the reinforcements that had been hurrying towards the sound of the shots. Only when they had poured through the yard, out of the main gate into the street, did Nigel notice that Gabriel Sorn was missing and the moaning of the boiler's safety-valve had ceased. His mind scarcely had time to register this, when Constable Gurney appeared, the body of Eustace Bunnett slung insensible over his shoulder. Bunnett had made a dash for the side door while his late pursuers were rushing out through the main gates. But Constable Gurney was not to be caught napping this time. Emerging from his concealment he had batoned Eustace Bunnett as he bent down to unlock the door: occupied with the key, Bunnett had not time to aim his revolver before the blow fell.

Ten minutes later, Gabriel Sorn was discovered, lying in a dead faint beside the boiler. He had raked out the furnace just in time to save all their lives.

# XV
# July 21, 8 p.m.

*Oh that this too, too solid flesh would melt!*
SHAKESPEARE, *Hamlet*

"YES, it was a remark of yours that first put me on to it, Sophie."

"Mine? I'm sure I didn't say anything——"

"Oh, but you did. You did indeed. Do you remember telling me about Joe's engaging little schoolboy tricks? Making figures out of fruit and matches, pretending his teeth had fallen into the soup?"

"Of course, but——"

"It was that last item which put it into my head that perhaps it was Joe and not Eustace whose body we'd found in the copper."

Herbert Cammison's swarthy face betrayed a certain impatience. "Why not start at the beginning," he suggested. "Less melodrama and more continuity is what we want."

"Sorry. I do so enjoy making an exhibitionist of myself. Well, then, I'll table the data in due order, starting at seven-thirty last night when I sat down upstairs to digest them."

"I thought it was beer you were digesting," said Sophie.

"So it was. I find it conducive to thought," replied

Nigel with dignity. "Well, as you mention it, I will have another glass. Better late than never. And you might as well leave the bottle beside me. Thank you."

Nigel drank deeply.

"Well," he continued, "when all was said and done, the really odd thing about this murder remained—why was the body put into the copper at all? The obvious reason seemed, to conceal the method of murder: which pointed, of course, to an expert professional killer—Herbert, in fact."

"Oh!" gasped Sophie, quite forgetting her knitting for a moment; "surely you never suspected *him*?"

"Didn't I just!"

Herbert gazed at him with mild curiosity. "Yes, you would. Why not?" he said dispassionately.

"We aim to explore every avenue. I thought of him first as a soloist, so to speak: then, when it became evident that Joe had planned to murder Eustace, I considered Herbert as a possible accomplice—very favourably, I may say. He had the motive, the brain, the technical knowledge, and the nerve."

"Thank you," said Herbert.

"Not at all."

"What are you talking about?" complained Sophie. "First you say Eustace murdered Joe and then you say Joe planned to murder Eustace. I think you're boozed up."

"That's just what did happen. *The wrong murder was committed.* As I say, there seemed no possible reason why, if Joe's plan had been successful—and the fragment of ring I found proved that it had gone pretty far towards success, he should have transferred the body from the refrigerator-room to the pressure-copper. Any injury he had done to Eustace in the course of stuffing him into that room could surely have been explained by Eustace's struggles to get out. Then I suddenly remembered what you said about Joe's teeth. Pretending your teeth have fallen into the soup implies that you have false teeth."

"But, damn it, the dentist reconstructed the plates found in the hop-back: he has no doubt they're Eustace's. I don't see——"

"Nor did I at first. Then it suddenly occurred to me—and I verified it by ringing up the dentist last night—that the teeth had been identified as Eustace's, but no one had thought of comparing them with the jaws of the body. It was a scandalous error, I admit, but we none of us had any doubt that the body was Eustace. The dentist had tried the sets on the plaster-cast he'd made of Eustace's jaws when the sets were originally constructed. He told me he had casts for Joe and Mrs. Bunnett, too, which corroborated my idea that Joe had false teeth."

"Yes, of course, I see," Dr. Cammison said softly.

"So I asked myself—supposing Eustace turned the tables on his brother and killed him? He could exchange clothes with Joe, remove Joe's plates, throw the body into the copper and chuck his *own* teeth in after it. He could rely on the plates getting pretty well bashed about in the boiling process; they would be recognised by his dentist as Eustace's teeth, but there was a good chance that they could not be reconstructed accurately enough to show that they didn't fit the jaws of the body and so give the substitution away. But surely, I thought next, our efficient medico, Herbert Cammison, F.R.C.S., would not be misled into confusing Joe's body with Eustace's. Then I remembered. There was nothing but bone and hair left: and I had seen Joe's passport, which stated that he was five foot eight—that is, within an inch of Eustace's height; and Herbert had told me that in reconstructing the skeleton one had to allow a margin of error of two inches. The passport also said that Joe had light hair. You must remember I'd only seen a photograph of him, in which the brilliantine of his hair made it look dark; I'd assumed all along that he had dark hair. Very well: the remains in the copper were of roughly the same stature and of the same-coloured hair as Joe. Eustace, by the way, had to cut off Joe's moustache before he dumped him in the copper. Oh, yes, he was very thorough, and cold-blooded as a fish; he needed to be.

"Well, my mind running on teeth—racing on them, in fact—jumped to another tiny bit of evidence. The crumbs in Joe's attic. Now, Eustace had got rid of his own teeth; he would not be able to eat anything but soft stuff. Again, if he put Joe into the copper, it must have been he who burgled his own house and was hiding out in Joe's. It was interesting, therefore, that I found the remains only of bread and cake in Joe's attic—no trace of any other kind of food. With this on my mind, I rang up Mrs. Bunnett's house and got on to the cook. She said that only bread and cake had disappeared from the larder: the Sunday joint was left. That obviously pointed to Eustace. Whoever took the food must have brought a bag or some sort to put it in. Why shouldn't he take the joint too? Because, if it was Eustace, the joint was no use to him—he had no teeth to chew up the meat with."

"What about the crusts of the bread, then?" asked Herbert.

"Crusts become soft if you mumble them in your mouth long enough. Well, then, what with the teeth, the crumbs and the passport, a case against Eustace was beginning to build itself up. Another little point occurred to me. Lock, questioned as to the person he had surprised outside Joe Bunnett's office in the brewery on Sunday night, said first that he'd thought it must be a ghost. Now that was an odd thing for a night-watchman to say quite seriously: night-watchmen are not imaginative; they couldn't stand their jobs if they were in the least susceptible to 'ghoulies and ghosties and things that go woomph in the night.' So mightn't it be that subconsciously, from the brief encounter he had with this mysterious figure, he had registered the impression of Eustace Bunnett?

"You see, up to midnight on Thursday last, the actions of Joe and Eustace were the actions of murderer and murderee respectively. There was no possible doubt that Joe had planned a murder and gone to commit it. Supposing, I said to myself, Joe had attacked Eustace in the brewery and Eustace had killed him instead: supposing then, that Eustace for some reason decided the best thing was to swop identities with Joe; he must have discovered, in the course of conversation with his brother, that *The Gannet* was lying in Basket Cove: later he would realise that this had been planned by Joe as an alibi. Therefore if Joe was to be made out as the murderer, something must be done to explain why he had not made use of this alibi. If the police found *The Gannet* floating in Basket Cove, with a bewildered Bloxam on board, they would ask themselves—why didn't Joe return and go off in the boat? It was indicated, therefore, that *The Gannet* should be scuppered.

"We now come to the evidence of the tramp. He said that about two or three on Friday morning he heard a motor-bike going inland and saw a glow in the sky. I began to realise the times were all wrong. You see, if Joe murdered Eustace, he scheduled to get back to the cove soon after one o'clock. On the theory that Joe committed the murder successfully, one would have to presume that, by the time he returned to *The Gannet*, it had already accidentally caught fire and was blazing so merrily that he couldn't put it out. But petrol-caused fires burn up fiercely and consume quickly. So, if the fire was at its height when Joe arrived at 1.10 a.m., it was unlikely that between two and three a.m. it would still be blazing so ferociously as to make the glow in the sky which the tramp saw. On the other hand, if Eustace had killed Joe, thought out a plan of action, changed clothes with the body, etc., and ridden off on Joe's motor-bike, he couldn't arrive at the cove much before 2 a.m. The glow in the sky, and the sound of the motor-bike, therefore, were much more consistent with Eustace's responsibility for the whole thing.

"All that, of course, was highly theoretical. It depended upon the tramp's having a fairly accurate sense of time—which was likely, and on *The Gannet* not having caught fire accidentally—which was more than likely: it was obviously vital for Joe to drug Bloxam effectively, and this put out of court the idea that Bloxam could have set fire to the boat through carelessness.

"Everything so far was consistent with Eustace as murderer and Joe as victim. Proof of the latter could be obtained soon enough by comparing the reconstructed sets of teeth with the jaws of the body.

Equally, if the victim was found to be Joe, then it followed almost certainly that the murderer was Eustace; for Eustace had disappeared, and no one else—except Sorn—had an interest in its being established that Eustace was dead. But I didn't suspect Gabriel Sorn: after all, it was too far-fetched altogether to imagine that he would kill Joe in order to dress him up as Eustace and then throw suspicion on him. Any lingering doubts I had of Sorn were dispelled when he came to see me last night. He evidently believed that it was Joe who had done the murder, was in concealment and had just telephoned him to help in a getaway. Sorn hated Eustace, hated him all the more when he realised he was his father: he had no compunction in helping the man he thought was Eustace's murderer to escape. Unfortunately, he told his story in a sadly unconvincing way."

"But I can't understand why Eustace wanted to disappear like that, to change places with Joe. Making up Joe like himself and putting him in the copper—why, it was sentencing himself to death," Sophie said.

"Yes, it worried me, that. When Sorn told me that his mother was a proud creature, I began to understand; and Eustace's confession has cleared it up. Still, we must gratify your husband's indecent craving for continuity. Having satisfied myself that Joe was the one who had got murdered, and Eustace the one who'd done it, I was in a much better position to explain subsequent events. You see, I was prepared to believe that Gabriel Sorn, or Mr. Barnes, or Herbert were capable of murdering Joe: but I couldn't believe that any of them would proceed so remorselessly to plant incriminating evidence against him. Only a Eustace Bunnett would murder a chap and then try to prove the chap guilty of his own murder. There was something vindictive in the way Joe's name was blackened after his death: and Ariadne Mellors was killed in a vindictive way; and worst of all was setting fire to *The Gannet* with that poor chap Bloxam on board."

"Good God! You think Eustace realised he was on board?" said Dr. Cammison.

"He has admitted it. This utterly remorseless and vindictive behaviour seemed to me to square up with none of the people connected with the crime except Eustace. It was this that trapped him in the end— poetic justice all right; if he'd not made that last incursion into the brewery on Sunday night, to call our attention to Joe's passport and emphasise Joe's guilt still further, he'd probably be a free man to-day crossing the seas and looking forward to living on the property he had bequeathed to Mrs. Sorn."

Dr. Cammison nodded his head slowly a number of times. "Ah, I see. Of course. I was wondering how—Yes, of course."

"Eustace's confession clears up the minor points. I'll just give you the gist of it. Extraordinary chap. The jury'll have a job deciding whether it's Broadmoor or the gallows."

"Yes," said Herbert crisply. "It's an interesting comment on our social system that a fellow like Bunnett, whose whole life was a series of more or less legalised crimes, has to kill three people before we put him where he can't do any more mischief."

"The confession, then. Eustace arrived at the brewery five minutes before midnight. Joe met him at the entrance, and spun a story about having received an anonymous letter *re* the night-watchman. Eustace says his suspicions were aroused at the very beginning by this; he asked Joe how he'd got there, where *The Gannet* was, and so on. Joe didn't mind telling him all this, because dead men tell no tales and it was necessary to give Eustace a reasonable explanation of his movements if he was to get him into the brewery. Eustace pretended to accept all this; but he kept a wary eye on Joe from then on. The two entered the brewery and went along towards the bottom of the staircase that leads up to the office: Joe had suggested they should wait in his room till Lock should have finished his rounds. Suddenly Joe whispered, 'Look out! He's coming this way,' and made a dash into the refrigerator-room which was the nearest hiding-place. Eustace followed him, taken in for a moment by the trick: if he'd stopped to think, he'd have realised, of course—what Joe knew very well—that by this time Lock's round had taken him a long way from that part of the premises.

"As soon as they were both inside the refrigerator-room, Joe struck at Eustace, aiming to knock him out. But in the darkness he missed and hit his knuckles hard on that refrigerator by the door. Eustace's suspicions became certainty. He struck back, knocking Joe down with a lucky blow. Then he saw red. This weakling of a brother, whom he had despised and downtrodden all his life, having the audacity to turn upon him! In a sheer frenzy of rage he flung himself at Joe and strangled him before he had time to recover from the effect of the blow.

"So now Eustace was faced with the question that has worried every murderer from Cain downwards—what shall I do with the body? He didn't dare risk walking straight out and saying to Lock, 'My brother has just attacked me and I had to kill him in self-defence.' No doubt it would have been the best thing to do; and, backed by evidence they might have found on *The Gannet,* it might have convinced the police. On the other hand, a good case might have been made out for Eustace having lured Joe into the brewery: unconsciously, too, Eustace probably realised that nobody would take his word against that of the dead man—a dead man as popular as Joe was. Anyway, he hadn't the nerve just then to tell the truth. His mind was habituated to dealing tortuously rather than straightforwardly with any given situation. What shall I do with the body? he asked himself. And then, so he says—a rather patronising interest in literature was one of his minor unpleasing traits, as you know—two lines of *Hamlet* came unbidden into his head.

> *"Oh, that this too, too solid flesh would melt,*
> *Thaw, and resolve itself into a dew!"*

And at once he remembered what had become of Truffles. He would put the body into the pressure-copper. But that was not enough. Next day the remains would be found: it would be recognised at once as murder: awkward questions would be asked: somebody *might* have seen Eustace stealing out of his house into the brewery. It was at this point that the brilliant idea struck him of exchanging identities with Joe. Joe had planned to murder him, had devised an alibi, had inadvertently left some clues, maybe, pointing to himself. Very well then, Joe had done everything necessary to incriminate himself except commit the murder. The logical thing was to make it seem that Joe *had* committed the murder. A simple, coldly logical piece of reasoning. I must say I admire it very much. A pity Eustace spoilt it by over-complication later.

"Very well, Eustace was to be murdered. A change of clothes, some gruesome business with the teeth, and the pressure-copper would do the rest. Joe was of the same physique and height as Eustace. But what would happen to Eustace? He must disappear, and leave not a wrack behind. He could not draw cheques in his own name. Banks will not accept the signature of a ghost. At once his thoughts turned to Mrs. Sorn. In his young days, when she was a pretty and inexperienced girl, he had met her abroad and had an affair with her. A child, Gabriel, was born. But Eustace refused to marry her, then: he was ambitious, and she had no money. Deserted by him, disowned by her family, she settled down with her child in the south of France and scraped along by giving English lessons. In due course, Eustace built up the business here and became a rich man. Mrs. Sorn, who had always given it out that she was a widow, heard of Eustace's success and wrote suggesting that he should do something for their child. Whether it went as far as blackmail, I don't know. Possibly not, but Eustace had become a respectable man: he could not afford to let it be known that he had an illegitimate son and had treated the mother so badly. So he paid for Gabriel's education, and later—perhaps under pressure—took him into the brewery.

"When Mrs. Sorn got into communication with him again he remembered her beauty and charm; he could afford to marry her now, and asked her; but she—very sensibly—wasn't taking it. She did not conceal her contempt for him and his past conduct, and in a fit of pique he went off and married the present Emily Bunnett, who was a barmaid in one of his pubs and a fetching enough creature physically in those days. He soon got tired of Emily; but she managed the house all right and was an adequate punching-ball when Eustace was in one of his vindictive, bullying moods. But Mrs. Sorn remained his thorn in the flesh. She was his one failure, the one person over whom he could not domineer. And I think it was a grudging admiration for her independence, plus maybe a certain remorse for his past treatment of her, that made him leave her the bulk of his property in his will.

"Now, at any rate, with the body of his brother before him, he was thankful he had made that will; for it solved the whole financial problem. All he had to do was to get out of the country, turn up after a decent interval at Mrs. Sorn's villa, assume another identity and live on the inheritance he had left her. He could rely on her not daring to give him up to the police. Her family pride, of which Gabriel Sorn told me, her passionate love for Gabriel himself, would—Eustace judged—make it impossible for her to betray him. If Eustace was handed over to justice, everything would come out. Gabriel would be branded for life as the bastard son of a murderer. Eustace as a murderer, in fact, would have a far stronger hold over Mrs. Sorn than Eustace, the respectable brewer, ever had.

"So that was that. Eustace turned on his electric torch, changed clothes, ring, etc., with Joe's body, carried it to the pressure-copper and tipped it in. The only things of his own he kept were twenty pounds in notes and the duplicate keys. We'll see why he needed them in a minute. He then went off on Joe's motor-bike; it was he whom Sorn heard riding away from the brewery at 12.40 a.m. It naturally took him longer than it would have taken Joe to reach the cove; he knew its position, but he didn't know the quickest way to it; nor had he ridden a motor-bike since his youth. So he didn't get to Basket Down till between one-fifteen and one-thirty. He left the bike at the top of the cliff, found the bridle path (he had Joe's torch), found the dinghy, and rowed out to *The Gannet*. His idea was to pour petrol over the stern of the vessel and set fire to it, thus— as he hoped—giving the impression that the engine had caught fire accidentally. It was a bit weak, all that, but he hadn't the time or the skill for an expert piece of incendiarism. Anyway, the main thing was to get rid of the yacht so that the police would be kept guessing for several days about Joe's whereabouts. He found the spare petrol tins and doused the stern. Then he discovered that he had no matches. He went into the cabin to get some, and saw Bloxam lying there in his drugged sleep. It was a bit of a shock to Eustace. However, he was not to be diverted from his purpose by a trifle like that. He got a box of matches—incidentally laying hands on some soft food, Joe's revolver, and all Joe's money he could find—set fire to the boat, left her and Bloxam to burn, rowed ashore, hid the dinghy in the cave, and returned to Maiden Astbury. He concealed the motor-bike in Honeycombe Wood, hoping it would eventually be found and provide a clue against Joe. He had been wearing Joe's gloves throughout, to guard against leaving fingerprints. He walked down Honeycombe Hill, let himself into Joe's house with the keys he had taken from Joe's body, and retired to the attic.

"A rather ticklish problem now presented itself.

He had to stay long enough to lay a number of false clues against Joe—to impress the police with the idea that Joe was alive and behaving in a suspicious way: he must not leave the country till the body in the copper was established as Eustace's, for otherwise inquiries for Eustace might still be proceeding at the English ports: at the same time, every day he stayed increased the risk of his being more or less accidentally found. On Saturday night he crept out and burgled his own house. That's what he'd kept his duplicate keys for. He stole the Roxby's papers, but left the file to call attention to Joe's motive for murder: he stole food, for his own benefit—there was none in Joe's house, of course: he also got his own passport. Nobody knew of its existence, and therefore nobody missed it. I ought to have thought of it, though: Mrs. Bunnett told us he used to go off on rather furtive holidays abroad. The middle-aged gentleman who disported himself in an improper manner on the Continent must not by any chance be identified with the upright brewer of Maiden Astbury. So Eustace had wangled a passport in another name—we found it on him—the name of James Henderson; and it was as James Henderson that he proposed to enter France and arrive at Mrs. Sorn's villa.

"On Sunday he, very suitably, rested—except for a few little matters like smearing Joe's brilliantine on the cushion in the attic. That night, judging that the police guard on the brewery would have been withdrawn by now, he intended to enter the brewery and leave a few more clues against Joe. His state of mind, as far as we can gather, was very interesting at this point. Brooding over the whole business in his solitary confinement, he'd begun to imagine himself as the hidden hand of justice. Joe, after all, was the real murderer—the murderer in intention: Eustace had killed him only in self-defence: Joe was the real criminal, and it was Eustace's duty to see that the police should be made to realise this. Eustace, of course, was always self-righteous enough for three, and all this was merely a rationalisation of his bitter hatred of Joe for having dared to turn upon him and put him in such a perilous position. But it was a powerful enough rationalisation, for all that. Joe must be pursued, even in death: his good name must be blackened: he must be exposed as the cowardly murderer that he had tried to be.

"It was this that caused Eustace to over-reach himself. He should have made his getaway that night, instead of visiting the brewery; especially after he'd killed Miss Mellors. He had just climbed down from the attic when he heard somebody entering the house and coming upstairs. He'd not time to climb back into the attic; so he darted into the study and picked up the poker. Miss Mellors came in, and that sealed her fate, poor thing. Eustace got another of his fits of blind, panicky rage, and went on battering her long after it had ceased to be necessary. After a pause to recover himself, he went on to the brewery; there he was surprised by Lock before he could get into Joe's room. He nipped downstairs, but found his escape cut off by the constable, whom he heard running in: so he slipped down the passage and hid in the store-room.

"So there he was, properly trapped; all through his overzealousness for justice. Tollworthy missed him in his search: he didn't examine each sack, and I don't really wonder. So Eustace got a reprieve of a sort—if you call standing up inside a sack for the best part of twenty-four hours a reprieve. He could shift his position as much as he wanted, of course; the store-room is not constantly visited during the day. Still, it must have been a painful enough business—and serve him damn well right. At about eight-thirty, when the coast was likely to be clear and he knew Lock would be elsewhere, he slipped out, went up to his private room and telephoned Sorn. He disguised his voice, of course, and accounted for the curious sounds he must have made by saying that he had to whisper. He told Sorn he was Joe Bunnett speaking from Mrs. Bunnett's house, played up to his sympathies, and begged him to make a diversion which should aid him to escape. It was a hell of a gamble, of course. But he banked on Sorn's romantic agin-the-law nature, his hatred of Eustace and his affection for Joe. He safeguarded himself up to a point by pretending that Mrs. Bunnett had given him sanctuary. If Sorn split to the police, they would search there first. However, Sorn ate it all right. He agreed to come to me with a story—in which Eustace coached him over the phone—that the murderer was hiding in Honeycombe Wood and proposed to make a getaway with the aid of Sorn's car, that night. This, of course, was to draw the police away from the brewery, and it would certainly have succeeded if I'd swallowed Sorn's story.

"What Eustace—in the character of Joe—told Sorn he was really going to do was to dash off in the opposite direction in Eustace's car, make for Southampton, and get a boat abroad. To do this, he said, he must have his passport. He'd made one attempt to get it and failed. So he asked Sorn to get it for him and bring it to Eustace's house. That was a very clever move on Eustace's part. If Sorn succeeded in getting Joe's passport, it would be because the coast was clear, and, therefore, Eustace would already be on his way to Southampton: he was intending to use his own car all right. If, on the other hand, the police were not tricked by Sorn's story, they would catch him as he entered Joe's room and that would provide a diversion during which Eustace might manage to escape.

"Well, as you know, it was the latter that happened: or nearly. Sorn signally failed to suck me in with his story. We had every bolthole from the brewery blocked up; so, when Sorn crept in by the side door, took the master-key from the office, and let himself into Joe Bunnett's room, he got the fright of his life. In fact, he acted up better than Eustace could have hoped: he lost his nerve and kicked up such a shindy that Eustace very nearly got away under cover of it. He as near as nothing got past the constable at the side door. Failing there, he shot back into the brewery and led us a dance that makes a good many gangster films look like cold mutton. But you know about that."

"It must have given you a turn when you heard the boiler safety valve begin to blow off. We could hear it from here," said Herbert.

"Yes, that was a pretty unsavoury moment. Sorn ought to get a medal for what he did: it was about ten to one on his being blown into hundreds and thousands: he told me this morning that he had often imagined in phantasy this situation arising and himself playing the hero who should draw the fires from under the boiler, so when it did actually happen in real life he jumped to it automatically—shows you there's something to be said for phantasy-building. But the worst moment, I think, was when Eustace emerged from the well—he'd hidden behind that iron gate and got himself covered with cobwebs. The combination of cobwebs and sunken mouth—it's extraordinary how much the absence of teeth alters the human face for the worse—made him so disagreeably resemble a risen corpse that my stomach turned over like a catherine wheel. And of course that gun in his hand didn't improve one's morale either. You'd never think an oldish man like him would have the stamina to do all he did. It suggests he must have been insane since Joe attacked him in the refrigerator-room: it's what you'd expect when a man who has wielded almost unlimited power suddenly finds himself outlawed from society."

Nigel took a turn or two round the room, absent-mindedly picking up ornaments and putting them down again.

"No," he said, "it's been a dirty, untidy case in most ways, even though it does add force to a certain well-worn phrase."

"Namely?"

"There's trouble brewing."

# THE PERENNIAL LIBRARY MYSTERY SERIES

### E. C. Bentley

**TRENT'S LAST CASE**
"One of the three best detective stories ever written."
— Agatha Christie

**TRENT'S OWN CASE**
"I won't waste time saying that the plot is sound and the detection satisfying. Trent has not altered a scrap and reappears with all his old humor and charm."
— Dorothy L. Sayers

### Gavin Black

**A DRAGON FOR CHRISTMAS**
"Potent excitement!"
— New York Herald Tribune

**THE EYES AROUND ME**
"I stayed up until all hours last night reading *The Eyes Around Me,* which is something I do not do very often, but I was so intrigued by the ingeniousness of Mr. Black's plotting and the witty way in which he spins his mystery. I can only say that I enjoyed the book enormously."
— F. van Wyck Mason

**YOU WANT TO DIE, JOHNNY?**
"Gavin Black doesn't just develop a pressure plot in suspense, he adds uninfected wit, character, charm, and sharp knowledge of the Far East to make rereading as keen as the first race-through." — Book Week

### Nicholas Blake

**THE BEAST MUST DIE**
"It remains one more proof that in the hands of a really first-class writer the detective novel can safely challenge comparison with any other variety of fiction."
— The Manchester Guardian

**THE CORPSE IN THE SNOWMAN**
"If there is a distinction between the novel and the detective story (which we do not admit), then this book deserves a high place in both categories."
— The New York Times

**THE DREADFUL HOLLOW**
"Pace unhurried, characters excellent, reasoning solid."
— San Francisco Chronicle

*Nicholas Blake (cont'd)*

**END OF CHAPTER**
". . . admirably solid . . . an adroit formal detective puzzle backed up by firm characterization and a knowing picture of London publishing."
—*The New York Times*

**HEAD OF A TRAVELER**
"Another grade A detective story of the right old jigsaw persuasion."
—*New York Herald Tribune Book Review*

**MINUTE FOR MURDER**
"An outstanding mystery novel. Mr. Blake's writing is a delight in itself."
—*The New York Times*

**THE MORNING AFTER DEATH**
"One of Blake's best."
—Rex Warner

**A PENKNIFE IN MY HEART**
"Style brilliant . . . and suspenseful."
—*San Francisco Chronicle*

**THE PRIVATE WOUND**
[Blake's] best novel in a dozen years . . . . An intensely penetrating study of sexual passion . . . . A powerful story of murder and its aftermath."
—Anthony Boucher, *The New York Times*

**A QUESTION OF PROOF**
"The characters in this story are unusually well drawn, and the suspense is well sustained."
—*The New York Times*

**THE SAD VARIETY**
"It is a stunner. I read it instead of eating, instead of sleeping."
—Dorothy Salisbury Davis

**THERE'S TROUBLE BREWING**
"Nigel Strangeways is a puzzling mixture of simplicity and penetration, but all the more real for that."
—*The Times Literary Supplement*

**THOU SHELL OF DEATH**
"It has all the virtues of culture, intelligence and sensibility that the most exacting connoisseur could ask of detective fiction."
—*The Times* [London] *Literary Supplement*

**THE WHISPER IN THE GLOOM**
"One of the most entertaining suspense-pursuit novels in many seasons."
—*The New York Times*

## Nicholas Blake (cont'd)

### THE WIDOW'S CRUISE
"A stirring suspense. . . . The thrilling tale leaves nothing to be desired."
—*Springfield Republican*

### THE WORM OF DEATH
"It [The Worm of Death] is one of Blake's very best—and his best is better than almost anyone's." —Louis Untermeyer

## John & Emery Bonett

### A BANNER FOR PEGASUS (*available 2/82*)
"A gem! Beautifully plotted and set. . . . Not only is the murder adroit and deserved, and the detection competent, but the love story is charming." —Jacques Barzun and Wendell Hertig Taylor

### DEAD LION (*available 2/82*)
"A clever plot, authentic background and interesting characters highly recommended this one." —*New Republic*

## Christianna Brand

### GREEN FOR DANGER
"You have to reach for the greatest of Great Names (Christie, Carr, Queen . . .) to find Brand's rivals in the devious subtleties of the trade."
—Anthony Boucher

### TOUR DE FORCE (*available 3/82*)
"Complete with traps for the over-ingenious, a double-reverse surprise ending and a key clue planted so fairly and obviously that you completely overlook it. If that's your idea of perfect entertainment, then seize at once upon *Tour de Force*." —Anthony Boucher, *The New York Times*

## Marjorie Carleton

### VANISHED
"Exceptional . . . a minor triumph."
—Jacques Barzun and Wendell Hertig Taylor, *A Catalogue of Crime*

## George Harmon Coxe

### MURDER WITH PICTURES
"[Coxe] has hit the bull's-eye with his first shot."
—*The New York Times*

*Edmund Crispin*

## BURIED FOR PLEASURE
"Absolute and unalloyed delight."
—Anthony Boucher, *The New York Times*

*D. M. Devine*

## MY BROTHER'S KILLER
"A most enjoyable crime story which I enjoyed reading down to the last moment."
—Agatha Christie

*Kenneth Fearing*

## THE BIG CLOCK
"It will be some time before chill-hungry clients meet again so rare a compound of irony, satire, and icy-fingered narrative. *The Big Clock* is . . . a psychothriller you won't put down." —*Weekly Book Review*

*Andrew Garve*

## THE ASHES OF LODA
"Garve . . . embellishes a fine fast adventure story with a more credible picture of the U.S.S.R. than is offered in most thrillers."
—*The New York Times Book Review*

## THE CUCKOO LINE AFFAIR
". . . an agreeable and ingenious piece of work." —*The New Yorker*

## A HERO FOR LEANDA
"One can trust Mr. Garve to put a fresh twist to any situation, and the ending is really a lovely surprise." —*The Manchester Guardian*

## MURDER THROUGH THE LOOKING GLASS
". . . refreshingly out-of-the-way and enjoyable . . . highly recommended to all comers." —*Saturday Review*

## NO TEARS FOR HILDA
"It starts fine and finishes finer. I got behind on breathing watching Max get not only his man but his woman, too." —Rex Stout

## THE RIDDLE OF SAMSON
"The story is an excellent one, the people are quite likable, and the writing is superior." —*Springfield Republican*

### Michael Gilbert

**BLOOD AND JUDGMENT**
"Gilbert readers need scarcely be told that the characters all come alive at first sight, and that his surpassing talent for narration enhances any plot. . . . Don't miss."                    —*San Francisco Chronicle*

**THE BODY OF A GIRL**
"Does what a good mystery should do: open up into all kinds of ramifications, with untold menace behind the action. At the end, there is a bang-up climax, and it is a pleasure to see how skilfully Gilbert wraps everything up."                    —*The New York Times Book Review*

**THE DANGER WITHIN**
"Michael Gilbert has nicely combined some elements of the straight detective story with plenty of action, suspense, and adventure, to produce a superior thriller."                    —*Saturday Review*

**DEATH HAS DEEP ROOTS**
"Trial scenes superb; prowl along Loire vivid chase stuff; funny in right places; a fine performance throughout."                    —*Saturday Review*

**FEAR TO TREAD**
"Merits serious consideration as a work of art."
                    —*The New York Times*

### C. W. Grafton

**BEYOND A REASONABLE DOUBT**
"A very ingenious tale of murder . . . a brilliant and gripping narrative."
                    —Jacques Barzun and Wendell Hertig Taylor

### Edward Grierson

**THE SECOND MAN**
"One of the best trial-testimony books to have come along in quite a while."                    —*The New Yorker*

### Cyril Hare

**DEATH IS NO SPORTSMAN**
"You will be thrilled because it succeeds in placing an ingenious story in a new and refreshing setting. . . . The identity of the murderer is really a surprise."                    —*Daily Mirror*

## Cyril Hare (cont'd)

### DEATH WALKS THE WOODS
"Here is a fine formal detective story, with a technically brilliant solution demanding the attention of all connoisseurs of construction."
—Anthony Boucher, *The New York Times Book Review*

### AN ENGLISH MURDER
"By a long shot, the best crime story I have read for a long time. Everything is traditional, but originality does not suffer. The setting is perfect. Full marks to Mr. Hare." —*Irish Press*

### TRAGEDY AT LAW
"An extremely urbane and well-written detective story."
—*The New York Times*

### UNTIMELY DEATH
"The English detective story at its quiet best, meticulously underplayed, rich in perceivings of the droll human animal and ready at the last with a neat surprise which has been there all the while had we but wits to see it." —*New York Herald Tribune Book Review*

### WITH A BARE BODKIN
"One of the best detective stories published for a long time."
—*The Spectator*

## Robert Harling

### THE ENORMOUS SHADOW
"In some ways the best spy story of the modern period. . . . The writing is terse and vivid . . . the ending full of action . . . altogether first-rate."
—Jacques Barzun and Wendell Hertig Taylor, *A Catalogue of Crime*

## Matthew Head

### THE CABINDA AFFAIR
"An absorbing whodunit and a distinguished novel of atmosphere."
—Anthony Boucher, *The New York Times*

### MURDER AT THE FLEA CLUB
"The true delight is in Head's style, its limpid ease combined with humor and an awesome precision of phrase." —*San Francisco Chronicle*

### M. V. Heberden

**ENGAGED TO MURDER**
"Smooth plotting."

*—The New York Times*

### James Hilton

**WAS IT MURDER?**
"The story is well planned and well written."

*—The New York Times*

### P. M. Hubbard

**HIGH TIDE** *(available 3/82)*
"A smooth elaboration of mounting horror and danger."

*—Library Journal*

### Elspeth Huxley

**THE AFRICAN POISON MURDERS**
"Obscure venom, manical mutilations, deadly bush fire, thrilling climax compose major opus.... Top-flight."

*—Saturday Review of Literature*

### Francis Iles

**BEFORE THE FACT**
"Not many 'serious' novelists have produced character studies to compare with Iles's internally terrifying portrait of the murderer in *Before the Fact,* his masterpiece and a work truly deserving the appellation of unique and beyond price."
*—Howard Haycraft*

**MALICE AFORETHOUGHT**
"It is a long time since I have read anything so good as *Malice Aforethought,* with its cynical humour, acute criminology, plausible detail and rapid movement. It makes you hug yourself with pleasure."

*—H. C. Harwood, Saturday Review*

### Michael Innes

**DEATH BY WATER** *(available 4/82)*
"The amount of ironic social criticism and deft characterization of scenes and people would serve another author for six books."

*—Jacques Barzun and Wendell Hertig Taylor*

## Michael Innes *(cont'd)*

**THE LONG FAREWELL** *(available 4/82)*
"A model of the deft, classic detective story, told in the most wittily diverting prose."
                                    —*The New York Times*

## Mary Kelly

**THE SPOILT KILL**
"Mary Kelly is a new Dorothy Sayers. . . . [An] exciting new novel."
                                    —*Evening News*

## Lange Lewis

**THE BIRTHDAY MURDER**
"Almost perfect in its playlike purity and delightful prose."
                                    —Jacques Barzun and Wendell Hertig Taylor

## Arthur Maling

**LUCKY DEVIL**
"The plot unravels at a fast clip, the writing is breezy and Maling's approach is as fresh as today's stockmarket quotes."
                                    —*Louisville Courier Journal*

**RIPOFF**
"A swiftly paced story of today's big business is larded with intrigue as a Ralph Nader-type investigates an insurance scandal and is soon on the run from a hired gun and his brother. . . . Engrossing and credible."
                                    —*Booklist*

**SCHROEDER'S GAME**
"As the title indicates, this Schroeder is up to something, and the unravelling of his game is a diverting and sufficiently blood-soaked entertainment."
                                    —*The New Yorker*

## Thomas Sterling

**THE EVIL OF THE DAY**
"Prose as witty and subtle as it is sharp and clear. . .characters unconventionally conceived and richly bodied forth . . . . In short, a novel to be treasured."
                                    —Anthony Boucher, *The New York Times*

*Julian Symons*

## THE BELTING INHERITANCE
"A superb whodunit in the best tradition of the detective story."
—August Derleth, *Madison Capital Times*

## BLAND BEGINNING
"Mr. Symons displays a deft storytelling skill, a quiet and literate wit, a nice feeling for character, and detectival ingenuity of a high order."
—Anthony Boucher, *The New York Times*

## BOGUE'S FORTUNE
"There's a touch of the old sardonic humour, and more than a touch of style."
—*The Spectator*

## THE BROKEN PENNY
"The most exciting, astonishing and believable spy story to appear in years.
—Anthony Boucher, *The New York Times Book Review*

## THE COLOR OF MURDER
"A singularly unostentatious and memorably brilliant detective story."
—*New York Herald Tribune Book Review*

## THE 31ST OF FEBRUARY
"Nobody has painted a more gruesome picture of the advertising business since Dorothy Sayers wrote 'Murder Must Advertise', and very few people have written a more entertaining or dramatic mystery story."
—*The New Yorker*

*Dorothy Stockbridge Tillet*
*(John Stephen Strange)*

## THE MAN WHO KILLED FORTESCUE
"Better than average."
—*Saturday Review of Literature*

*Simon Troy*

## SWIFT TO ITS CLOSE
"A nicely literate British mystery . . . the atmosphere and the plot are exceptionally well wrought, the dialogue excellent."
—*Best Sellers*

### Henry Wade

**A DYING FALL**
"One of those expert British suspense jobs . . . it crackles with undercurrents of blackmail, violent passion and murder. Topnotch in its class."
—*Time*

**THE HANGING CAPTAIN**
"This is a detective story for connoisseurs, for those who value clear thinking and good writing above mere ingenuity and easy thrills."
—*Times Literary Supplement*

### Hillary Waugh

**LAST SEEN WEARING . . .**
"A brilliant tour de force."
—Julian Symons

**THE MISSING MAN**
"The quiet detailed police work of Chief Fred C. Fellows, Stockford, Conn., is at its best in *The Missing Man* . . . one of the Chief's toughest cases and one of the best handled."
—Anthony Boucher, *The New York Times Book Review*

### Henry Kitchell Webster

**WHO IS THE NEXT?**
"A double murder, private-plane piloting, a neat impersonation, and a delicate courtship are adroitly combined by a writer who knows how to use the language."
—Jacques Barzun and Wendell Hertig Taylor

### Anna Mary Wells

**MURDERER'S CHOICE**
"Good writing, ample action, and excellent character work."
—*Saturday Review of Literature*

**A TALENT FOR MURDER**
"The discovery of the villain is a decided shock."
—*Books*

### Edward Young

**THE FIFTH PASSENGER**
"Clever and adroit . . . excellent thriller . . ."
—*Library Journal*

**If you enjoyed this book you'll want to know about
THE PERENNIAL LIBRARY MYSTERY SERIES**

### Nicholas Blake

### Gavin Black

☐ P 473 A DRAGON FOR CHRISTMAS $1.95
☐ P 485 THE EYES AROUND ME $1.95
☐ P 472 YOU WANT TO DIE, JOHNNY? $1.95

### John & Emery Bonett

☐ P 554 A BANNER FOR PEGASUS
*(available 2/82)* $2.50
☐ P 563 DEAD LION *(available 2/82)* $2.50

### Christianna Brand

☐ P 551 GREEN FOR DANGER $2.50
☐ P 572 TOUR DE FORCE *(available 3/82)* $2.50

### Marjorie Carleton

☐ P 559 VANISHED $2.50

### George Harmon Coxe

☐ P 527 MURDER WITH PICTURES $2.25

### Edmund Crispin

☐ P 506 BURIED FOR PLEASURE $1.95

### D. M. Devine

☐ P 558 MY BROTHER'S KILLER $2.50

Buy them at your local bookstore or use this coupon for ordering:

### Kenneth Fearing

| ☐ | P 500 | THE BIG CLOCK | $1.95 |

### Andrew Garve

| ☐ | P 430 | THE ASHES OF LODA | $1.50 |
| ☐ | P 451 | THE CUCKOO LINE AFFAIR | $1.95 |
| ☐ | P 429 | A HERO FOR LEANDA | $1.50 |
| ☐ | P 449 | MURDER THROUGH THE LOOKING GLASS | $1.95 |
| ☐ | P 441 | NO TEARS FOR HILDA | $1.95 |
| ☐ | P 450 | THE RIDDLE OF SAMSON | $1.95 |

### Michael Gilbert

| ☐ | P 446 | BLOOD AND JUDGMENT | $1.95 |
| ☐ | P 459 | THE BODY OF A GIRL | $1.95 |
| ☐ | P 448 | THE DANGER WITHIN | $1.95 |
| ☐ | P 447 | DEATH HAS DEEP ROOTS | $1.95 |
| ☐ | P 458 | FEAR TO TREAD | $1.95 |

### C. W. Grafton

| ☐ | P 519 | BEYOND A REASONABLE DOUBT | $1.95 |

### Edward Grierson

| ☐ | P 528 | THE SECOND MAN | $2.25 |

Buy them at your local bookstore or use this coupon for ordering:

### Cyril Hare

| | | | |
|---|---|---|---|
| ☐ | P 555 | DEATH IS NO SPORTSMAN | $2.50 |
| ☐ | P 556 | DEATH WALKS THE WOODS | $2.50 |
| ☐ | P 455 | AN ENGLISH MURDER | $1.95 |
| ☐ | P 522 | TRAGEDY AT LAW | $2.25 |
| ☐ | P 514 | UNTIMELY DEATH | $2.25 |
| ☐ | P 523 | WITH A BARE BODKIN | $2.25 |

### Robert Harling

| | | | |
|---|---|---|---|
| ☐ | P 545 | THE ENORMOUS SHADOW | $2.25 |

### Matthew Head

| | | | |
|---|---|---|---|
| ☐ | P 541 | THE CABINDA AFFAIR | $2.25 |
| ☐ | P 542 | MURDER AT THE FLEA CLUB | $2.25 |

### M. V. Heberden

| | | | |
|---|---|---|---|
| ☐ | P 533 | ENGAGED TO MURDER | $2.25 |

### James Hilton

| | | | |
|---|---|---|---|
| ☐ | P 501 | WAS IT MURDER? | $1.95 |

### P. M. Hubbard

| | | | |
|---|---|---|---|
| ☐ | P 571 | HIGH TIDE *(available 3/82)* | $2.50 |

Buy them at your local bookstore or use this coupon for ordering:

**HARPER & ROW, Mail Order Dept. #PMS, 10 East 53rd St., New York, N.Y. 10022.**

Please send me the books I have checked above. I am enclosing $ _____ which includes a postage and handling charge of $1.00 for the first book and 25¢ for each additional book. Send check or money order. No cash or C.O.D.'s please.

Name _____

Address _____

City _____ State _____ Zip _____

Please allow 4 weeks for delivery. USA and Canada only. This offer expires 11/1/82. Please add applicable sales tax.

*Elspeth Huxley*

☐ P 540  THE AFRICAN POISON MURDERS          $2.25

*Francis Iles*

☐ P 517  BEFORE THE FACT                     $1.95
☐ P 532  MALICE AFORETHOUGHT                 $1.95

*Michael Innes*

☐ P 574  DEATH BY WATER *(available 4/82)*   $2.50
☐ P 575  THE LONG FAREWELL *(available 4/82)* $2.50

*Mary Kelly*

☐ P 565  THE SPOILT KILL                     $2.50

*Lange Lewis*

☐ P 518  THE BIRTHDAY MURDER                 $1.95

*Arthur Maling*

☐ P 482  LUCKY DEVIL                         $1.95
☐ P 483  RIPOFF                              $1.95
☐ P 484  SCHROEDER'S GAME                    $1.95

*Austin Ripley*

☐ P 387  MINUTE MYSTERIES                    $1.95

Buy them at your local bookstore or use this coupon for ordering:

---

**HARPER & ROW, Mail Order Dept. #PMS, 10 East 53rd St., New York, N.Y. 10022.**
Please send me the books I have checked above. I am enclosing $ _____
which includes a postage and handling charge of $1.00 for the first book and
25¢ for each additional book. Send check or money order. No cash or
C.O.D.'s please.

Name _____

Address _____

City _____ State _____ Zip _____

Please allow 4 weeks for delivery. USA and Canada only. This offer expires
11/1/82. Please add applicable sales tax.

*Thomas Sterling*

| | | | |
|---|---|---|---|
| ☐ | P 529 | THE EVIL OF THE DAY | $2.25 |

*Julian Symons*

| | | | |
|---|---|---|---|
| ☐ | P 468 | THE BELTING INHERITANCE | $1.95 |
| ☐ | P 469 | BLAND BEGINNING | $1.95 |
| ☐ | P 481 | BOGUE'S FORTUNE | $1.95 |
| ☐ | P 480 | THE BROKEN PENNY | $1.95 |
| ☐ | P 461 | THE COLOR OF MURDER | $1.95 |
| ☐ | P 460 | THE 31ST OF FEBRUARY | $1.95 |

*Dorothy Stockbridge Tillet*
*(John Stephen Strange)*

| | | | |
|---|---|---|---|
| ☐ | P 536 | THE MAN WHO KILLED FORTESCUE | $2.25 |

*Simon Troy*

| | | | |
|---|---|---|---|
| ☐ | P 546 | SWIFT TO ITS CLOSE | $2.50 |

*Henry Wade*

| | | | |
|---|---|---|---|
| ☐ | P 543 | A DYING FALL | $2.25 |
| ☐ | P 548 | THE HANGING CAPTAIN | $2.25 |

*Hillary Waugh*

| | | | |
|---|---|---|---|
| ☐ | P 552 | LAST SEEN WEARING . . . | $2.50 |
| ☐ | P 553 | THE MISSING MAN | $2.50 |

Buy them at your local bookstore or use this coupon for ordering:

---

**HARPER & ROW, Mail Order Dept. #PMS, 10 East 53rd St., New York, N.Y. 10022.**

Please send me the books I have checked above. I am enclosing $ _____ which includes a postage and handling charge of $1.00 for the first book and 25¢ for each additional book. Send check or money order. No cash or C.O.D.'s please.

Name _____

Address _____

City _____ State _____ Zip _____

Please allow 4 weeks for delivery. USA and Canada only. This offer expires 11/1/82. Please add applicable sales tax.

*Henry Kitchell Webster*

☐ P 539   WHO IS THE NEXT?                    $2.25

*Anna Mary Wells*

☐ P 534   MURDERER'S CHOICE                   $2.25
☐ P 535   A TALENT FOR MURDER                 $2.25

*Edward Young*

☐ P 544   THE FIFTH PASSENGER                 $2.25

Buy them at your local bookstore or use this coupon for ordering: